# Save Clagtoft!

by

# Ken Pearson

First Published in 2005


PUBLISHED BY
PAUL MOULD PUBLISHING UK

IN ASSOCIATION WITH
EMPIRE PUBLISHING SERVICES, USA

ISBN 1-904959-20-2


Printed in Great Britain by
CLE Print Limited

# Chapter One

Stringy, pale Abraham Chimble came out of Clagtoft post office and down the wooden steps, bearing a basin in which lay a torch and a dollop of Plasticine.

Liz Otmill, who had come out first, turned to watch. "Why do you always come down the steps backwards?"

"It's me gout. Frontards, you have to bend toe-knuckles and that hurts. Backards, you can do it flat foot. Folks might laugh but they wouldn't if they had gout."

"I notice you didn't lock the door."

"No. One customer allus comes in for his pools postal order Wednesday afternoon. Left it out for him."

Liz chuckled. "Never seen a post office like this before. Wooden caravan, door left open for customers to help themselves…"

"You nivver see Clagtoft afore. We do things our way."

They crossed Main Road and headed for the church. "What's the Plasticine for?"

"Ah. The reason I'm off up the tower, the vicar keeps on about it raining in. Some lead got nicked of the roof and I did a bodge-up with corrugated iron. Where it don't fit very snug, this clays handy for bunging up. Only bother is bloody pigeons pick it out again."

"I hope they don't eat it"

"Bung them up an' all if they did. Mebbe they make little clay men, chuck 'em up to shoot at."

He opened the church door. "Its dark and spooky going up the tower steps. You sure you want to go up?"

"Sure. I've been up tower steps before."

"You go fost if you like, then if you fall I can catch you."

"Not likely. Not having you shining that torch up my skirt."

"Dammit. Foiled again."

"Anyway my twelve stone would bring you down with it."

1

When she saw the cramped stone spiral and the blackness above, she changed her mind. "I think I will go first but I'll take the torch if you don't mind."

"Up you go. Ignore the first door it's the clock chamber."

She began climbing cautiously. "D'you use these steps backwards?"

"More like sidewards. Keep to the outside and do sort of cross over steps."

"Pity I can't see it. There's a ballet routine very similar."

She stopped climbing. Chimble continued but stopped when he felt something warm against his ear. "Switch the torch on!"

"It is on," said Liz.

"I've gone blind!"

"Back up. Your heads inside my skirt. I can feel the ends of your moustache tickling."

Chimble reversed by two steps. "Hah, enjoyed that whilst it lasted."

"I've got to a blank wall."

"Above left. Little wooden door with a bolt, opens outward."

With some effort they emerged at the top into bright daylight.

"Oh, this is terrific," said Liz "Wonderful. I'll be up here with a camera lots of times. And a sketch pad." She edged around the narrow space between the battlements and the little spire, exclaiming at the vast expanse of land around the village, totally flat as far as the eye could see in all directions.

Chimble busied himself poking Plasticine into crevices. These artists, he thought, they see pictures where there ain't any. Fen country, what sort of picture can you make, straight line across, then blue at the top for sky and brown at the bottom for muck...

"I hadn't realised," said Liz "How much variation there is in soil colour."

"There's bits where it's clay near the top; that yellowish, mainly as you go towards the Wash. Other way, there's patches of blackland as we call it. Peat fen." He poked too hard and something fell heavily inside. "Hope that didn't brain the vicar. How'd you come to be in Lincolnshire, thought Norfolk was more like artist's country."

"I came to a wedding at Stumpleton. An old friend from art college days. Damn good wedding, never been so thoroughly pissed

2

for ages. One guest was from Clagtoft. Little Rube. Ruby Fasswelt..."

"Big Rube's youngest."

"...And about 2 o'clock next morning I was on the back of her motorbike heading this way."

"Didn't know she had a pavilion-seat."

"Probably hasn't. I wouldn't have noticed. Slept on Big Rube's settee. Woke up with the sun, went upstairs to their loo, looked out of their landing window and saw Clagtoft for the first time. Decided I wanted to stay and Big Rube offered me a berth. Little Rube was just due to move out and she'd have been left on her own."

"Not a gret deal to see I'd have thought. Not for a professional artist. That's what you are ain't you?"

"Earned a living from it, oh, nearly 12 years. Just starting to get known, I hope."

She moved round to where she could see Clagtoft Drain snaking across the landscape two lush green banks and occasional flash of bright water, spurts of willow and reeds and keck; houses dotted around, some near roads and some apparently not. No way of telling Chimble what she had felt that first morning. Of her realisation that here was a landscape largely overlooked by artists. So starkly simple to the casual eye, its subtleties cunningly hidden. Of her secret resolution to turn herself into a Constable of the fenland. And people, a whole way of life, virtually unrecorded.

Her love-affair with the place and its people began as she stayed with big Rube, sleeping in the spare bedroom of her council house at 16 Duchess of York Drive. She had taken two days to go back to Dorset to fetch her painting gear and a call in London to explain to her agent, and then back to Clagtoft. Back to tramping around some of the richest agricultural land in existence, trying to will her canvases to express what she felt about its raw power, won from the wild over centuries; about these people and their isolated daily lives.

"Tom!" bellowed Chimble. He had seen his customer going into the post office. "Left it out. Get yoursen a stamp if you need one."

"Doesn't anything get pinched?" asked Liz.

The bushy ginger eyebrows lifted. "Tom Chaunter? Never pinched owt in his life."

"I meant... strangers, people passing through."

3

He laughed. "Passing through? Where the 'ell to?" he waved an arm northward. "Squadderby road goes to Squadderby. Nowt past there bar tairty fields. Pudding Lane comes out on Conker Drove. That gets to Iggerby then stops at the West Forty-foot Drain." He limped to the corner of the tower and waved again. "Piggery Lane to Clagtoft Fen and Slaumy Gowt. Stumpleton Road, mile and a half to the ramper. So anybody as is here is where they should be. If they've no business here they stand out a mile."

"Do I stand out a mile?"

He lowered his face, his pale blue eyes shining over his little steel-rimmed glasses at Liz's amply-filled shirt. "I'd say you stand out just about the right amount."

She laughed and pointed. "Is that Clagtoft Hall?"

"No that's Goatskin Hall Councillor Herbert Brangle's place. Clagtoft Hall's yonder, amongst all them trees. Empty, just about ready to fall down, I reckon. Some Yank was supposed to be buying it through Brangle's estate agency but when he see the difference between it and what Brangle had told him, he jumped back over the Atlantic."

"And that one, along side the Drain, that's Wassing's isn't it?"

"Right. The Manor House. William deMondford Wassing. Rhymes wi' passing not tossing. Last of a long line of Wassings, bin there since fourteen hundred and summat, he reckons. And no more to come, unless a strapping lass like yoursen can provide him with some kids."

"Ugh. Don't fancy him. Looks a bit queer. Eerie queer, I mean, not… queer queer. Does he live in that old place alone?"

"Old Mrs. Hammel, Henrietta Hammel, his house keeper. And Dangle. But Dangle lives in the Granary, above where they keep the Rolls-Royce."

Liz pondered a moment "Is… Dangle a nickname?"

"He's Italian. Proper name's Benito D'Angelis but everybody calls him Dangle. Bin chauffeur to the Wassings since just after the war. He was a p.o.w. but never went back to Italy. I've often wondered what kept him here – never married or owt. Never lont our language, just jabbers away in Italian when you speak to him. Right then, that should keep the rain out." He patted the spire. "Wanted to pairnt it but the vicar said no. Was off to use red and white, like a medieval traffic-cone."

4

He lifted the little trap-door to the stair-well and began lowering his legs inside.

"Listen" said Liz. From somewhere in the village below an amplified female voice was booming and echoing.

Chimble said "That's Proggle with her loud-hailer. Uses it for advertising things, meetings, jumble-sales, all that. D'you know Proggle?"

"Lives next door."

"Oh aye. 14 Duchess of York Drive. Postmaster ought to know. Can you hear what she's on about?"

She listened for a minute, shook her head. "Poor old Cassandra, gets worked up about things, she told me she got on to the parish council so she can wake it up and get things done in the village. Are you a councillor?"

He chuckled. "Aye and it's me she keeps waking up. Two or three times some meetings. No good, I can't concentrate, just doorze of wi'out knowing I'm going. Only really come to life wi' a spanner and a bit of machinery to work on." He lowered himself onto the stairway "Now you sit on the edge and lower yoursen through, I'll guide your foot onto the top step. Shan't look up, scouts honour."

"They're pale blue, in case you're interested."

When they merged into the churchyard they could still hear Cassandra Proggle's electrically-processed voice from the direction of Ketchup Terrace.

"No good" said Chimble. "Allus have to wait till she switches off and you can ask her what she's on about. Don't know what the Yanks made of it."

"Yanks?"

"At Greenham Common. She went to that there women's demonstration camp, protesting about new clear weapons. Come back after one winter, six months pregnant. Brought back this loud hailer she'd been using to holler at the Yanks through the barbed wire."

They crossed the road to the post office. "Come in for a cup of tea?"

Liz followed him in and noticed for the first time that the post office was only a part of the huge van. Chimble led the way through the partition and she saw with surprise a comfortable-furnished room.

5

"Do you live in here?"

"Sort o' temporary. Temporary's been about three year up to now. When I fost took over, the post office was in my house, next door to this, front room job. Then one night a bloody great tree fell on it."

"With you inside?"

"I was but I knew nowt till I wock up next morning with rain dripping on my face. And a note on the calendar reminding me to fix up some insurance, which I'd forgotten to do."

He explained that before coming to Clagtoft he had been running an iron mongery business in near by Stodgington for many years but trade had dwindled to a point where he would shortly have to duck out. When people began running cars and the weekly shopping trip into town became part of normal life, they didn't want to know about Chimble's Hardware anymore.

Then had come a stroke of luck; a road transport firm nearby suddenly wanted space and buildings urgently and made him an offer he'd have been foolish to refuse.

"It was a double stroke of luck. In the same week as I signed that deal Clagtoft post office came up for sale. Went for it hammer and tongues."

"Fulfilling a boy hood ambition to be a postmaster?"

He laughed. "Steam, that was the attraction. A previous owner had been a ploughing contractor using them big steam tractions you only see at rallies now. And they'd left tonnes of machinery behind, all included in the deal. Nivver been so happy since me first Meccano. Workshop, lathe, lots of engines and parts, two big barns and o'course Diana."

"I suppose I ought to know who Diana is?"

"My Sentinel. Steam road wagon. Ever seen a Sentinel?"

Liz shook her head. She was fascinated, even stirred, by his tangible enthusiasm.

"After we've had our tea I'll introduce you. Beautiful lorry. Solid tyres mind, so she's not what you'd call, a luxury ride. And just at the moment her boiler's a bit dicky. Oh and I've brought remaining stock of hardware with me; put it in these barns. Anytime you need a mangle or a flat-iron or a skillet, owt like that…"

"Sounds like stuff for the Antiques Road Show."

6

"Some on it will be. But there's folks in Clagtoft as still uses mangles. And oil lamps; onny recently I selled a chimney for an oil lamp, Tich Ounge down the fen. Got the 'lectric but he still likes he's ode oil-lamp."

They went out into the yard.

"Did the gypsy caravan come with the deal?" asked Liz.

"Ah back of the yard, half hid in weeds. It's not a gypsy caravan. It's what the engine men use to live in when they went out ploughing or threshing with the steamers. Drew it behind one of the engines. So when me roof got busted, I pulled the van up near the road and moved in, post office an' all."

"What do the post office people think to it?"

He laughed. "Not a deal. They was already threatening to shut me down afore it happened. Now they keep on at me to move back in. I tell 'em I could do but it'd mean selling damp stamps. I put two stack-sheets over the house roof, as you can see but they don't keep it all out. So without insurance money I'm just staying put till I can find some good unbroken tiles to match and enough fine weather…"

"If you've got a builders estimate, you might raise a loan."

"Builders estimate? You're talking hundreds..."

"Or some more corrugated iron, maybe?" Liz was grinning. "And a Diana-load of Plasticine?"

His grin matched hers. "I'll think of summat. Meanwhile… ay up Proggle's coming this way."

There was a sudden blare of noise like a station announcement as Proggle stopped her bicycle at Chimble's yard entrance and pointed her hailer.

"AAA PUDINA RAA OOR ARMOO ER EE BANBAN."

"Switch that damn thing off and tell us what you're on about."

She propped her bike against the van wheel and came across. "I'm on about Europe and the total extinction of Clagtoft."

There was a moments silence.

Liz said "Perhaps you should run it through the machine. It sounded like 'Europe and the total extinction of Clagtoft'."

"That's exactly right. Them Brussels buggers have thought up a scheme that involves using a six-mile stretch of Lincolnshire fenland totally flattened. And that includes where we're standing on."

"They couldn't do that," said Chimble. "Not totally flatten."

7

"What's it supposed to be for?" asked Liz.

"Runway for landing space shuttles. European Space Agency wants to run a shuttle like the Yanks do. They'll be launched in South America, then landed here."

"They mean the old wartime airfield surely," said Chimble "Out yonaway, off Squadderby Road, the Yanks had an emergency landing strip for Liberators. Run alongside Chaunter's land, up as far as Kelter's Jitty. They used to put paraffin flares on it at night. Onny thing ever landed on it was one of our Wellingtons and it run off the end and busted up."

As he spoke a tractor drew up at the post office. "Yon's Fred Cletch" said Chimble. "If anybody knows owt about it he will. Farms some o' the land up there."

Fred jumped down and pointed to the post office "Come on post master, lets have some service."

While Abe was gone, the two women looked around the treasures in his yard. Proggle said, "Frightens me that Diana thing. Sentinel. Last winter he connected the boiler up to the caravan for heating. Hissing and rumbling away just behind, some folks daren't go in for a stamp."

There was a Robin three-wheeler Chimble used as an everyday runabout and another, gutted and looking derelict, in an open-fronted shed.

"He reckons he's going to convert that to steam-driven."

Liz laughed. "A steam Robin? I'd like to see that. Is he putting a chimney on it?"

"He's got it all worked out. Does it all on paper first. Not quite as potty as he looks our Abraham. Trained as a mechanical engineer."

"Where did you hear about this space idea?"

"Local radio. Had the news on but I was only half listening until I heard Clagtoft mentioned. Quite definite it was, total demolition. Diverting and filling in all the land drains."

"Sounds expensive. All Europe to choose from, there's surely somewhere easier than this?"

"You know how bureaucrats work," said Proggle "Draw a line on a map and that's your lot. People's lives don't matter to them... there's Fred come out. I want a word with him.

She crossed the yard in a few strides, her seemingly endless legs vanishing at the knee into a dress that in Clagtoft terms fitted

8

where it touched. A tall, willowy figure with long dark hair, she had tireless energy when motivated, alternating, as Liz knew, with bouts of languorous fatigue. Today she had been galvanised into the mother and father of all spells of indignant energy.

"Fred Cletch! You're a farmer – how many shotguns you got on your premises?"

Fred stopped with one hand on his tractor. "Shotguns? Two mebbe. Or three, if you count an antique one as was Dad's."

"Any other firearms or weapons?" he laughed. "Don't think so. Who wants to know?"

"I do. Starting now I intend organising the defence of Clagtoft. We may not need guns until the very last minute, when all else has failed…"

"Hang on a bit Cassie. This business is only at proposal stage, they may have several possible sites in mind. I'm sure, when they realise the value of this agricultural land…"

"Their assessment of this lands value," said Proggle "Can be put into one word – set-aside. If they think great areas of it can be left idle, they'll think nothing of taking a six-mile swathe for one of their lunatic schemes."

Fred stood silent, his mind churning over an interview with his bank manager only that morning, when he had discussed a loan to buy some more land.

# Chapter Two

Skinny, pompous William deMondford Wassing ascended the broad staircase of the Manor House, bearing a tray on which lay a note in the unreadable handwriting of his housekeeper, Henrietta Hammel. He forgot to tread leftward on the eleventh step, which sometimes cracked loudly if he didn't. It went off like a pistol-shot and he winced and groaned as if a bullet had gone in somewhere.

He paused at the large window of the landing, from where he could see Clagtoft Drain, the footbridge taking Snogging Lane over past The Pound and on to Squadderby Road, and the allotment shed belonging to Dangle. Further back were Chimble's barns, the Stamping Cat, the old brewery, the vicarage and the church. Two figures were moving about on the church tower; probably, he guessed, the vicar and the District Nurse. The more distant view of Clagtoft Fen and the ruler-straight bank of the West Forty-foot Drain never caught his attention. He was vaguely conscious of living on a vast plain of former seabed but his imagination was not stirred by it. Just now he was listening and wondering.

There it was again, that strange noise outdoors. A bit like a deep-voiced wireless with Joyce Grenfell talking. He knew Hammel had a wireless but it made tinny sounds. Dangle had one that he stood on the roof of the Rolls when he polished it, singing Italian words to the pseudo-American pop-music. But it was Dangle's day off; he'd be in his allotment shed, probably with several other men. Wonder what they...

There it went again. He reached up to turn the catch of the window sash, then stopped as he remembered the window was still taped up to keep out last winters draughts.

A clue appeared. Cassandra Proggle on her bicycle, rounding the bend into Squadderby Road, aiming her electric megaphone at

Mrs. Chaunter's house as she cruised by, bellowing again as she passed the Old Slaughterhouse, targeting bramble Cottage. He waited to see if he could decipher it, but it remained as inscrutable as Mrs. Hammel's writing. The sound came again but muffled and distant. She had turned into Pudding Lane.

A floorboard creaked in the corridor below.

"Mrs. Hammel. Did you hear what Miss Proggle was announcing?"

She appeared at the foot of the stairs, seventy-year-old jaws chomping at nothing. "Sounded like… don't let the fillies get ripe on the mat."

A muffled bell rang in William's fifty-year old brain. "Village, was it?"

Pause. "Aye. Coulda bin that."

She stared blankly as he came down, pointing to her note on the tray. "Mrs. Hammel, when you took that call, can't you remember who it sounded like?"

Chomp, chomp. "Bit like Grunsell, 'im at the pub."

"He's never rung me before. On this note, it looks like European Spare Agony. Any idea what it means?"

The jaws stopped and the eyes switched on. "It was Mr. Brangle. He said the Yew Ropian Space Agency was off to knock Clagtoft down."

"Ah. Wiped off the map, what Miss Proggle said." He put the tray back on the hall table. "Thank you, Mrs. Hammel. That will be all."

She resumed chomping and stood still. Often did so nowadays, as if not having heard. Damned annoying. When his father, the Colonel, had said 'that will be all' to servants they vanished immediately. Hammel was here then. Housemaid, while his mother was alive. She understood then.

"I'll be in my study." he said crossing the hall. Could use the extension in there, though there was no certainty she wouldn't quietly lift the other one and listen.

He contacted Councillor Herbert Brangle, chairman of Clagtoft Parish Council, at his office in Stumpleton where he wan an Auctioneer and Estate Agent.

"Thank you for returning the call William. I tried to impress on your housekeeper that the information I was passing on was strictly confidential. I hope she understood."

11

"I'm not sure that I got it right. Something about knocking Clagtoft down, was it?"

"Incredible as it sounds, yes. This will, of course, become common knowledge in due course but meantime..."

"Hang on old boy. Cassandra Proggle is cycling around the village bawling it through her electric megaphone."

"Proggle? How the hell did she get to know? Been a serious leak somewhere. This was given to me in the strictest of confidence by the Town Clerk here. He was given advance notice in case it affected their plans."

"Is Stumpleton going down as well?"

"No, no. But he looks after planning for the whole area. These European monsters want somewhere to land their silly rockets, and apparently intend to compulsorily – compulsorily, mind you – purchase a six-mile stretch to do it on. And our village stands right in the middle."

"Can they do that, legally?"

"They can seem to do anything they want. Make up the rules as they go along. I was letting you in early, as I thought, because I know you have plans in hand for alterations at the Manor House. No point in spending a lot, then seeing it go down in dust."

William chocked. "B... but it's a listed building, surely. The Wassings have held the manor for four hundred..."

"All the more reason, in some people's eyes, why it should go. There's little respect for anything old these days unless it's got a big price tag. My advice William, would be to get it valued, double it when you apply for compensation and tell 'em the extra's for the history. They'll have got funds put aside for compensation in addition to land purchase. Bleed the buggers, I say. I reckon on getting at least twice what I paid for Goatskin Hall – that's just between you and me of course."

"Of course." He cleared his throat. "There's more than money in it for me though. I was born in this house..."

"That could mean more money still if you played it right. Genuine distress, say, on the edge of nervous breakdown, eh? Might end up with something at least as grand as the Manor House and a damned sight cheaper to run."

"There's the land on the estate as well. Top grade arable, let out to farmers... well, mostly top-grade.

"There you go then. Sitting on a gold mine. Remember though, there's bound to be a big public shindig over this."

"That's what Proggle's got her teeth into. Don't let them wipe us off the map, all that. I suppose we shall, as councillors, lend our support to such a campaign?"

"Naturally. Not lying in front of bulldozers, any of that nonsense. But we shall appear on platforms, applaud and say wise things…"

\* \* \*

Jack Grunsell, landlord of the Stamping Cat, felt himself salivating as he pulled a pint for Harry Gozzard. Could do with one himself. Seen bits on films where customers said 'Have one for yourself, landlord', but it never happened here. And you knew damn well some could afford it. This Gozzard, barely in his twenties and rolling in it. Gangmaster. Many as fifty on his payroll at times; licence to print your own, that business.

"Cheers Jack. Bit better this. New barrel on?"

"Same one. Mebbe settling down a bit."

Harry looked around, didn't see anybody he wanted, stayed at the bar. "Did you hear what Spindleshanks was on about?"

"Spindleshanks?"

"Councillor Proggle. Flying round on her bike with that there shouting machine."

"Oh aye. Summat about they want to flatten Clagtoft to make room for space things. European job."

Harry looked at him suspiciously; he was not known for his leg-pulling.

"Is there owt in it d'you reckon?"

Jack picked up a glass, breathed on it, and rubbed it with a greyish cloth. "Nivver know these days. Them lot set behind big desks in Brussels and that, we're only a dot on the map to them."

"But we're supposed to be represented, ain't we? My job, I dooan't allus git time to go and vote, but I seem to remember we elected an extra M.P. for that."

"Ain't the same mate. Once old Heathy got us signed up for that lot, that was it. We toe the line, or else."

Harry took a mouthful of Gallstone's Bitter; for him, the best part of a cupful. "Won't bother me any road living down the fen."

13

"Wouldn't be too sure about that. Coming from outer space, going like the clappers, they'll want a widish bit to airm at."

The door opened and admitted a policeman in full uniform, traditional helmet at one end and trouser-clips at the other. Jack Grunsell glanced at the clock. Not open out of time.

"Just a routine call Mr. Grunsell. Nothing to worry about. Can I have a brief word in private?"

Jack led the way through to the living-room where his wife Edie was watching her video of Teletubbies. "Hello Albert. I'll get you a drink."

"Now then Edie, not supposed to on duty, y'know."

She turned the TV sound off and produced a whisky and water. "What's it this time? Drug dealing? Young Gozzard driving over the limit?"

Albert sipped and rolled it around "This time I'm afraid, it's about your boy, Clive."

"Ah, well," said Jack. "Since we come here, as you know, we've tried our level best to keep him at school. But he just cannot stomach that Trudgen bloke. So we thought with the school mebbe getting shut down and him coming up to leaving age anyway…"

"It's not about that." P.C. Tussock took out his notebook and began turning pages. "This concerns a complaint about him. From a member of the public."

Silence fell, Edie's eyes firmly fixed on the Teletubbies' silent gyrations.

"What sort if complaint?" asked Jack.

"Flashing."

Jack said "Ah." He waved his hand. "Boys his age, y'know, they do tend to get a bit, y'know…"

"There was mention of other things, like the racket from his guitar and that yodelling noise he makes in public places, but they were not the substance…"

"Mebbe just forgot to zip up."

"Apparently not. The complainant reported a remark made by Clive, co-inside-ent with the, er, exposure… where are we now…" more pages were turned. "Oh, yes. How about that then. You must know Jack, this is not the first time. It's been mentioned to me before, but this time it was a formal complaint."

"Tell us who it was, I'll go and apologise."

Tussock put his notebook away. "Better if he did the apologising; mebbe would if you told him." He put his glass down and licked his lips. "Just wanted you to understand it was a criminal offence."

Edie said, "We do, but I doubt if you could make Clive…"

"Educationally subnormal they said at Stumpleton" Jack said. "They managed to keep him going to school most of the time, but this twat Trudgen, I've seen better teachers crawl out of woodwork."

Tussock's hand was on the door.

"Ain't you telling us who complained?" asked Jack.

"Mrs. Glenda Hovel, Pudding Lane, Clagtoft."

"Oh, that cow…"

"Steady on Jack." Said Edie. "She was entitled to."

The policeman opened the door, went back through the bar and out.

"Come on Jack," Gozzard's voice. "Let's have some service here. Ne' mind fussing the bobby up wi' free booze."

Jack returned to his station.

"What was he on about?"

"Oh, just about this… Europe business. Says I shall have to apply for a fresh licence for the new Stamping Cat, wherever they build it."

Gozzard studied Jack's face, wondering if elongatory force was being applied to his member. "Lying sod," he decided. "Gi' us a pint."

\* \* \*

Mrs. Olive Ossack had earache. Some unkind Clagtoft people would have remarked no wonder, considering the noise that comes out a few inches away. She was called 'The Mouth'. It was said that when she was at work in the field, as she had been for most of her long working life, the casual remarks she made to her fellow-workers could be heard by workers in five or six other fields.

The energy thus expended took away nothing from her prowess as a land-worker. She was known as the fastest tatie-picker in the kingdom, in the days before that vegetable was harvested by machinery. Even when the first machines arrived, many people swore that the job would be done quicker by hand if only there were enough Olive Ossacks.

15

She was still fit as a flea at well over seventy, so an earache was unusual. "Go see the quack then," said Sam, her husband. "It's her day ain't it?"

Dr. Fanny Mulfry held a twice-weekly surgery at Clagtoft, in a building converted for the purpose. It had always been known as the Old Slaughterhouse and the name stuck when it entered its new phase of usage. More so in fact.

It was a little more than a half-mile from Olive's house at Lollycock Bridge to the Old Slaughter House on Main Road, but in fine weather her journey could take up to an hour. There were more people outdoors needing to be addressed. Anybody in a front garden would hear the introductory "Nah then duck" from a range of thirty yards, and unless they had a hide thick enough for them to give a cheery wave and vanish indoors, they were stuck with Olive for at least ten minutes.

Today, the news of the earache being over shadowed by that of pending destruction, the journey took even longer. Along Duchess of York Drive stood knots of people at front gates; Olive heard the news at the first and delivered her verdict to the rest as she passed along.

"Load o' balls innit? One o' Proggle's stories she picked up in London. Just look for summat to mek a fuss about, some does. Dooan't you tek no notice duck, they'll not bother at Clagtoft. Bin there longer'n them sods and it'll still be here when they've gone."

The Drive listened tolerantly; she was part of the village's passing pageantry. Its children mimicked her little-woman bustling walk. Elbows tucked in and head back as they strove to match the volume.

"Got earache duck. Off to see the quack – fost time nigh on ten year. Not since that there ancient flu; nearly a goner then I was."

Heads appeared at windows as she progressed past the village hall, her voice bouncing off its corrugated iron, bringing the startled face of Mr. H.W.M. Trudgen, Headmaster, to the window of the school opposite. Ketchup Terrace and the almshouses thought it was a second Proggle bulletin and rushed out to listen.

The long thin figure of Clive Grunsell, almost hidden behind his big guitar, emerged from the Stamping Cat. When he saw Olive he began strumming away, swaying and yodelling, doing a little foot-dance at each crossing of the voice-boundary.

16

"Ought to be in school you did," she bawled. "Them others is all set in there learning and you should be an' all."

Clive screwed up his face and did her a special double-yodel.

As she passed the post office and got the Old Slaughterhouse in her sights, she stopped suddenly and put her hands on her hips. "Well, I'll be..." Dr. Mulfy's car emerged from behind the surgery, turned into Main Road, accelerated past Olive and vanished in the direction of Stumpleton.

"Look at that," she told nobody and everybody. "Me with damn earache and she clears off."

Chimble opened the door of the post office. "Have to get here sooner Olive. Finishes at four and won't be here again while Saturday. You'd onny get antibiotics any road. That's all they know these days."

"If I 'ev sleepless nights while Sat'day..."

"Go down and see Mrs. Hovel instead. She'll mebbe do you more good."

* * *

Glenda Hovel described herself as a phytotherapist, a word which brought from the average Clagtoftian the response, "What the 'ell's that when it's at home?" At past times of her life she could truthfully have described herself as a parliamentary candidate (failed), a revolutionary socialist, a Butlin Redcoat, and a wife and mother.

The mother of two boys, the other elements had faded into the past, or, in the case of her husband, into the mists of the North Sea. He had left his job on Fred Cletch's farm and gone to work on an oil-rig, leaving Glenda and the boys in the rented cottage in Pudding Lane. Confronted by the large garden, Glenda had plunged into phytotherapy, or medical treatment with plants. Not mere dabbling in folk-remedies; she had studied the practice of herbal medicine with the same zest as she had lost a by-election. Now, a steady trickle of customers called at her cottage with sundry pains, bumps, scratches and bellyaches.

She was busy at the cooker, boiling up a concoction of yarrow and downy hemp-nettle.

17

"Cor, that pongs mum" called Gavin, her eldest son. He was 17 and nominally job-hunting. Much of his time was spent at home, working on a scale model of the proposed Piggery Lane Shopping Precinct, which Councillor Glenda was to present to the parish council as a contribution to the New Greater Clagtoft Plan.

She went into the living-room where he was at work. "Thought you'd be used to herbal smells by now." She watched his paint-brush move across the front of a supermarket. "That looks suspiciously like a Tesco."

"It is a Tesco."

"But we're not letting the giants in. Not initially. First chance goes to local enterprise."

Gavin laughed. "What – Hunkings, in Ketchup Terrace? One front room of a house with a few fags and tins of beans? What chance they got?"

"They can grow. They will when the population grows. There's access to capital for rural enterprise."

He looked at his model fondly. "Not easy to change it. Can't I leave that high bit and put Hunking instead of Tesco?"

"Should be O.K. What's that bit left rough for?"

"That's the pond."

"Oh yes, I've got ideas for that. How about a fountain, nicely concreted all round, with seats. Umbrellas, all that.

He sat silent, staring at the model.

"Glenda said 'If you don't agree, say so.'"

"It's a wild-life sanctuary as it is now. Birds, frogs, water-rats. Are humans entitled to..."

The door burst open and David came in from school, dumped a bursting satchel perilously close to Tesco's wet paint. "Need the table. Loads of homework; French, maths, history..." Gavin's face darkened and Glenda noticed. "Put the model on my desk please Gavin. Remember the agreement; first priority is education."

David spread enough work to cover the table. "Mum," he said. "They're going to knock Clagtoft down."

Four potatoes, she was thinking. Or, sports day, perhaps better make it five.

"D'you hear what I said?"

"This one of your funny jokes? O.K., why are they going to knock Clagtoft down?"

18

"I dunno. UFOs landing, summat like that."

"Something, not summat. An English exercise is it? Writing a fantasy story?"

Gavin was listening. "I told you that's what Miss Proggle was on about."

She stood with a potato in each hand looking at the tap running.

"European Space Authority." remembered David. "They need a runway right here. We'll see 'em zooming in."

Glenda put the potatoes down and went towards the phone but before she had dialled there was a knock at the door.

"'Allo duck." It was Olive Ossack. "Are you open? Got a rotten earache I have. Can you do owt with earaches?"

"How long has it been aching?"

"Yissday, and right through the night."

"You should have seen Dr. Mulfry. She was here today."

"Pissed off afore I got there she did. Shouted after her but she was gone like a scalded cock."

Maybe she saw you coming, thought Glenda. "Come across to the barn, see what we can find. Anything else hurting? Sore throat? Any bad teeth?"

"Them's all bad by now I should reckon. Spit the last 'un out into the garden ten year ago."

Down the centre of the barn were labelled drying racks and around the walls shelves loaded with packeted remedies.

"Good Lor'," said Olive. "Where d'you get all his stuff?"

"Most of it I grow. Some times I collect off the drain-banks and hedgerows in summer. As long as I know there's been no chemical sprays used."

"Aye. Bloody poison some o' that. Used to upset my ol' man when he was wocking. Come home all red once he did. Not just his face, all over. Even 'is prick." She lowered her voice slightly for once. "You ain't got owt here as'll perk 'im up a bit like, 'ave yer? You know what I mean."

Glenda's face stayed straight. "How old is Mr. Ossack?"

"Fower year older'n me. Seventy-six."

Glenda cleared her throat. "If his general health is O.K., he should manage a bit of activity now and then." She handed a packet over. "This doesn't work for everybody mind but it's worth a try. So long as, er, everything's in working order."

19

"It's that all right." Olive chuckled "Just wants a bit o' gingering up. How much is this?"

Glenda waved a hand. "I don't charge O.A.Ps. Only loaded ones. I'd just like to know whether he notices any difference."

Theold eyes gleamed. "Or whether I do. I'll let you know." She turned to go out.

"Hang on, you've got nothing for your earache. Here, try this one. It's horse chestnut, ground ivy, comfrey, golden rod, and one or two other things. Make it like tea and drink it an hour before bedtime. I'll mark that one, so you know which is which."

Olive went off with a spring in her step, eyes already peeled for somebody to shout the news at. She paused at the gate and turned.

"What d'you reckon to this 'ere space business?"

"Don't know. I've only heard what my son brought from school."

"I dooan't believe a word on it. Neether does anybody else wi' any sense."

# Chapter Three

Sweaty, portly the Reverend Crispin Owery ascended the stairs of Clagtoft Vicarage, bearing a bowl of hot water for his morning shave. A bachelor of frugal habits, he used the vicarage's ancient hot water system only when intending to bath. On other days he used a kettle for all purposes. He set a bowl on the bathroom windowsill and adjusted the mirror.

Through the frosted window-glass his eye caught the blurred image of something bright green moving against the grey backcloth of the Church of St. Dismas, across the graveyard. Odd, for somebody to be in the church-yard at this time of morning.

He attempted to open the window but he couldn't. It had been stuck closed since the last time it was painted, seven years ago. Have a look from the bedroom, he thought, and padded round into there. Drew back the curtains, and caught his breath.

There was a girl wearing a green shirt and slacks. She was bending, apparently trying to read a grave stone inscription, rubbing at it with her fingertips. Her brilliant red hair tumbled past her face.

For a few seconds the Rev. stood opened-mouthed. He knew every Clagtoft female in the age-range 10-50, having made detailed mental studies of their changing shapes year by year. This was most certainly a stranger.

He suddenly realised that he wore nothing but his pink y-fronts and that he was on full view. At exactly the same moment she straightened, turned, and looked directly at the vicarage. He took a hasty step back, trod on a boot, overbalanced and rolled across the bedroom floor in a mass of windmilling limbs and unreverend language. He scrambled to his feet and tested his moving parts, found everything working, and began climbing into his clothes. She might want to see me. Might want to complain about... nothing went right the first time – arms and legs in wrong holes, head into armholes...

By the first ring of the doorbell he was dripping with sweat. Maybe it wasn't her. Could be the milkman... no, this is Thursday. Foot in wrong boot, Gawd damn it. Tried to call "There in a minute" but managed only a croak. When he finally got the door open he was a gibbering wreck.

"Good morning. The Reverend Owery?" the voice was cool and musical.

"Ah – goo, ubber orn." His frantic nodding shook a bead of sweat from his nose on to the bare wood floor of the hall.

She seemed not to notice. "I'm Violet Wask. I'm doing post-graduate research into the archaeology of some fenland villages, including your parish. Some time in the next few weeks, if you can spare the time..."

"Ah – abba – come in, er, Miss... I..." he was mentally unable to cope with the red hair, that pale, smiling face, that...

He almost led her into the kitchen, where his breakfast egg would soon be boiled solid, swerved in time, aimed at the sitting-room, kicked the doorpost and swung the door open.

She sensed his confusion. "Sorry to have caught you at a busy time. Perhaps if I came back later..."

"No, no. Oh, no. Please sit down, Miss er." It was a bachelor's dream and he desperately wanted it to continue. He was aware of not doing the things bachelors did in dreams, but maybe if she stayed long enough...

He mopped his face. "Arch – arch – eology?"

"Yes. I just graduated, and got a grant for a year's work from the Eastern Trust. For a few weeks I shall be finding out about Clagtoft's history, what archaeological work has been done already. Particularly about the castle site – what's underneath all those mounds."

"Castle... oh. Do you actually, er, dig?"

She smiled, and his heart missed a beat. "Yes. I'm not very big, but I'm a demon with a spade."

He scraped his mind desperately for things to say. He still didn't know whether she had seen him in his y-fronts. "C..can I get you some tea? Tea? Or..."

"No, really, I've already interrupted your morning routine enough. I just thought I ought to explain why I was nosing around in your churchyard."

So she had seen. "I'm sorry…"

She stood up and held out a hand. "Now, I've got loads to do this morning and I'm sure you have. I'll be in touch again and perhaps you'll be kind enough to show me your church and tell me about its history."

Her hand was dry and firm, his damp and flabby. He showed her out and even as she walked briskly back along the path his mind was buzzing with things he might have said. When she vanished round Waddie's Corner he shut the door quietly, looked at it for a minute then kicked it hard and said "Damn, damn, damn, damn." When he got to the kitchen he was met by a cloud of acrid smoke and found he had left the gas on under the kettle, which had boiled dry and melted its plastic handle. At that moment, the smoke alarm began shrieking, and the milkman was knocking…

Violet fished a paper out of her shirt pocket and looked at a list. The next name on it was George W. Hunking, Parish Clerk, No. 1 Ketchup Terrace. She passed the almshouses, noting the date on a chimney stack, 1654. From across the road came the sound of children singing in the school. There were six houses in Ketchup Terrace, all painted dull red, and the first had a sign in its front window: Hunking's Stores, open daily. Over the door it said, G. W. and R. Hunking, Licensed to Sell Tobacco. A spring-mounted shop-bell sang a merry peal as Violet entered, and brought R. Hunking from a back room.

"Hello. Is it possible to see Mr. George Hunking, please?"

Rose pondered. "Are you from a newspaper? About this Europe business?"

"No. I'm a community archaeologist, and I want to see him in his capacity as Parish Clerk. Are you Mrs. Hunking?

Rose looked relieved. "Yes. I'm sorry, but George expected all sorts to be swarming in – television and the media and all them, over this demolition job."

"I see. No. I've no connection with whatever it is. What's going to be demolished?"

"Clagtoft."

Any uneasy silence. "I see," said Violet. "Er... is Mr. Hunking available?"

"For council business, I suppose, yes. Normally he's not here in day-time but he had a union meeting till late last night so he's took a morning off to work on his Open University thing."

"Good for him."

"Hang on, I'll get him."

Her footsteps mounted stairs, then two sets descended and George's large pale face appeared. He wore the first suit Violet had seen in Clagtoft, and it supported a battery of pens across the top pocket. He invited her into the living-room.

When they were settled he said, "I didn't know we had any archaeology in Clagtoft."

"There's some, practically wherever you go in England. All those thousands of years people lived here, something's been left behind from every age."

"I see. Do you think we're sitting on King John's treasure, something like that?"

"Who knows? But that's not what we're looking for, most of the time. It's the information about how people lived in the past."

"Land-wock, as they say round here. That sums up Clagtoft's past."

She smiled and George responded. It was suddenly a better day than its early promise. "I'd always imagined archaeologists to be ancient male professors, with beards."

"There are some like that, for those who prefer them."

"Not me. I'm more than happy with the one we have."

"Good. Can you put on your Parish Clerk hat and tell me about the castle site? Does the council own it and is public access allowed? Most important to me, could I have permission to explore below ground?"

"It is permitted for the public to go on it, yes. And it is public property, in the care of the council. That was established last year, when we were working out a strategy for tourism."

"Tourism?" Violet's face registered disbelief.

"Some people find it hard to believe but our chairman is sure that with expert handling of publicity, Clagtoft could become a venue for certain types of tourist. Mainly those with an interest in fenland

24

history. So if you do find the remains of a castle, it would give a boost."

"So you think I might be O.K. for digging?"

"It's not in my power to say yes but I might be able to cut a few corners, without having to wait for monthly meetings."

"What's all this about the village being demolished?"

"Oh that. I can't believe it would happen. Not a whole village. Perhaps the high buildings like the church tower and the windmill."

"Whose idea is it?"

"European Space. They're landing their Herpes shuttles in Europe now but they want a fresh place. They think they can just walk in and buy land wherever and whenever they want."

"Public outcry over that I'd guess."

"Proggle – councillor Miss Proggle – is organising a protest. She's done a lot of that..."

"It occurs to me, if this castle site does turn out important, it could be a factor on the side of the campaign. At least for delaying it."

"I think you're right, Miss... er, I'm sorry..."

"Look, Mr. Hunking..."

"Call me George, please."

"...George. I'll make this an earlier priority, if you can get my permission to dig through. And if you think of anything else in Clagtoft history."

"There's Maltrouser. And Hereward the Wake, according to Mr. Wassing."

"I've got notes of those. What about Clagtoft Hall?"

"That's where Maltrouser lived. Since then, it's a bit shrouded in mystery. Have you seen the state of it?"

"No, but I was warned off going to it. Something to do with squatters or travelling people."

George glimpsed an opportunity. "Can be risky. Tell you what, if you're here at the weekend sometime, I'll have a walk up there with you."

* * *

The next name on Violet's list was Mr. Horace W.M. Trudgen, Head Teacher, Clagtoft School. She had heard that the school was threatened with closure, due to cuts in the education budget, and that the children would have to be bussed to Stumpleton, eight miles away. She had heard that Trudgen was bitterly unhappy about it, as it would mean his losing Head Teacher status. She anticipated meeting a very unhappy man.

Before she reached the school, she was diverted. From somewhere nearby came a weird noise, almost if an animal were in great pain from being chastised with a musical instrument. She followed the sound until she came to the village pump, set in its own little yard between the almshouses and the churchyard. Clive stood precariously on top of the pump, energetically strumming his untuned guitar, yodelling, and executing a perilous knee-dance.

"Watch you don't fall off there." said Violet into a gap in the noise.

He immediately leaped off and rolled over on the hard gravel. When he recovered and stood up, he stared wide-eyed at her red-hair and bright green outfit. "Bugger you. Med me jump."

"Sorry, I didn't mean to, but it looked a bit dangerous. Can I have a look at your guitar?"

He glared suspiciously for a few seconds, then held it out. She looked all round it. "Not bad, wants a bit of attention. Fret loose there, needs to be seen to." She adjusted one string to a guessed note, then retuned the others from it. Something approximating a proper chord was the result. Clive watched wide-eyed as the sound was transformed under her delicate-looking hands. When she handed it back and said, "try that." His slack face brightened.

"You'll have to find somebody to teach you. Didn't you do music at school?"

He shook his head dumbly. She guessed at his mental condition, decided she hadn't more time to spare, and turned across to the school.

"Hey up," called Clive. "Want to show you summat." She turned and looked. He walked across the road to just beyond a house called Waddie's Cottage. He looked back and beckoned. She followed slowly and saw him turn off into a footpath beyond the house. He looked back again and saw her hesitating. "Come on," he called. "Got summat to show yer." He was beckoning with one hand but she saw what he was doing with the other.

"Busy now," she said. "I'll have a look another time."

"Don't get involved with that little monster," were almost his first words when Violet had introduced herself to Trudgen. He had seen

26

her talking to Clive. "I had him here for the first few weeks when they came and I've never seen so much disruption from one child before. No wonder they call him the village idiot."

"Is he still school age?"

"A few weeks to go. But he's not coming back into my school."

"I thought provision was made for problem children?"

"Theoretically, yes. But the arrangements seldom get applied in remote places like Clagtoft."

They turned to Violet's reason for being in the village, and Trudgen brightened visibly when heard that she might be around for several weeks and even months.

"Clagtoft, I would say, is a virgin territory for an archaeologist." And found himself mentally reversing what he had said; Archaeological territory for a virgin? Likely to be one of those who look virginal, even after a spasm of rough-and-tumble.

"What do you know about the history of the castle?" she was asking.

"A bit of folklore codswallop, that's my guess. One of those stories made up in the year dot and passed down, embroidered and decorated, from grandfathers to grandchildren."

"All the same, I'd like to hear what the stories are. Surprising how much apparent codswallop has been found to have a tiny foundation of truth."

They were in his small office in the school, and he pointed through the window. "Through that gap between Ketchup Terrace and the village hall, you see a lot of trees. Inside there, remains of Clagtoft Hall. One-time home of Samuel Dreadnought Maltrouser. One story is that the so-called castle was actually a folly, built by one of the Hall's owners."

Violet was taking notes. "I'll dig into the archives on that one. What do the older people in the village say about the castle?"

He laughed. "Some fantastic tales. One is that there were four monster stone towers, visible from Lincoln cathedral. And another that there's an underground tunnel from Clagtoft to Tattershall Castle."

"Some tunnel," said Violet. "Always has to be one. Any ghosts?"

"Riddled with 'em. One of the popular ones is a phantom pig. A local farmer's dead body was fished out of Clagtoft Drain a hundred years ago and the story was that he had gone for a midnight walk

27

along the bank, past the castle site, and it had charged out and butted him into the water."

They talked until Trudgen had to go to a class, then she got her second invitation. "Let me know if you want to see Clagtoft Hall any time. It's got a reputation for vagrants and suchlike congregations there. I'll go with you."

She thanked him and left. What with flashing village idiots and offers of male escorts into dangerous places, Clagtoft looked promising. She had five fenland villages on her research itinerary, and this was listed fourth; her present visit was merely a preliminary skirmish. With this threat of demolition hanging over, perhaps she should promote it to the top of the list.

Next thing was a look around the castle site. Remembering the map she had studied, she went along Conker Drove to Lollylock Bridge then turned off to the bank of the drain. The grounds of Goatskin Hall were to her left initially, and over the drain, the mass of wild trees which all but concealed Clagtoft Hall. She caught a glimpse of a roof and some chimneys. There was certainly a mysterious atmosphere about it; maybe she'd be glad of an escort when the time came.

She fought through some hawthorn and an area of aggressive nettles, and came to the site. A few trees grew on it, but not ancient ones. She guessed it to have been a managed site until recently. It looked interesting; there were humps and bumps over a defined area, and from her slightly elevated viewpoint she could make out at least two right-angles. Perhaps when the digging starts, they would be good starting points.

West of the site was an area of flat grassland the map called Cut-throat Paddock. Skirting the paddock so as to get different views of the mounds, she passed along the western boundary, beyond which were the gardens of the council houses in Duchess of York Drive. In one, a woman was hanging out washing. It was Big Rube Fasswelt, and as Violet came into view she peered at her suspiciously. "'Ello duck," she called.

"Good morning. I'm not out to pinch anything. Just having a look where they say the castle used to be. You might see me several times over the next few weeks."

"Is it owt to do with this 'ere space business?"

"No. This was planned before that came out. I might have to work fast if it's true about the demolition. Don't want to be here when they start zooming in."

"Course, we've seen people in there afore." Rube came down to the thorn boundary hedge.

"What is it, a courting venue?"

"It's that all right. One o' my boys used to keep binocklers in the bedroom, reckoned he could see 'em at it. No, I mean years back, people in there measuring up and that."

"Were they archaeologists?"

"Easy might have bin. Somebody said it was to do with the railway. New line coming through, and a station on Conker Drove next to Brangle's place. Is your job to do with railway?"

"No, I'm an archaeologist. Only interested in what used to be here, years ago. I might be digging some holes, see if anything's left of a castle."

"You be careful duck. They say there was a tunnel from there, used to come out under Lincoln Cathedral. You unblock that, you nivver know what might rush out at yer."

"I'll be careful. Were you born in Clagtoft?"

"Oh, no. Stumpleton. Onny come here when I got married."

"Did older village people tell any stories about the castle?"

Big Rube laughed. "One or two women has tales to tell about what happened to 'em in there. There's one as points to her two boys and says straight out they were started in there."

"Sounds like a dangerous place for a woman."

"Don't hang about there on yer own duck. Are you stopping in Clagtoft to sleep?"

"No. Back to Stumpleton by car."

"I was off to say, I've got a spare bed if you change your mind. Already got one lodger, Liz. She's an artist."

"Can I make a note of your address, just in case?"

"Number 16 Duchess of York Drive." She laughed. "Used to be Piggery Lane East, till the council built these. Some folks objected, but I reckon the owd name was better."

"What about the name of this field, Cut-throat Paddock?"

"Nobody grumbles about that. Mebbe to do wi' pig-killing. Years ago most folk kep a pig, and that might have bin where the pig-killer

29

did his job. Handy for the drain, let all the blood and stuff run down into it."

"Yuck. I'm starting to have second thoughts about digging."

"Could be you'll not get a chance. If this space thing comes we'll all be out on our necks any road. Shouldn't be sorry. Get back in town, get to bingo wi'out a bus journey both ways. Hallo, there goes Cassie again…"

The loud-hailer was booming out again.

"BAAA ROOOMBA AAR FODMUND OOL REEMOLE!"

"That's my neighbour. When she comes back I'll ask her what's the latest."

# Chapter Four

Every house in Clagtoft, decided Proggle, would get a notice of the first general meeting of the Save Clagtoft! Campaign. She would write them all herself if necessary. She sat down in the evening to do that. An attempt to recruit her son, Nelson Mandela Proggle, had failed on a plea of homework; as she set her stall out on the kitchen table she could hear the TV going in his bedroom. In the middle of the third leaflet she decided to change the wording and scrapped what was already done. Starting again on the edited version, her felt tip pen ran out and she couldn't find another. She gave up.

Next morning she rang three printers in Stumpleton but failed to reach the contract stage with any, chiefly perhaps because she thought they ought to be passionate enough about the threatened injustice to work for nothing.

Then she remembered the Parish News Letter. It had flourished briefly some years back, as a means of keeping people in touch with what the council was doing on their behalf. It had also stumbled on printing costs but had limped on by means of a partnership with the church, which possessed a hand-wound duplicator. That machine, she thought, might still be around. A month's church activity would no longer fill one side of a sheet, and in any case the vicar's poorly knee prevented his doing the deliveries. He got a mention at the foot of the council's News Letter in the return for the use of the machine. The last edition had been left in Hunking's Stores under a "Please Take One" notice and had ended up as four squadrons of paper aeroplanes on Bosh Green.

Proggle descended on the Rev. Crispin Owery and challenged him to produce the machine.

"Now, let me see. The last time I saw that machine it was in the loft above the vestry. I'm not sure, however, whether the churchwardens would agree to selling it."

31

"I don't want to buy it. I want to put it to good use – saving the church, and the rest of Clagtoft, from total extinction. And you; have you thought of where you'll go when they bash the vicarage down?"

"Oh dear. Is it really going to happen? One hears so many tales. Though I've still got Iggleby and Squadderby parishes, if they are spared from this terrible disaster…"

"This is no disaster mate. Disasters are acts of God; this is a purely man-made cock-up. Therefore avoidable. And the duplicator could be an important weapon."

In a few minutes they were rummaging in a dusty cupboard. By some miracle everything had survived – the machine, stencils, ink, and enough foolscap paper to circularise Clagtoft several times over.

Proggle loaded her bicycle basket, sat the machine perilously on the saddle, and trundled it briskly homeward.

"Must remember to inform the churchwardens." Owery was muttering. His problem was that he could no longer remember who the churchwardens were.

Mass Meeting of the
SAVE CLAGTOFT! CAMPAIGN
Your home, your school, your pub, your church, your job,
YOUR VILLAGE and YOUR WAY OF LIFE are
THREATENED WITH OBLITERANCE
by the VANDALS of the EUROPIAN UNION!
We must ACT NOW to save all we have and hold dear.
Your attendance is urgently needed at the inaugural meeting;
THURSDAY, 17th JUNE, 7 p.m. AT THE VILLAGE HALL.
(Please bring a list of firearms and other weapons in your
possession)

The posters carried, in addition to the message, a quantity of blobs, which would have interested a psychologist using such things for testing daftness. Similar blobs appeared on Proggle but she cared not. She mounted her bicycle and began zooming around at high speed, pushing the posters through letterboxes, taping them to telegraph poles, and thrusting them into the hands of anybody she happened to meet.

She was unsure of how far out of the central area she needed to go, as nothing had been said about the width of the proposed runway. There was a cluster of six houses in Clagtoft Fen, and a random sprinkling along the roads leading to Iggleby, Slaumy Gowt and Peamoor Water. Eventually, having come to the last poster, she turned wearily for home.

As she turned into Main Road and passed the post office, she heard Chimble call, "Aye up Cassie!" She stopped. He was standing at he door waving the poster she had delivered earlier.

"No can do." he said.

He pointed to the poster. "It says here Village Hall, Thursday 17th June, 7 p.m. you ain't booked the hall for that." As chairman of the council's Village Hall Committee, he was in charge of bookings.

"For God's sake man, this is an emergency. We're on about the hall and everything else…"

"We still have to honour our bookings. This is the W.I. Crafte Fayre, raising money to pay off their Millennium Fund debts. Can't turn away a good customer."

"They'll have to postpone it."

"That would be between you and them. You go and see Mrs. Trudgen, their chairperson, and see how you get on."

Proggle pondered. "O.K., I'll change our venue. Same date and time but we'll make it an open-air meeting on Bosh Green. And Mrs. Clever-dick Trudgen'll find nobody at her Crafte Fayre, they'll all be at our meeting."

"Wouldn't bank on it."

She stared at him, realising he was no more than luke-warmly with her. "Can't you see the danger of this, Abe? The need for us to shout and shout, loud and early, to make ourselves heard?"

He gave both sides of his moustache an affectionate hand-brush. "Reckon we'll all look a bit silly if we jump up and down and create a gret fuss, then it all turns out to be a load of media codswallop."

"Not half as daft as we'd look loading up furniture vans ready to go into some slum back-street in Stumpleton. It could even be that they've put the story out to test reaction – if nobody fusses, then they go ahead and buy the land. No, I'll leave the notice as it is, then on the day I'll put one outside the hall saying that due to pressure on space the meeting has been moved to Bosh Green."

\* \* \*

33

At a quarter to seven on 17th June, Proggle arrived at Bosh Green. This was Clagtoft's equivalent of Hyde Park, a place of congregation and recreation for all citizens. Its Serpentine was a stretch of Clagtoft Drain, here shaded from the evening sun by a line of willows. Its three other boundaries were Main Road, the vicar's garden, and an undetermined line, which nominally separated it from Cut-throat Paddock. At earlier times that boundary line had been hotly disputed between the council and Albert Chaunter, owner of Cut-throat Paddock. To much disappointment the dispute had been side-stepped by Albert selling the Paddock to the council.

For the delight of young Clagtoftians, Bosh Green was thoughtfully provided with two broken swings, a broken seesaw, a tree-stump to stand, sit or dance on, a derelict bus, and a shed containing the Parish Lawnmower. The last-mentioned building was sited conveniently close to the Drain, enabling Saturday-night revellers to topple it in. They did so frequently, cheering loudly at the satisfying splash. Cheering again next morning, at the spectacle of Chimble's Sentinel pulling it out again.

Proggle leaned her bike on the tree-stump, parked her loud-hailer on it, and scanned the landscape. The only humanity in sight was Clive Grunsell, who had followed her along Main Road and now stood a few feet away, eyeing the loud-hailer.

"Would you like to sing through it?" she asked him.

His eyes lit up. She switched it on and pointed it across at the post office. "Come here, then."

He sidled up, brought his face near it gave a tentative moo. "Louder," said Proggle. "Give us a good strong yodel." Clive took a deep breath, flung out his arms, and brought off such an ear-splitting howl that the twenty-two rooks in the churchyard trees scrambled simultaneously and raced off towards the coast, the vicar's cat shot up an apple-tree, and Chimble was out the post-office door and down the steps before he noticed his gout.

"That should be enough," said Proggle, her trembling hand switching it off. "Should fetch 'em out."

At five past seven, just as the church clock struck six, the Mercedes of Coucillor Herbert Brangle drew up. The Rolls-Royce of Councillor Wassing had already gone past on its way to turn round.

The stout, bespectacled figure of Brangle hatched from the Merc, checked the stability of its pork-pie hat, reached back inside for its walking-stick, and progressed regally towards the tree-stump. He began speaking ten yards away; he had a country auctioneer's voice reputed to have broken shop-windows adjacent to Stumpleton's open-air auction market.

"Pitched it a bit early I reckon Cassie. Be sitting watching the news still."

"They'll come. It's hardly sunk in yet. Once they realise what's at stake they'll be howling for somebody's blood."

"Ah, here come Chimble and Wassing. Not howling yet. And Mrs. Ossack; maybe she'll oblige."

"Would you do us the favour of acting as Chairman?" asked Proggle.

"Of course." As if nothing else were thinkable.

By half past seven a little knot of twelve or thirteen stood within yards of the stump and the immediate horizon was deserted. Proggle hid the loud-hailer behind her bike-wheel, as if had been brought in by mistake.

"I had anticipated the media being here," she said. "I sent them notices, then rang and reminded them this morning."

At that moment a girl reporter from a country newspaper was chatting to the W.I. secretary in the village hall; somebody had knocked down the switching notice and the girl thought she must have misunderstood her briefing. And a few miles away, on the wrong side of the Forty-foot and two miles from the nearest bridge, a man from Eastern Telly was studying a map, which bore no mention of Clagtoft.

"Anybody here possess a video camera?" said Proggle. She got two sorts of head-shakes, one from those who hadn't and one from those who didn't know what one was.

"I've got a Brownie," said Olive Ossack. "But you have to order the films special."

Brangle rapped his stick on the tree-stump. "Declare this meeting open. Having to start without the press, otherwise'll be here after dark. You know what it's about, thanks to Miss Proggle's sterling work in printing and distributing leaflets. Your village under threat. Hand over to Miss Proggle."

Proggle didn't rap on the stump, she jumped on it, towering over the audience as though the back row were fifty feet away.

Liz Otmill, standing a few feet apart from the main group, moved even further away to avoid the church spire appearing to sprout from Proggle's head. Not for the first time, Cassie reminded her of Queen Boudicca, rallying her soldiers before some great battle against the Romans. She began sketching, making Proggle more fiercely dominant, Brangle more of a pudding faced zombie. She shifted his Mercedes to appear behind him, and she put Wassing's Rolls-Royce where it contrasted sharply with Proggle's decrepit old bicycle.

They are all of this place, she thought, in their different ways. Yet in spite of Proggle's stirring address, how much fighting spirit really existed? She had read of Lords of Manors or squires or whatever shifting houses, even whole hamlets, to improve the view from their mansion windows. But those had been known, touchable enemies, in the days when it happened. It was somebody they could shout defiance and curses at. Clagtoft faced an almost intangible enemy, one they couldn't even spit at.

Glancing secretly about, she captured face after face with her pencil, trying to show something of the worry, the bafflement, the amusement she saw reflected.

Wassing looked slightly annoyed at first. So he was; Dangle, his chauffeur, had parked the Rolls with two wheels on the grass of Bosh Green, something he had strict instructions, dating from the Colonel's time, never to do. Worse, he had appeared in public without his peaked cap, no doubt considering this to be an 'out of hours' job. Now he had switched on his tinny radio and it could be heard from where Wassing stood.

But Liz the artist saw William's face change when Proggle leaped up to address the tiny assembly. Perhaps he, too, felt as a British soldier might have felt at the sight of the intrepid Queen. Here indeed might be an attraction of opposites.

Chimble, a figure she had sketched before, never appeared as anything but the slightly comic, eccentric buffoon he undoubtedly was. As her pencil evoked the detail of the bushy eyebrows and moustache, she surprised herself with an irrational feeling of affection for the man. Must be sixtyish, she thought, twenty years ahead of me. Lanky, slightly bowed, always looking as if worried over some piece of reluctant machinery. She already had one sketch of him doing something to the engine of the Boeing, as he called his Robin; almost like a doctor, alert for the symptoms in a sick child.

36

Clive Grunsell was evidently puzzled at this meeting, kept circling it and eyeing it with suspicion. Any minute now, she thought, he'll do a quick flash and then run away.

The Rev. Crispin Owery had not been a subject for Liz's pencil or brush, mainly because he was so seldom seen in the village. His parish had been extended to cover Iggleby and Squadderby, but even when his ministrations had focussed on Clagtoft alone they had been so feeble as to be unnoticeable. Their first encounter had been wrong-footed. She had asked permission to do some sketching of the church's interior and it had been granted apparently grudgingly. He had implied that people ought not to go in there for any purpose other than prayer; nettled, she had offered him the key back saying "Forget it mate, you won't want an atheist in your church then." However, she had worked in there on two wet days, only to brush with him again when he came in and made an oblique reference to her having had the lights on a long time. She immediately pressed a tenner into his clammy hand, which she had intended giving to the church anyway and told him what to do with his precious building. After that her visits had been confined to tower-climbing, for which she had borrowed Chimble's key.

Proggle was warming up. "This is a completely crazy idea. The E.S.A. already has a landing site for its shuttles, so why do they need another? And aren't there places in plenty which would do without destroying an ancient community? Why does Europe have to have a shuttle anyway? I'll tell you why; out of sheer envy of the Yanks. Just to show that Europe can go one better. Not only that but out of sheer contempt for the English, just because we dragged our feet at the beginning of the Space Agency we've got to sacrifice some of our richest agricultural land.

"It's not going to happen. They think they can ride roughshod but they'll find out they're wrong. They think they can push a few yokels out of their homes, give 'em a few pennies and some square boxes to live in somewhere else..."

"Where are we off to then?" asked Olive Ossack.

"Oh, they won't tell anybody that..."

"I'm tekking my dog wi'me. Ain't off nowhere wi'out 'im."

Another voice said, "You tek 'im Olive but leave the fleas be'ind."

When the laughter died, Proggle went on, "Believe me, this is a serious threat. Once the bureaucrats get their teeth in they don't let go easily. Let's give 'em a shock. They'll be up against Lincolnshire fen folk for the first time – the folk who produced Hereward the Wake and..."

"Hunking Slodge," said a voice, and the crowd dissolved into more laughter. This was a pop band, its leader, Jump Hunking, brother to the Clagloft's Parish Clerk. It had shot into the charts with one single then faded into obscurity. Jump became a successful record producer.

"ORDER PLEASE, ladies and gentleman," Brangle's voice thundered across Bosh Green, struck the church tower and came rolling back for those who missed it the first time. "Let Councillor Proggle have her say, then we'll open up for general discussion."

"Thank you Mr. Chairperson. What I'm proposing now is the immediate formation of a Clagtoft Fighting Force. A body of citizens who will make it clear to Europe, the world and anybody else that has any attempt to lay a finger on Clagtoft will be met by outright, unyielding resistance. Physical resistance if need be. This place hasn't stood here all these hundreds of years to be snuffed out just because some bird-brained pillock in Paris happened to draw a line through it on a map."

"Hear, hear." There was a ripple of applause.

"'As owt been said about compensation?" asked Albert Chaunter. He made a living from a few scrappy pieces of land and some rickety cottages.

"I don't know," said Proggle, "And I'm not due to find out. No compensation is going to be paid because nobody is losing anything they've got. We are here to ensure the total preservation of a fine village, one which some of us have been working to make even better. Now, I suggest we make a start by electing a leader for this Clagtoft Fighting Force. Are there any nominations?"

The only audible response was a crescendo chorus from the rooks in the churchyard trees, who were apparently holding a parallel meeting. When that died away, Bosh Green was momentarily silent.

Wassing spoke: "Councillor Miss Proggle has, I believe, summed up the situation in admirable fashion and I venture to suggest that no-one else could better serve the interests of the, ah, sort of thing she has in mind. I propose, therefore, that she be elected leader of..."

Somebody clapped loudly and the clapping spread until the whole audience was at it. It was something to do, much easier than trying to say something when you didn't have anything to say.

Brangle said, "I think it can be taken as passed by popular acclaim that Miss Proggle has been..."

"Hang on!" bawled Proggle. She had noticed that a few at the back of the meeting, considering it all over bar formalities, had begun drifting away in the direction of the Stamping Cat. A dominoes tournament was nearing a critical stage.

"Don't bother," said Brangle. "None of them'd be a deal of use anyway."

Proggle couldn't resist a final yell: "All right, you pathetic shower of spineless buggers. If you won't fight we'll do it for you."

She descended from the stump and came closer to the remaining group, as if in recognition that the Mass Meeting was now over and they had gone into committee.

"As I see my job," she said, "I shall be co-ordinating activities on four separate fronts. First, those in the form of demonstrations, meetings, marches and so on, which I propose organising myself. O.K.?"

Nods of relief all round.

"Second, there's media representation, getting our protest over to as wide a public as possible via newspapers, radio and television. Who'll take on that job?"

Glenda Hovel, hitherto silent said, "I think that's the decisive aspect of such a campaign. I still have one or two contacts from when I stood in the by-election. I'd be willing to have a go."

"Good on you, thanks," said Proggle. "Then there's parliament itself, which ought to be actively concerned without any prodding from us but with what we've got for a member..."

"Perhaps I can help," said Wassing. "I have had the pleasure of meeting our Member, Mr. Roland Clunch and I'm sure he would be only too glad to make vigorous representations on our behalf."

"See that idle sod doing owt vigorous," said Chimble in a loud mutter, "That'll be the day."

"Thank you Mr. Wassing," said Proggle. And to the meeting in general "All this, you understand, wants to begin first thing in the morning. The sooner we make ourselves heard and felt, the better chance we have of forcing them to hesitate before acting. Now, there's the fourth front, which is the European parliament. Not that that it seems to have even as much clout as our own, but..."

"I'll see what I can do in that respect," said Brangle. "I must admit, I can't even remember the name of our M.E.P., but leave it with me, I'll be on the blower in the morning."

"Good. Now there's the logistics aspect, mainly concerned with transport; getting crowds of people to where the marches and demonstrations are to be held. I suggest we do a trial protest march here at Clagtoft, then a full-scale effort through the middle of Stumpleton. That should get us on regional telly at least. After that, we'll be thinking in terms of a Westminster protest, with a petition to hand in at Number 10. After that, if the battle still isn't won, we come down to the Last Resort activities – keeping the bulldozers out by sheer physical obstruction. All this entails some engineering and I believe we have someone who can rise to the challenge. Abraham, will you take it on?"

"Eh? Oh, sorry Cassie. Wool-gathering as usual. Engineering, oh, aye. Owt of that nature. Just tell us what's needed..." The sun had fallen bellow the churchyard tree; the rooks were still arguing hammer and tongs, but the humans decided to call it a day after first arranging to have their next meeting in the village hall.

Brangle declared the meeting closed, shouldered his walking stick and aimed himself at his Mercedes. The Rev. Owery said, "Goodnight all and may God lend you strength in your endeavours."

Chimble responded, "Ah bloody men."

As Liz went out on to Main Road she heard Wassing telling Dangle to take the Rolls home as he intended to walk. She was puzzled; it was a common belief in the village that Wassings were never seen walking. The Rolls had been part of the local scene since 1932, as much part of the place as the church, the windmill tower and the Ebenezer Chapel. Liz walked a few paces then stopped and looked back.

Proggle had not left Bosh Green; she still stood near the tree-stump, holding her bike handlebar in one hand and the loud-hailer in the other. Then, apparently sure that all had departed, she began walking slowly in the dusk in the opposite direction towards Cut-throat Paddock.

Liz shrugged and began making her own way. She rounded the bend into Stumpleton Road and as she passed the gap between the almshouses and Ketchup Terrace, glanced across and saw that a second figure was now crossing Cut-throat Paddock in the same direction as Proggle.

# Chapter Five

Before the village was threatened with extinction, life in Clagtoft was as hectic as in most rural communities. The pace was governed by the temperamental seasons and by the persistent refusal of crops to become ready for harvesting at a time to suit the grower's convenience. The weather never favoured human activity; if it was dry it was too cold and as it warmed up it was too wet. The "Wonder of Christmas", to most people a celebratory festival, was to a fen farmer a time of stunned amazement that he had survived another year without a major catastrophe.

Fred Cletch had inherited Woad Farm, a one hundred per cent arable business, from his father. Unlike most sons of farmers he had not at first worked on the family farm; his father had a notion that relations should not become each other's employers. Fred had gone to Louth in the north of the country and worked on a mixed farm. When the old man became too ill to cope, he came back to take over, bringing his wife and family.

Some of the land Fred farmed belonged to the Wassing estate and was rented through a Stumpleton solicitor. William deMoundford Wassing, whose living depended on the income from the estate, was in trouble. His father's investments in other directions had not been updated with the changing times and were much less productive than in the days when the Rolls was bought. The Manor House showed distinct signs of crumbling into dust. William's reaction to the gathering darkness around his financial affairs was to instruct his solicitors, Pillage and Rumpus, to raise the rents paid by farmers.

Just before the demolition news hit Clagtoft, Fred Cletch had received his notice of the increase. He explained the situation to his wife. "Old Wassing's in dead trouble, that's common knowledge. Dangle and old Henrietta are both several weeks behind in wages

42

and one of his chimney-stacks is threatening to come down through the roof and get into the bed wi' him."

"Silly old devil ought to sell out and buy a smaller place."

"That he'll never do. Wouldn't be Lord of the Manor any longer. But I reckon this letter might do us a bit of good in the long run. It gives me an idea. We've had several good years on the trot and I reckon it'd be a good plan to buy some of the land off him. That'd give him enough for urgent repairs and once I'd paid off the loan it'd be ours rent-free."

"Mmm. I'll leave that to you. Can't help thinking, it would leave him with less income in the long run."

"Why should we worry? Never done a hand's turn of work in his life, what right has he to live on the work I do? I'll make an offer for them two fields off Squadderby Road."

So Fred had talked the matter over with his banker, though not committing himself to anything yet. He had looked back at the prices made in recent land sales, phoned a friend for advice, then put in what he considered a shrewd offer to Pillage and Rumpus.

There the matter stood when the news broke about the hare-brained scheme of the European Space Agency. Like many Clagtoftians, Fred believed that nothing much would really happen. That people like Proggle would do their thing, create a fuss, get their pictures in the papers and then the whole affair would die as natural a death as Stumpleton F.C.'s bid for the F.A. Cup a few years back.

Then one morning he opened his newspaper and saw something, which gave him second thoughts. "Shuttles over East Anglia," said the headline. It went on: "When Herpes 22, the new Space Vehicle, begins operating, the flight-path of its landing run will be from south-east to north-west over Suffolk and Norfolk. Much of it is open countryside but concern is being expressed over urban clusters like Ipswich, Bury St. Edmunds and King's Lynn, which lie under the flight-path. The actual landing strip is an open fen-country in Lincolnshire with only tiny hamlet of Clagtoft to be cleared away."

"Tiny hamlet?" roared Fred. "Makes it sound like half a dozen houses. Why don't the silly devils lift their arses off them office chairs and look at the place, see what they're doing?"

"Maybe we should have gone to Proggle's meeting after all," said Mrs. Cletch. "They reckon she's getting protest marches up. Doing one in the village first, then another in town."

Fred put his paper down. "Tek more than marching to stop owt like that. Remember that by-pass business, they went up trees and down rabbit-holes? They still got the road built in the end."

"Right. What's your remedy then?"

"Oil."

She stared at him for a second, then remembered, and laughed.

A few years before, Clagtoft Drain and its tributary Glugwell Creek had been seen to have a film of oil on them. The matter had been reported to the parish Council. They in turn had reported it to the Drainage Authority who had thanked them and asked them to keep an eye on it.

The oil persisted. Even after a long rainy spell it was still there. At a meeting of the Council a letter was read from Mr. Albert Chaunter, suggesting that a sample of the oil should be sent for analysis, as he was convinced that there were rich deposits under the village.

Chimble said it was perfectly true; long before they got on to North Sea oil, the government had come to this area in wartime and put a row of them nodding donkeys across Sid Sneck's eighteen-acre. They wouldn't go to that expense for nowt.

Councillors Chimble and Miss Proggle volunteered to trace the slick to its origin and get a sample to send away for analysis. "If it looks to be good stuff," said Chimble, "They'll be down on Clagtoft like a ton o' bricks. Everybody as owns a plot of land'll be a millionaire. They'll want to build a refinery on the council allotments, save running lorries to Immingham."

The two councillors set out on a warm afternoon and found a place along Snogging Lane where the concentration of oil seemed strongest. Proggle had brought an empty sauce bottle and attempted to reach down to the drain to skim a sample off the surface. Chimble held one of her hands as she bent over but his foot slipped, she overbalanced, lost her hold on his hand and fell full length into the water.

When she scrambled out she expressed a brief but emphatic opinion on the intelligence and probable parentage of Abraham Chimble. Then she took off her dress and handed it to him saying that if he still wanted a sample he could wring one out of it. She turned and walked rapidly back to the village in her underwear, Chimble limping goutily along behind with the dripping dress.

"Nothing more was done about it," Fred Cletch told his wife. "But there are oil-wells on the mainland, there's one near Lincoln. And this could be a way of getting the scheme delayed at least while somebody looks into it. I'll ring Brangle, see if he can get owt moving."

Brangle remembered the oil business, chiefly because of a pleasant recollection of having stood in the vicarage garden talking to the vicar one afternoon and seeing the half-clad Proggle sail serenely by. And Chimble carrying her dress, slinking into the post office, looking furtively over his shoulder.

"But you're a day or two late with the idea Fred. We're on to oil already. I've been on to our Euro M.P., and believe it or not he knew nothing about the shuttle business until I told him. Doesn't that say something about this Europe nonsense? Sooner we're out of it all the better, if you ask me. However…"

"What's the next stage then? I mean, over the oil."

"This Euro M.P. bloke… got his name down somewhere… he's got a contact in one of the oil companies, and he's suggesting they send a geologist out, see if they can concoct some sort of expert opinion to put to the Public Inquiry."

"Public Inquiry? Hadn't heard about that one."

"Oh, aye. It's not on yet but it's in the air. Wassing contacted Clunch, the Westminster M.P., got him interested. Hadn't realised it was happening on his patch till William told him. He says a Public Inquiry is our best way of showing people and the agriculture minister…"

"Reckon I've got a good big slice of the farmland concerned. There's other farmers of course; Chaunter, Sneck, Frank Wowser."

"Ah – one thing Fred, does some of your land go as far as Slaumy Gowt?"

"Includes it."

"Does it, begow! Now that could be important."

"There's little or no value there. It's all wetland. Overgrown raw fen."

"That's just it! Exactly what these environment people are keen on. Any wildlife in there – endangered species, rare plants or even trees, they'll come down on our side in the inquiry."

"Don't know about rare. There's some sodding great thistles in there, as I know to my cost. Spend a fortune spraying."

"Don't buy any more for a while. Let it have its head until all this blows over. I've asked Glenda Hovel to look down there – hope it's O.K. with you – see if she can spot any rare plants."

"Far as I'm concerned she can have it. Grow her crackpot remedies in it if she likes. Tell you another thing; it's slow-running water in there, and I reckon I've seen a badger."

"Great stuff. I'll tell Glenda to take a camera."

* * *

Proggle was standing at the edge of Gandle's Pit, gazing with awe into its murky water.

"Ain't no bottom to it y'know. Anybody as tumbles in the middle, they just keep on going down." Olive Ossack was explaining its significance. It was a well-known local landmark, reputedly never known to have dried up, even in the driest of summers. It possessed the obligatory ghost, in this case the well-known Black Dog. Its water was said to rise and fall with the tide, though the sea was more than ten miles away.

Proggle listened patiently to Olive's stories, though as a native of the village she had heard them all before. "What I want to know about is them wanting to turn Clagtoft into another Woodhall Spa."

Woodhall was a village north of Clagtoft, which had indeed been turned into a prosperous spa town because of the healing properties of the water found when somebody made a bore in search of coal. The story was that the men employed on the boring liked the work so much that they brought lumps of coal in their pockets to drop down the hole when the boss wasn't looking, encouraging him to dig deeper and keep their jobs going. In the end, it was the special water which brought prosperity.

"It was true all right," said Olive. "Off to call it Clagtoft Spa they was. I ought to know. It was my Auntie Meg as got cures and started it all off."

"What did the water cure?"

"Wasn't the watter, it was the mud. That Charlie Culvert as used to run the bus, 'im and 'is missis used to fill jars with it, had market stalls all ower Lincolnshire down to King's Lynn selling it. 'Culvert's Healing Mud' they had on it, fancy printed labels. All they did was fetch bucketfuls from here. Med no end of money the old bugger did.

46

And when Cletch, Fred's dad, stopped 'em coming here they used to fetch mud off the salt marshes, put the same labels on."

"What was Auntie Meg's complaint?"

"Screws. Had 'em something chronic. Walking wi' two sticks for years she'd bin. Traipsing to a rheumatic clinic but they couldn't cure her any more than they could fly. It wasn't till she fell in Gandle's Pit…"

Proggle couldn't avoid laughing. "Sorry. I shouldn't laugh about it. How did she fall in?"

"Brought 'er granddaughter to git some struts in a jam-jar. Sluthered on the mud and went down. Grabbed a lump o' gress to keep hersen out the middle. End up lolloped all ower wi' mud, struggling. Reckoned she'd brock her ankle, so they left her laid out in it while they fetched an ambulance. Mud up to her arse she was while they got her to Stumpleton. Then it was nowt, onny a sprain. Telled her to try her weight on it and there she was walking about. 'Ay up' she says. 'I can walk wi' out me sticks! Must be that mud!'"

"Who had the Clagtoft Spa idea?" asked Proggle.

"The Council I reckon. That was when owd Charlie Culvert latched on to it, crafty sod. Left ower three thousand when he died and made most it out o' Gandle's Pit."

"Don't know whether we can use mud in the campaign," said Proggle. "Other than for throwing. Anyway, I'll see if I can trace this clinic and find out whether they got it analysed."

\* \* \*

As Community Archaeologist, Violet Wask was aware that the threat to Clagtoft rendered her examination of it more urgent and she focussed on the Manor House as a place of primary importance. She had arranged by telephone to call in the morning and sat chatting to Wassing in his study for some time.

She was surprised to find him somewhat less than knowledgeable about the history of the place; he was fiercely voluble about its past and present importance but when she asked specific questions such as the date of its construction or whether there had been a previous house on the site, he evasively failed to answer. However, he promised that she could have access to the family papers, which his father had lodged with the family solicitors, Pillage

47

and Rumpus. He had never looked at them himself. Meanwhile, perhaps she would like to look around outside?

When Dangle was originally appointed, his title was 'chauffeur and gardener'. He chauffed reasonably well but as a gardener he was a distinct no-starter. In the days when the Colonel provided a sit-on mower the lawns got cut at high speed and with unnecessary frequency because Dangle enjoyed zooming around on it. Inevitably the machine collapsed through sheer exhaustion and it happened at a time when the Wassing fortunes were at a low ebb. Its replacement was a walk-behind, and as walking was the one pursuit Dangle hated with deep Italian fervour, the lawns became lucky to get trimmed twice in a season.

"Quite a romantic-looking garden." remarked Violet.

"Er, yes, isn't it?" said William, not sure what she meant.

It was a tangled mass of weeds, overgrown shrubs and the remains of trees, which had either been felled or had fallen; somebody had begun the task of sawing them into manageable logs.

"I have a gardener," said William. "But sadly he's getting rather old and unable to cope. I suppose he ought to retire but he's been here so long…"

"Was that him I saw when I came in? I noticed he said 'buono morning' which is half Italian."

"He is, I regret, all Italian. Came after the war as a chauffeur and gardener and despite all my efforts he has still not mastered our language."

They followed a path through to the end of the garden, where it met the bank of Clagtoft Drain. Violet immediately climbed to the top of the bank, casting her archaeologist's eye around… " Any idea what that might be?" It was a place where the bank had evidently been altered and on the water side there were some heavy, evidently quite old, timbers.

William came up and looked. "I really don't know. Perhaps somebody had a boat tied up here…"

Violet went down perilously close to the water, peering at the structure more closely.

"I played in this garden as a child but never came up here. Perhaps my parents warned me…"

48

She had come up the bank again and was looking closely at the garden. She pointed. "Do you get flooded along there?"

"Er, it's always a bit soggy. Come to think of it, yes, in winter especially."

"I believe what you have here is the remains of a moat."

"A moat? Good Lord! Do you really think so?"

"Wouldn't be too unusual, given the apparent age of the site, and the fact that it's called a Manor. Was there a large hall inside, since split into several rooms?"

"I remember the Colonel saying that the inside had been drastically altered at some stage."

"Is there a clear roof-space above the bedroom ceilings?"

He stared at her blankly. He was out of his depth with this knowledgeable slip of a girl. "There's a loft of some sort up there but I've never seen into it."

She wanted to potter around the garden looking for more traces of the moat so he left her to do her own thing and went back into the house.

As soon as he had vanished Dangle appeared. "I noticed you have spotted the moat," he said.

"Oh! You do speak English then. Somebody told me…"

A toothless smile lit up the wrinkled face. "Sometimes it is better if people don't know I speak English. In the village they talk about me as if I am not there. If they ask of me anything I answer Italian…" he laughed. "They don't know what I am calling them."

She decided she liked him. "I'll keep your secret. But why did you trust me with it?"

"I heard about you, and why you are at Clagtoft for a short time…" he waved an arm around. "You are the first person taking interest in the history. You are right, it was a moated manor. On the bank was the sluice gate to fill the moat from the Drain."

"Have you seen the family papers?"

"No, no, no. These are not for a chauffeur to see. Mostly from the library in Stumpleton. When we had a bus service I went to spend my days off in there looking at the history for these villages. In my room I have notebooks filled up."

"I'm surprised Mr. Wassing knows so little about it."

He shook his head sadly. "Like so many from university, he thinks education stops then…"

49

"Hang on," laughed Violet, "I've just come from university."

"Ah, but you are intelligent, and... curious, is it? And beautiful."

"Thank you. I wonder – would you be kind enough to show me your notebooks?"

She found that Dangle lived in his bachelor bed-sit, created by himself, in the upper floor of the coach-house, which had been a granary. The 1932 Rolls-Royce, the only car ever owned by the Wassings was housed immediately below him. Before the car came they had travelled by horse-drawn coach or gig.

The previous chauffeur-gardener had been the husband of Henrietta Hammel and the couple had lived in the main house. Dan Hammel had gone into the army in 1943 and got himself killed; the Colonel had driven himself, somewhat erratically, for several years. When Dangle came he was offered a small bedroom inside the house but he quickly abandoned it and made it understood that he preferred to doss down in the granary. He was supposed to eat in the kitchen with Mrs. Hammel but he invariably collected his meal and carried it across the yard to his own lair. Mrs. Hammel, who "couldn't stand the sight of that there wop", went along with the arrangement.

"I'll fetch the notebooks for you," said Dangle. "I dare not take you up there. Wassing watches like a hawk. Also does Hammel."

When he brought them she promised to tell him all her own discoveries in the Clagtoft area. They had been talking out of sight of the house but as soon as Violet approached it alone, Wassing came bustling out.

"I say, Miss... er, d'you think it would be possible for my moat to be reconstructed?"

She almost laughed but realised in time that he was quite serious. "It would certainly be possible. But somewhat expensive I would guess. Have to be piped under the drive I suppose, unless you intend having a drawbridge."

"Why not? Dammit, we are fighting to keep these nameless vandals from destroying the village. What would be wrong with using ancient methods like... like portcullises and..."

"Boiling oil?"

"Why not?"

"You might run into difficulties with the planning department."

"I would do it first then argue after. At least it would demonstrate my determination to keep what is lawfully mine."

As she turned away a thought occurred to her. "Perhaps Mr. Chimble could help. He's got masses of ancient machinery. Might be something there for digging moats."

"Brilliant idea, thank you. I'll telephone him right away."

* * *

Chimble and Proggle were together in the post office when the call came from Wassing. "I believe I have the very thing for that job," said Abraham. "It was left behind here when I took over. A dragline excavator, originally oil-engined but I spent most o' last winter converting 'er to steam. I could do your job as a test run."

He put the phone down and rubbed his hands. "Wassing wants a moat dug around the Manor House."

"Good for him. And we may need such a machine for other things, if it works." said Proggle.

"Course it'll work. Had it going on compressed air; all it needs is boiler and firebox. What else wants doing?"

She stood for dramatic emphasis. "If all else fails and we are forced to take physical action to stop the destroyers moving in, I envisage Clagtoft in the state of total siege. All the ways leading in blocked by massive earthen barriers. The Clagtoft Fighting Force, armed to the teeth, waiting to repel anybody attempting to gain entry."

"Have to get Dangle enlisted. He was a soldier."

"An Italian soldier. They were on the losing side."

"Have to get stocked up wi' grub an' all. I'll measure up yon shed, see how many tins of bairked beans it'll tek."

"What I see is Clagtoft gone back to a time when it was self-sufficient. Killing our own pigs, keeping our own cows and chickens…"

# Chapter Six

The bar of the Stamping Cat had been specially re-arranged for the Press Conference. Two tables had been put together under the dartboard and behind them sat Cassanda Proggle (centre), flanked by William deMondford Wassing and Herbert Brangle on one side with Glenda Hovel and Abraham Chimble on the other. Each sat behind a neatly-printed name-card.

Facing the table were ten chairs for the Press. They were empty.

"I told 'em all seven o'clock," said Glenda. "Can't understand what's keeping 'em."

"Might be some world-shattering story on the go," said Chimble. "World War broke out, royal engagement, owt of that sort."

Jack Grunsell appeared behind the counter. "Can I get anybody a drink?"

Brangle said, "I think we'd prefer to keep it dry till they arrive."

Jack came out and sat on one of the Press seats.

"That's a Press seat," said Proggle.

"I am Press," answered Jack. "Stumpleton Chronicle and Advertiser, village correspondent for Clagtoft <u>and</u> Iggleby."

The door opened and Liz Otmill came in beaming. "Your young flasher's at work out there," she said to Jack. "I pointed my camera at him but he jumped over the churchyard wall when he saw it. Seems to be shy."

Jack went out. Liz surveyed the line of dignitaries. "Looks like an industrial tribunal. Can I have a photograph please?"

Might as well," said Proggle. "Doesn't look as if the Sun's coming out. Or even Eastern Telly. They told me they sent somebody out for the mass meeting and he couldn't find Clagtoft. We're on the map, aren't we?"

"On some but not on others," said Brangle. "I wrote very sharply to the A.A. about it once. Next one they issued they put us in but I'm damned if they hadn't got us six mile yon side of Dogstead."

The door opened again and a girl came in. "This the Shuttle Protest thing? Is? Am I too late? Betty Gawster, Fenland Voice."

"You're welcome Betty. Have a seat. The others got held up somewhere so you've got us to yourself at the moment. As you probably know, the people of this village are braced to fight against losing it to this daft scheme for landing space..."

"Anybody been evicted yet?"

"No, but we don't intend..."

"Any eviction notices served?"

"If we waited till things got that far..."

"Right. Are you lobbying parliament? Getting a petition up? Building tree-houses, anything of that nature?"

"We're organising two protest marches."

"Somebody in the village told me they can't do it round here because it's where King John's treasure is buried. Anything been found?"

Chimble said, "I dug up a 1793 penny last year when I was planting marigolds."

Betty snapped her notebook shut. "Well, thanks everyone. You've been most helpful. I must push off now; I've still got a funeral and a snooker final to do. Best of luck with your campaign." She went.

They sat uneasily for another twenty minutes then Brangle said, "Don't know about anyone else but I'm thirsty."

When all were served, Proggle said, "This is disappointing but I'm not letting it get me down. While we're still together I suggest we knock up a Press Statement, put in all the things we wanted to say, and send copies out to all the media."

"Actually," said Wassing, "If the Press had turned up – the proper Press – I was ready to tell that young lady but she hurried off..."

"Tell us then," said Proggle.

"This afternoon, I took a telephone call at the Manor House. The caller was the Space Commissioner at the European Space Agency. He was speaking in English with a strong foreign accent but I could tell every word he said. He was speaking from Headquarters, he said, and had to tell me that the demolition of Clagtoft was to begin

53

with the oldest buildings. I was advised to begin getting my 'sticks' together – some European term, I suppose – ready to move out of the Manor House at a moment's notice. Temporary accommodation would be provided in Stumpleton. He mentioned something, an address. Was it Camilla Close?"

"That's right," said Chimble. "Old folks' bungalows, down Shanghai district."

Wassing glared at him. "This would only be for a short time, until something more fitting could be found for me elsewhere. I was about to tell him of the Old Rectory at Dogstead but he rang off."

There was an uneasy silence. They glanced at each other, wondering who was going to break down first into laughter. Glenda said, "Did you try 1471?"

"What do you mean?"

"The code for finding out where the call came from."

"I know where it came from. The Space Commissioner."

Everybody left it to everybody else and nobody did it. They were all agog to know who made the call.

"Are you actually packing, ready to move?" asked Brangle.

"Certainly not," said Wassing indignantly. "We are all fighting to keep Clagtoft, are we not? I feel a certain pride in having been singled out for the first definite attack and I intend displaying the utmost courage in defiance."

"Are you off to ring 'em back and tell 'em bollocks?" asked Jack.

Wassing ignored him. "The Manor House was, in medieval times, defended from marauders by a moat which surrounded it. I have engaged my colleague here, Councillor Chimble, to reconstruct the moat with one of his machines. When that work is completed I shall decide on the possible construction of a drawbridge. Possibly with a portcullis."

"Will it all be done in time?" asked Proggle.

"One can only hope. Meantime, you may be assured that if any person resembling a European approaches the Manor House, he will be met by a hail of bullets from an upper window."

An uneasy silence, then Brangle turned to Chmble. "Are you sure it'll work on steam?"

"For almost any mechanical purpose, Stearm beats owt else. It's onny a matter of tonning a shaft. Not like your fussy little car engines, you don't need a gearbox. Full power at low speed."

"Why isn't more of it used?"

"Git your 'ands mucky, that's why," replied Chimble. "Don't just press a button and sit back – 'ave to think about what you're doing. That's the painful bit for most folks nowadays, thinking…"

Wassing excused himself and left early because he had so much to do and as soon as the door closed they all fell about laughing and guessing who had made the phone call.

Clive, the flasher? No, he didn't know enough. Fred Cletch, one of Wassing's tenants? George Hunking, the parish Clerk? Most of those present favoured Harry Gozzard, the gangmaster. It was rumoured that he had done some tree-felling work at the Manor House and never got paid for it.

Before they broke up, however, Gozzard came in. As he walked to the bar he sensed a sudden silence. "What's up? All holding yer breath? Somebody dropped one?"

Glenda said, "Harry, can you imitate foreign accents?"

He narrowed his eyes at her. "What sort of foreign accents?"

"Any. French if you like." He shook his head. "Nah. Too Lincolnshire, me. Why? Somebody getting a play up? Fawlty Towers or summat?"

They told him about Wassing's phone call and he was highly amused. "Can't somebody follow up wi' another? Tell him to start knocking it down hissen?"

There was a general agreement that it would be sufficient fun to watch the medieval defences coming into being and Brangle speculated on possible battles with the Planning Department and with the Drainage Authority, who expected to be asked for permission to extract water from their drains.

"Ask me owt," said Gozzard, "They're all a load o' nut-cases down there at the Manor House. That there Iti, supposed to be gardener, nivver tonns a hand in the garden. And that ole gel as is housekeeper – is she married?"

"Widow," said Chimble. Her husband was killed in the war. Dangle took his job."

"Has she got a son as lives round here?"

"No. she had a kid but it died young. Her old man was away when it was born, then he nivver came back either."

"Strange that," said Harry. "I did some tree-wock for Wassing and he still owes me for it. So I'm claiming the logs as mine. Went down to fetch a van-load and that owd gel came out and ses, 'I thought for a minute you was Laurence'. I ast her who Laurence was and she ses 'My son Laurence.'"

Proggle said, "She must be going doolally. I've known her all my life and I've never heard of a son, Laurence or otherwise. Perhaps that's what she called the kid that died. Common delusion among the senile that. Thinking the kids they lost are still around..."

"While we're still together," said Brangle, "A few of us that's concerned with the Save Clagtoft! Campaign..."

"D'you want me out the road?" asked Harry.

"No, of course not. It's your concern just as much as anybody else's. The vicar asked me today whether, in view of the serious situation, he ought to go ahead with his annual Garden Fete."

"I think he should," said Glenda. "Anything that's normal should go ahead as if nothing's happened. As if nothing's going to happen. Once we admit that our normal way of life has been interrupted, we're halfway to losing the battle."

"Tell the vicar to mek it the biggest ever," said Chimble. "Tel him to cock a bloody great ecclesiastical snook at Brussels. Invite all them Euro-fanatics to it."

"Another thing" said Proggle. "We need funds for our campaign, even more urgently than the vicar does for his wheezy organ. Let's open it out into Bosh Green and have a car-boot sale at the same time."

"Last orders please," said Jack Grunsell. "To make it a real good do, you want the old Clagtoft Silver Band playing selections. Village dos is nivver owt wi'out a band."

"Brilliant," said Proggle. "I'll see if I can rake 'em out and we'll have 'em on the protest march as well."

Chimble said, "Playing 'Colonel Bogey', so we can all sing to it. Bollocks! And the same to you... oh, sorry Miss Otmill. forgot you was still here."

"Have another beer Abe. We'll make it an operatic duet. They come in pairs anyway."

* * *

The fenland had a strong fraternity of car-booters; people who habitually loaded up, not mere boot, but trailers, vans and in some

56

cases small lorries, and travelled over a wide radius to where the best pickings were likely to be. They knew each other, compared notes about the good, bad and indifferent venues and phoned each other with news of forthcoming events. They made themselves some useful pocket-money, provided a valuable service to the low-paid and unemployed who bought from them and were a source of niggling worry to a few "static" traders who imagined themselves being cheated.

Clagtoft didn't get many boot-sales but when one came round it did very well, booters from as distant as twenty miles alerting each other to get their pitches booked. Chimble was taking the bookings and three days before the event he told Proggle he already had 28 pitches booked at £3 a time. "There'll be a few more yet," he said. "Plus them as allus turns up on the day and pay a fiver. We'll be well over a ton."

The day turned out fine and warm and the Rev. Crispin Owery could scarcely believe his eyes when he saw the crowds swarming into the village. His annual garden fete, always held in his own garden, seldom attracted more than twenty-five or thirty people. Realising that the boot-sale was the major attraction, he got Tom Chaunter to dismantle a bit of the fencing between his garden and Bosh Green, in the hope that people would see his own little effort and wander through.

Two of the car-boot fraternity were sons of Big Rube of Duchess of York Drive. The boys now had their own partners and families, all living by land-work. They were popular among the regular stall-holders. One of the Fasswelts specialised in furniture and had a heavy trailer-load of choice pieces labelled "as new" in large letters, the labels covering the worst of the defects. Or in some cases "genuine antique", meaning obviously old and decrepit.

The second Fasswelt, more of a general dealer, had positioned his stall in a corner of Bosh Green, adjacent to a 'secret' entry into the vicarage garden – an entry known to most Clagtoft schoolboys through the ages, but not to the vicar.

When the Rev. Owery did his dutiful round of the boot-sale, he failed to recognise the Fasswelt boys as former parishioners. They both called him 'rev' and both earnestly pressed him to buy something.

"How about a dozen good healthy tomato plants rev? Top-class grub toms are. Keep yer on the run."

"No, no, thank you."

"Garden tools? Good petrol-driven lawn-mower? Let yer have this one cheap – only twenty quid."

"Oh, quite reasonable I'm sure. But I already have a similar one."

Clive Grunsell seemed bewildered by the large crowd milling around Bosh Green. For once neglecting to strum, yodel or dance, he ambled around trying to take it all in. One stall-holder had a radio playing and for a few minutes Clive gave the hidden musicians a helping hand with his guitar. It brought a little applause, but his heart wasn't in it and he resumed his wandering and gaping.

Wassing arrived in his conspicuous brown Rolls, saw the mass of common vehicles thronging the roads and open spaces and instructed Dangle to park in Chimble's yard alongside the Robin and the Sentinel. In that company the Rolls looked perfectly at home. Henrietta Hammel had come too, William always insisting on a full supporting cast for village events.

The Save Clagtoft! Campaign had it's own stall, a table borrowed from the village hall and set out mainly with Proggle's explanations of what the affair was in aid of, spelled out in block capitals on torn-open corn flakes packets. In case anybody couldn't read, a real possibility in Clagtoft, she repeated the explanations every ten minutes, speaking in block capitals through her loud-hailer. Glenda Hovel had bagged a space on the stall and was selling her herbal remedies, also with written explanations. One was headed "Why buy expensive Viagra?"

Occasionally riding the waves of the hubbub could be heard a boom from Herbert Brangle or an ear-splitting passing comment from The Mouth. "Pity they couldn't 'ave got the Clagtoft Band," said Olive. "Allus ed the band they did, when it was Clagtoft Show."

"We're hoping to get them on our protest marches," Proggle told her.

"Ah. Last I heard there was two trombones and two drummers. And them's mebbe too old for marching."

Abe Chimble heard what was said. "Needn't bother about that. Provide a mobile banstand for 'em to play on. Farm cart or summat. Better still, they could sit on the back o' Diana."

"Wouldn't the noise drown 'em out?"

58

"Meks less noise than a diesel. Just a gentle puffing. They could keep time by it."

Liz Otmill stood apart and watched the bright swirl of Clagtoft at leisure. She had begun sketching but there was too much change and movement, so she resorted to the camera. If the village was to be lost, she would at least have something of its people on record. Wonder if they would all stand still for a group photograph if Proggle asked on her machine? Maybe not; they wouldn't understand what she was saying. She kept repeating her message of doom but they continued their scrutiny of incredible bargains totally undisturbed.

She went to where the vicar had effected an entry into his garden fete. This was a pitiful remnant of what car boot sales had elbowed out, just as, a hundred years before, the rumbustious village feast days had been sanitised into staid churchy functions by pious Victorian vicars. Owery stood forlornly alone on his lawn, behind him the Jumble stall, the Cake stall and the Tea stall, each with its elderly helper. She felt a twinge of pity for him and brought a cup of tea. He told her that the Organ Fund had so far been enriched by £3.55 – half of what it had taken last year.

"Hardly enough to get one note mended I imagine," said Liz and doubled it in return for a snapshot of him and his helpers. She couldn't resist a final dig: "Perhaps it'll be working in time for a grand farewell service, just before the bulldozers arrive and reduce it to rubble."

His podgy face dropped and fear shone from his piggy eyes. "Do you think it's really going to happen?"

"Who knows? History marches on and some people inevitably get trampled underfoot." She took another photo of him, looking pathetic in his off-duty tweed jacket, his badge of office pinned to his shirt-front.

Henrietta Hammel came into the garden, almost running. "Vicar! He's come back! Isn't it wonderful? I knew he would come back to Clagtoft!"

Owery almost visibly wilted under the heat of her excitement.

"That, I… I am sure is a b.blessing for you dear lady. Who has come back did you say?"

"My boy. My Laurence. He's there." She pointed through the gap in the fence but all Liz could see was the drooping form of Clive,

59

mouth open, gazing, hand absently stroking across the guitar-strings.

"Must have got lost in the crowd," said Liz, wondering.

"Bring him in when you find him," said Owery. "Let him see our garden fete as well." He knew nothing of Hammel's loss of son and husband, nothing of her impending descent into senility.

Liz watched Hammel go back through the gap. Clive saw her approaching and quickly moved away. She realised what was happening and hurried after the old woman. Then checked herself. Ever since coming to Clagtoft she had avoided any close involvement. Had wanted to stand aside from their lives to watch and understand, to try to express her understanding through her pictures.

Hammel had Clive by the arm now and was parading him along the line of the stalls, presenting him proudly to astonished people who knew perfectly well who he was. "My Laurence has come back, after all these years. Off to stop in Clagtoft now, ain't you duck?"

When they got to her employer, Wassing had somehow become his own father. "Colonel, can I bring Laurence back to the house when we go? He's been gone so long, he'll hardly remember the place."

William desperately thrashed around for something to say and while he was still mumbling about it Clive broke lose and tore across in the direction of Cut-throat Paddock, yodelling with every ounce of power his lungs could provide.

* * *

Later that evening, when his little band of helpers had gone home, the Rev. Owery counted the takings of his annual garden fete. £8.23. It would have been rather more except that some of the coins from the tea-stall turned out to be pesetas. He took out the file and neatly entered the latest amount at the bottom of the list. In nine years of painstaking fund-raising the total now stood at £43.18. Also in the file was the letter from the firm specialising in organ repairs; they had been to inspect the Clagtoft instrument and had listed its defects. Their estimate of the cost or repairing it, now nearly ten years old, was £1,450.

With a weary sigh, he went back into the garden. The last of the stallholders had gone and Bosh Green was empty except for the vast amount of litter. If a wind sprang up, no doubt some would find its way through into his garden.

He leaned the piece of loose fencing back into place, although knowing it would take more than that to fool Clagtoft children. He crossed to his garden shed to fetch his watering-can; his tomato-plants would need a soaking after such a hot day. The can was not there. The shed was quite empty. No garden tools, no lawn-mower. Then he remembered, and went along to his greenhouse. No tomato-plants either.

# Chapter Seven

On the way back to the Manor House, Hammel was still babbling about her 'discovery' that her son Laurence had miraculously appeared in the village. Being a servant she naturally sat in the front seat of the Rolls but though the glass partition shielded Wassing from most of it, he guessed what she was on about. He was perplexed. Had he missed out on something in her history? He remembered having been told about her marriage and of her loss of both baby and husband in a short space of time; how on earth could she imagine, this long after, that a teenage village boy could be the same?

Impending senility was the only explanation, a forbidding possibility from which he cravenly shrank. When Dangle stopped the car at the front door, he opened the sliding partition before getting down and said, "Don't worry too much Mrs. Hammel. I'm sure everything will come right in the end." Both servants looked blank, as if even more senility threatened behind them.

As at all stressful times, William retired to his study. The threat to the village was bad enough; the more immediate and urgent assault by telephone on the Manor House had multiplied his anxiety. He wondered if he would ever sleep again. Brangle had advised him years ago to find Hammel a place to live out her retirement but nothing had been done. He slumped at his writing –desk for half an hour, looking miserably out at the wilderness of the garden.

Then his eye caught a folder at the back of the desk. It was labelled simply 'Claud'. He pulled it across and opened it. Claud Hereward Wassing was his younger brother who had left home quite suddenly at the age of 21. His parents had drawn an immediate veil over his existence and it had taken several years and the death of both their parents before William learned the story. The daughter of the Lord of a nearby Manor had somehow become pregnant by

Claud and he could not marry her because she was already married. As her husband was big and strong, Claud took the Wassing way out. He scarpered. Where to, William knew not for a long time. Then a letter had arrived from New Zealand. He had taken £500 and a steamer ticket given him by the Colonel, bought a partnership in a small dairy business and was doing very well thank you.

A scrappy correspondence had gone on between the brothers, the average wait for a reply often taking as long as two years. It was William's turn to write and he had begun the task several weeks ago. He read through what he had already written:

"Dear Claud, Thanks for your kind enquiry; yes, I am still a single person and look like remaining so for the foreseeable future. As for the ideas of marrying a housekeeper – well! Dear Hammel is still with me, getting a wee bit feeble now but where else could she go? The old Manor House has given her shelter for all these years and I think it fitting that it should continue to do so for as long as she needs it. Besides, one hears such frightening tales of employers having to pay out ludicrous sums for wrongful dismissal of staff.

Yes, there is one dear lady in Clagtoft whom I admire greatly and who undoubtedly would lend memorable distinction to the status of Mistress of Clagtoft Manor. She may well, in the fullness of time, find herself confronted with an opportunity to become that... her name is Cassandra, which I looked up and found that it means 'helper of men'.

She does sterling work in the village, to which she has returned after an absence on political work in London and elsewhere. She serves on the Parish Council, bringing to it a strong sense of urgency and purpose.

Unfortunately I have had little opportunity to plead my suit with her; she lives in Duchess of York Drive (mentioned in earlier letters), so you will understand that I am unable to call on her openly. However, she has on one or two occasions encouraged me to approach (in darkness, which I find incredibly exciting) via Cut-throat Paddock, where we used to play as boys, and enter via her back garden. The servants have been told that I go out to study astronomy. There we have sat, happily chatting and sipping cocoa, until well after midnight! I will let you know of developments, if any.

Plans for a Greater Clagtoft are still in the air and I hear that a scale model of the new shopping precinct, scheduled for the Piggery

Lane area, will be presented shortly to a meeting of the Council. The pond (where you blew up a frog, remember?) will be magically transformed into a fountain!

Alas, I got no further with my suggestion for a statue of Samuel Dreadnought Maltrouser to be placed in the forecourt of the Village Hall. Mr. Brangle, the chairman, thought that the expression of our admiration for the eminent Victorian engineer would not be best served against a background of corrugated iron. Even newly-painted bright blue, as it is now. Even our ancestor, Hereward the Wake, after whom you are named, receives little veneration in Clagtoft. Indeed, Trudgen, the present schoolmaster, actually suggested that when the Colonel paid someone to trace our ancestry, he 'had the wool pulled over his eyes'! I gave him a piece of my mind, I can tell you.

You guessed correctly; the 'pop group' called Hunking Slodge are connected with the Clagtoft Hunkings. Jump Hunking, their conductor (if that's the word) is the brother of George Hunking, our Parish Clerk. There was some talk of an annual Pop Festival being arranged here, though exactly where it would go in such an intensely arable area, I cannot imagine. George told me that his brother is now rich enough to start his own gramophone record company, but I find that hard to believe.

This old house is, I fear, in need of considerable repair, and I am at my wits end to know how."

At his desk, reading through what he had written, William noticed that the passage about the house had been left uncompleted. The reason became apparent by the urgency of what followed, dated some time after the beginning:

"STOP PRESS. 30th June. I wrote the above statement some time ago and since doing so a startling development has come to light. Clagtoft, our native village, home of our ancestors, is threatened with total extinction! In case you think this is one of my little jokes I am enclosing a cutting from the Stumpleton Chronicle and Advertiser. Similar items have appeared in some national daily newspapers can you believe it? That anybody, politician or otherwise, would even contemplate such an act of wanton vandalism? And this, incredible though it may sound, in the name of scientific advancement. What can it benefit mankind, if deeply rooted people of the soil are torn bodily from their homes and made to go and live in some urban slum? No doubt they will be compensated financially but how do you price anything as precious as heritage? Mr. Brangle thinks that the very age of the Manor House would enhance the compensation; it would certainly relieve me of the worry over its decay.

Very strenuous efforts are being made to stave off the threat and I am proud to say that the lovely Cassandra is in the forefront – a natural leader indeed! I am doing my utmost to press the case for our survival. I rang Mr. Brangle this morning and urged him, in his capacity as Chairman of the Parish Council, to petition H.M. the Queen, asking for her intervention. These European bureaucrats would certainly jump at a word from a British monarch! Start at the top, I say! I have myself attempted to contact our M.P., Roland Clunch (having once met him in a social context), but he seems a very busy man. However, I managed a longish discussion with his secretary.

Under Cassandra, many factors are being assembled towards our"

At this point, William's reading of his own epistle finally reached the end; he had broken off there only a few days previously. He switched on the desk lamp, reached wearily for his fountain pen and began writing:

"MORE STOP PRESS – and this, I am grieved to say, brings news of the ultimate catastrophe. Unless you are able to tear yourself away from your cows and leap on an aeroplane this minute, you may never see Clagtoft Manor House again. Were I the weeping sort, this letter, I tell you in all seriousness, would be tear stained.

At 10 a.m. today (4 July) I received personally a telephone call from the Commissioners of the European Space Agency (their role in this diabolical business is explained in the newspaper cutting), telling me that this dear old place has been singled out, being the eldest building, for almost immediate demolition.

I finish in haste; naturally, I intend to fight this with all the ferocity I can muster. I am having the moat reconstructed, and am seriously contemplating arming the servants. Before I post this in the morning, I shall look out photographs of the house and enclose it. Your boyhood home, trampled under the foot of brute science!

Your loving brother, William."

The Public Parks and Open Committee of Clagtoft Parish Council arranged a site meeting at Clagtoft Castle for Saturday afternoon. Councillor Herbert Brangle discovered that he was himself chairman of that committee, which according to the minute-book had not met since the purchase of Cut-throat Paddock, eight years ago. At this time, so the book said, it had been decided to change the name of the field to Hemlock Green but everybody had forgotten and it was still obstinately Cut-throat Paddock in the mind of everyone in the village.

As with most of the council's specialist committees, nobody was quite sure who were its members, so practically the whole council turned up just in case. The only absentee to send a message was Fred Cletch; he pleaded a sick tractor.

The purpose was to discuss the investigation of the site with Miss Wask and to decide whether permission to dig the trenches could be given. Others present were members of a local Archaeology Society, volunteers for the digging, Olive Ossack, who saw the meeting and wondered what it was about and Oscar Straddle. Oscar was a one-man archaeological society from Dogstead; he had brought his bicycle, complete with large pannier bags filled with tools, and a large black Labrador named Scargill.

"This is it," said Straddle raising two hands into the empty air. "An enormous stone keep, with four massive towers rising to the sky. They used to light fires on one tower to guide ships passing through he Wash. And a tunnel ran from here, all the way to Belvoir Castle in Leicestershire."

"I heard it was Lincoln Cathedral," said Mrs. Ossack.

"That was a branch off it."

Brangle said, "Like to call the meeting to order as there's a proposal before the committee. Proposed that permission be given to Miss Wask, who is the official Community Archaeologist, with full backing from the, er..."

"Eastern Trust." said Violet.

"Thank you. Miss Wask is investigating several sites in the area, but because of the European threat she is giving this priority. What might be found here could be a means of delaying the sale of the land. I know that some councillors were worried about large scale digging on council land, but when we compare what Miss Wask proposes with what those…"

"I propose we give Miss Wask permission to do whatever she wishes on the site." Said Proggle.

There was a chorus of "Hear, hears" and some raised hands.

Brangle cleared his throat, evidently a sound meaning something in dog language because Scargill pricked up his ears and glared at him.

"We can take that, I believe, as unanimous. To be written in as a minute George."

Chimble said, "I brought summat as might help." He held up an ancient metal-detector. "One I had in stock at the old shop, somebody ordered and never fetched. Gev it a battery and away it went." He switched it on and produced a buzz; Scargill backed off and eyed it suspiciously.

Violet said, "O.K., but there's only a limited use in archaeology…"

"Went down one side o' my yard, tonned up half a ston of owd ironwork." He began circling the meeting, swinging the machine from side to side.

Ah, thought Scargill, a new sort of game; he followed at a distance, nose to the ground, awaiting the next development.

Thirty yards away, the note changed and Scargill growled. "Ah, summat under here," called Chimble. "Mebbe King John's treasure."

"More likely an 'oss shoe," said Olive. "No end about."

"Hold it there Mr. Chimble," called Straddle. "I'll get a trowel." He finished in his bicycle bag, brought a tool across and began work.

Scargill's tail was going full revs; obviously his boss knew where bones were. I'm first in the queue.

A few inches down a piece of iron came into view. Straddle tapped it tentatively with his trowel but Chimble said decisively, "Ah. Jack-hoe tine. Selled hundreds in me time." He bent and yanked it up. "Ain't one o' mine though."

Is that all? Thought Scargill; switched off his tail and sat down.

Straddle made a few more exploratory pokes. "Something else here. Iron, or steel maybe. He worked around it for a few minutes, prised it clear of the soil, gingerly lifted it out and wiped it on the grass.

"Good God!" exclaimed Chimble. "It's an 'and-grenade. It might be alive!"

Straddle didn't hesitate; he threw it as high and as far as he could, over the heads of the meeting and into the bumps and hollows of the castle site. It bounced once on a mound, rolled down the side and disappeared into a mass of long grass and nettles.

"Get away everybody!" boomed Brangle. "It could still go off!"

The meeting retreated at a gallop across Cut-throat Paddock, some holding hands over ears.

So that's it, muttered Scargill. A new game, eh? Tail going in overdrive, he scampered across into the long grass and within seconds had located the bomb, got it firmly between his teeth and set off at high speed after the vanishing meeting. He overtook the slower members.

"Look out!" squeaked Wassing. "The dog's bringing it!"

They fanned out in all directions. This is great fun, thought Scargill, I'm supposed to guess which one wants it. Not you? No. How about you? He paused to drop it for a second, then got a better grip and shot after Brangle who was lumbering towards the parish hall. "Tell that damned animal to drop it," he wheezed. "Get inside here everybody!"

Hello, thought Scargill, fresh development. Not altogether an outdoor game after all. Dancing at the back of the crush in the doorway, he waited his turn to go in.

"Mr. Straddle," squawked Proggle. "Tell it to put it down."

Straddle heroically confronted his pet. "Down boy, down." Scargill obediently settled on his haunches, still holding the bomb. The last of the meeting disappeared inside and the door was slammed. Heart pounding, Straddle inched forward, hand held out. "Give us it here boy. Give. Give." They remained eyeball to eyeball for ten seconds, then Oscar made a frantic grab. Scargill gave a muffled woof and tore off towards Ketchup Terrace, along the front of which were all the people who lived there, trying to fathom out what was gong on.

"Live bomb!" howled Straddle. "The dog's got a live bomb!"

For a few seconds nobody moved, then a voice said, "It bloody 'as y'know." They all vanished indoors.

Jack Grunsell and two customers sat on cabbage-crates outside the Stamping Cat, drinking. They disappeared rapidly when the warning reached them, Straddle adding a rider, "Somebody ring 999!"

Jack rushed to his telephone and got Stumpleton police station. "Live dog loose in Clagtoft carrying a bomb!"

Phew, thought Scargill, all this yelling and running about, don't think a lot to this game for a warm day. Damn thing's making my jaws ache. Find a cool spot for a rest. He spotted the shade under the post office, went in and let the bomb roll out behind one of the wheels. Dropped his nose on to his paws and went to sleep. A deep silence settled over the village.

Straddle stood with hands on hips in the middle of Main Road, pondering an imagined newspaper headline, which read "Archaeologist hero saves the village." Then he heard Brangle's voice from behind him: "Don't just stand there you bloody idiot. You'll catch the full force if it goes off." The whole meeting had emerged from the village hall, crept at the double behind Ketchup Terrace, across the graveyard, and were crouching behind the solid churchyard wall. Straddle took cover inside the red telephone box at the front of Chimble's house.

"It's the scrapnel as does most damage," said Chimble. "Little bits o' scrap metal flies about."

The vicar emerged from his house open-mouthed. "Get back inside Rev." bellowed Brangle. "Open all your windows, keep the blast damage down." Owery looked even more puzzled but did as he was told.

Jack Grunsell folded like a jack-knife, scurried across the road and joined the meeting. "Rung the emergency," he reported. "Services on the way."

Even as he spoke, P.C. Albert Tussock came in sight round Squadderby Road corner, feet at the usual forty-five degree out from the pedals, whistling "Z-Cars" theme tunelessly. He evidently knew nothing of the emergency. When he saw the row of heads behind the wall, he braked heavily.

"What the 'ell's going on 'ere?"

"Constable," said Brangle, "A few yards always from you, under Chimble's van, there is a live bomb."

Tussock laughed heartily. "Irish bomb is it? IRA job? Looks more like a live Labrador to me."

"In front of the dog."

He looked again, frowned, then dismounted and leaned his bike against the wall. Walked slowly across and squatted, peering at the bomb. Went down on his knees, reached down and picked it up.

"Keep you heads down," hissed Brangle, as if the sound of his voice might cause an explosion. They all watched the policeman, Straddle coming out of the phone box and peering from behind it.

Tussock grinned and raised it as if to throw it over the wall. Every head vanished.

Scargill woke up and saw that somebody else had his toy, switched on his tail and scampered out. Tussock tossed it up and caught it, and Scargill did a frisky-lamb dance. Mebbe this bloke knows the game; meself, I can't make any sense of it.

"Tin money-box," said Tussock. "Had one just like it. Made to look like a first war hand-grenade." He shook it. "Still got something in it. Anybody got a thin-bladed knife?"

They all emerged sheep-faced and crossed Main Road to look. From a distance, the first of the sirens could be heard approaching along Stumpleton Road. Brangle began mentally rehearsing explanations.

* * *

Liz Otmill had taken advantage of a fine, warm day and walked into Clagtoft Fen carrying her gear and portable easel. She spotted a small house with a steeply-sloping roof, a cluster of old brick barns around two sides and a little plantation of ancient apple-trees behind. She selected a spot on the broad grass verge beside the lane and was soon at work on a sketch.

She was almost ready for paint when a van roared up and stopped beside her. Harry Gozzard got out and came to look. "Nah then duck. 'Ang on a few minutes, I'll go in and light a fire, then you can draw smoorke coming out the chimbly."

"Is it where you live Harry?"

"Aye, born in it an' nivver lived nowhere else. It was me dad's, so it come down to me as the oldest."

Liz studied the sky, rummaged in her box of paint tubes. "Have you got an oldest to leave it to when you go?"

70

"God, I ain't going yet duck. Got too much to do. Wouldn't be too sure there ain't an oldest knocking around somewhere, but if there is nobody's said owt to me about it."

"Live in there on your own?"

"Some o' the time." He grinned; a bit sheepishly she thought. "Tek a guest in now and then. Long as she's willing to pay rent as I ask."

"So I've heard."

"What – some bugger bin talking about me? You ain't heard nowt bad hev you? If you hev it's a pack o' lies. What'd they say?"

She grinned. "Something about keeping a mattress in the back of your van, for the girls that work in your gang."

He laughed loudly, went back to his van and looked inside. "I'm damned if there ain't one in there. You bin talking to Big Rube."

She added a tinge of red to her cerulean blue. "Rube says if she caught you across one of her daughters she would strangle you."

"I believe she would an' all. Ev to be careful shan't I?

"Another thing I heard was that you keep a list of all Clagtoft women under forty, and tick 'em off one at a time."

He laughed at the sky, walking around in a circle. "Christ, I 'ev got a reputation ain't I? Wonder you didn't hoof it across yon field when you see me comin'."

"I'm all right, I don't qualify."

His clear blue eyes swept her. "Oh, I don't know. Why not?"

"Not a Clagtoft woman and not under forty."

"Ain't you really? Could've fooled me." He went back towards his van. "Come in for a cup o' tea, when you want a break. If you dost."

"I dost. Be there in a few minutes. Put the kettle on."

She was surprised to find his living-room impeccably clean and tidy, tastefully furnished. The tea came in good china, along with a plate of tempting scones. "My sister's cooking, them. Brings me a tinful ivvery week."

"What about the rest of your cooking?"

"Do most on it me sen. If I'm too knackered I pop up to the place on the ramper and ev a treat."

"Not a bad life."

"Suits me. Nivver known owt else. Dad was a ganger an' all; I helped him, then took over when he died."

"And granddad? Was he a ganger?"

71

"No, he was a proper farmer. There was no gangers in his day. They all wocked for the farmer, casuals an' all. Used to git the Paddys in for the tairty harvest. They lev in the Paddy-huts up in the village. All this stretch o' land, from the road to the Forty-foot was grandad's. That's him up yonder." He indicated an enlarged monochrome photo in a frame over the mantle piece. It was taken in a field; enlargement had made it hazy but it was clearly a horse pulling a plough, a man behind holding the shafts. Liz almost dropped her cup.

"Hang on," she said and stood up for a closer look. "He's got no clothes on."

Harry rolled back in his chair and roared with laughter. "Daft as a boilt owl, th' owd bugger was. Started doing that when he were turned fifty, so I were told. Used to pick apples, did the garden, owt as he felt like doing. Nowt on but a pair o' boots. Folks used to come down this way just for a laugh. One time, landlord of the Cat wanted to change the nairm; The Naked Ploughman he wanted to call it. But the brewers wouldn't wear it. They thowt 'e was mekking it up."

"What happened to granddad?"

"Took 'im away in the end, locked 'im up somewhere. Them days there was no other way. If I did it now they'd give me some pills or summat."

"Have you tried doing it?"

"Often do when nobody's about. Out here you can see folks coming from far enough, so I keep near the house. That owd bugger used to go a mile off sometimes."

"What did grandma say?"

"Not a deal I shouldn't think. Bit fierce he was. I reckon she was relieved when they carted him off. Don't know who took that photo; I found it amongst Dad's stuff, got it enlarged. Mek a good picture for you that would. The Naked Ploughman. Fetch big money."

"I am planning to do some old-time land-workers, if I can find people willing to dress up as they used to dress. And find enough old implements."

"Old implements, good God, missis, yon barn's bosting wi' 'em. I bet the owd 'oss-plough as is on that photo's still in there. Tell you what – I'll borry Josh Kelter's owd hoss, bring it round here and yock it up. Then I'll strip off and model for you."

Liz laughed. "D'you know, I might just take you up on that."

"Onny one condition – I don't want my face on it. Might be bad for business.

"No problem," she said. "It'll be your body, beer-belly and all, and somebody else's face."

"How about Wassing's?"

"That wouldn't do. Doesn't look anything like a ploughman's face. Needs and Edwardian look. I think I'll make it Chimble's."

# Chapter Eight

For some time Chimble wondered if he had bitten off more than he could chew. Fitting a steam traction-engine power unit to the big dragline excavator had not been too difficult and he soon had it working on compressed air to prove that the mechanical parts functioned. When it came to adding a boiler, firebox and chimney however, nothing seemed to go right.

"If I could, I'd have it on a trailer and pull it behind." Abe told Clive, who had been hanging around watching proceedings.

To his surprise, the boy made a sensible suggestion. "Can't you weld a shelf across the back and put it on sideways?"

It worked. It added a foot or two to the width of the already large machine but then, as Abe remarked, it wont need to go through anybody's pantry door. Being a track-layer, the extra weight didn't matter.

When smoke was seen coming from the chimney, a little crowd gathered, and Chimble addressed them.

"Not since the early days of railway building 'as anything like this 'ere machine been seen in action. Mebbe not even then."

"You off to build us a railway Mr. Chimble?" asked Clive.

"Not today son. Got a big job down at the Manor House fost. Just wait for steam up, then you'll see what she can do."

Before anybody saw what she could do however, a lot of leaky joints had to be fixed and last-minute adjustments made. By the time Abe got it working, the crowd had lost interest and dispersed. For half an hour he sat at the control, raising, lowering and swivelling the jib and scooping large helpings of fresh air above the surface of the yard. In the end, he couldn't resist taking it out on the road for a trial run. Track-laying tractors often used the road through the village, and he knew his outfit made much less noise then they did. He manoeuvered gently into the middle of Main Road, aimed at

Waddies corner, and eased the regulator open. Get to the Stamping Cat, he thought, I'll give 'em a toot on the whistle; that'll bring 'em out to look.

He didn't get that far. Just as he drew level with the vicarage there was a sudden roar of escaping steam as the pipe between the boiler and engine fractured. The tracks clanked to a stop and the big cabin containing Chimble and the controls vanished in a cloud of steam. Not knowing what had happened. He panicked and waggled every lever his hands encountered until finally all went quiet and the leakage subsided to a gentle wisp.

As a result of his frantic manipulation, the flywheels's momentum had swivelled the jib across the vicarage front garden, swung the grab over and neatly scooped out one of the vicar's highly prized hydrangea bushes. With its bright red blooms still smiling at the summer sky, it was now perched six feet above its former home, patiently awaiting the next move.

"<u>Oh</u> dear," muttered Chimble. "The vicar won't like that."

He didn't. As Chimble climbed shakily down from the monster, the Rev. emerged from his front door with a face like thunder.

"Ah, vicar. I was just coming to ask you where you wanted it."

"Damn you Chimble. I wanted it where it was. Took four years to raise that from a cutting – what on earth possessed you to do a stupid trick like that?"

"Accident mate. Pure accident. Summat's gone wrong. Soon as I find out what, I'll have her puffing again and let your bush down. Got plenty o' soil on the roots, should be all right..."

As he turned to look at the machine, a thought struck him. "Mind you, that was nowt to what the Yew Ropians'll do when they come, if they do. Pick up your vicarage by the roots they will, spread it all the way from here to Iggleby.

It took two and a half hours to repair the damage and raise steam again, during which time Main Road was effectively blocked. Two cars and eight tractors had to make detours via Conker Drove and Pudding Lane; an articulated lorry had to turn around in the Stamping Cat yard and, unable to cross Lollycock Bridge, make a detour of four miles via Dogstead and Squadderby. The various comments made by eleven drivers rolled off Chimble like water off a duck's back.

He told Clive: "Forgot to allow for expansion, that's the trouble."

Clive nodded wisely. "Need a loop in it Mr. Chimble."

Abe's whiskery face came round, the eyes bright over the glasses. "I'm beginning to wonder who's supposed to be the village idiot, you or me."

Clive did a little dance. "Me! Me! I got the job fost." He skipped away, punishing the guitar and yodelling like a demented farmyard cock.

The repair finally done, Chimble relit the fire then went back to the van for a cheese sandwich and a cup of tea. The hydrangea was rescued and put back in place, looking as if nothing had happened. When steam was up he raised the jib and swung it to travelling position, knocking a branch off a laburnum in the process. The vicar didn't emerge this time, so Chimble retrieved the amputated limb and poked it back into the tree.

Clive had seen the activity and returned. "What you off to do next Mr. Chimble?"

"Tekking 'er down to the Manor House, ready to start wock in the morning. You can be stoker, if you like."

"Can I drive it an' all?"

"No. You ain't got a licence. You'll walk behind wi' a bucket o' coal in each hand. If you're lucky, I might have a yoke in stock."

"What's a yoke?"

"Thing to put on your shoulders so by as you can carry two buckets o' coal an' light yer pipe at the same time."

"Yer a rum sod you are."

By nightfall the traffic in the centre of Clagtoft was flowing freely once more (mainly two cars bound for the Stamping Cat), and the monster was safely parked on what was left of the north lawn at the Manor House. The top of its chimney was a few feet away from Hammel's bedroom window; she spent an uneasy night alternately listening to the gurgling and groaning of the cooling boiler, and having dreams involving vast explosions.

\* \* \*

Next morning, Proggle got a letter from a large international medical company: "Dear Miss Proggle, Thank you for your enquiry regarding the private rheumatism clinic at Dogstead, which our Company Historian tells us was taken over by one of our satellite

76

companies several years ago. The clinic no longer exists, but its records certainly include a mention of mud-packs used in experimental treatment. There are no laboratory reports carrying analyses of the mud; we doubt if the clinic had a laboratory. Our historian noticed, and this may be of passing interest to yourself, that a solicitor was instructed by the clinic to draft an official complaint under the Trades Descriptions Act, against a product labelled "Culvert's Healing Mud", described as 'a sure-fire cure for all arthritic and rheumatic conditions', and sold at markets. Again, there were no scientific details and the matter seems to have been dropped."

Proggle rang Brangle and read the letter to him. "Looks like we lost out on that one," she said.

"Not necessarily," said Brangle. "Keep that letter. Anything with an impressive letter-head is potentially useful. You don't put on record what it says – you just wave it at the Public Inquiry, read out the company's name and say it refers to the valuable properties of the mud in Gandle's Pit. That's not lying. It's using negative truth to positive advantage."

"Yes. Well, I'll pass the letter on for you to wave."

Later that morning Proggle was passing near Olive Ossack's house, so she called to tell her the outcome of the investigation. She was surprised to find the house door shut and locked; unusual for ten o'clock in the morning. Olive and Sam must have gone out together. She was turning away but then had a second thought. Wonder if they're all right? She knocked louder and shouted. "Anybody in? Olive?" she looked into the window of the kitchen, and it was deserted. Called and knocked again, and this time she heard voices inside.

A bedroom window opened and Olive's face appeared, her coarse steel-grey hair pointing in all directions. "Who the 'ell's that?"

"Oh sorry Olive. Were you still in bed?"

Olive giggled. "We bin up once and ed some breakfast. Then we come back."

"Are you all right?"

"Course I am. Nivver felt better since I was a gal." She lowered her voice to about half a shout. "It's some stuff Hovel gev me for the owd man. Got 'im going again good and proper. Hang on, I'll come down."

"It's all right, if you don't…"

Olive had shut the window and a minute later had unlocked the door and asked Proggle in. She was wearing an old raincoat over her nightie. "Time he was up an' about any road."

"I was passing by, so I called to tell you that the magic mud from Gandle's Pit never made the big-time. In fact, somebody complained that Charlie Culvert's stuff was a swizz."

"Ay, the buggers allus do say that, if they can't mek it in a factory and owercharge for it. They reckon nowt's any good as is natural." She reached up to the mantelpiece, took down the two packets Glenda Hovel had given her, shook them. "That's natural stuff. Proper herbs what Glenda grows, not chemical rubbish. That one was for my earache an' it bloody cured it one night, no bother. All as I'd have got from Mulfry would a bin anti-biotics and I'd still 'ave earache. And this stuff…"

"Looks revolting. What is it?"

"Don't know. It's what she gev me for the owd man. Nivver seen owt like it; bin up and down them stairs like yo-yos we have last couple o' days. Must've just dozed off when you…"

"Hang on Olive. This one's not his.  It's got your name on it. Look."

"Olive's jaw dropped. "Oh gawd. It has." She stared at Proggle, eyes horrified. "I bin giving him the earache stuff, and I had…"

They both collapsed in laughter.

Proggle's next call was on Mrs. Amelia Chaunter, who lived in a small house on Main Road, near to Chimble's original post office. Amelia was a widow, a former land-worker, still in sprightly condition "Apart from a bit o' the owd screws in me hands. All them code mornings cutting cabbages."

"Ought to be classified as an industrial disease," said Proggle. "There's skiving sods in some jobs get thousands in compensation for less disability than that."

"I suppose so. Any road, I'm all raight. Comfy in here, git me glass o' stout and a bit o' snooker on telly."

"I came to ask you about the Old Clagtoft Silver Band."

Amelia's eyes lit momentarily. "Oh, aye. Know a bit about that. Ain't bin on the go, oh, donkey's years."

"Your husband was in it, wasn't he?"

"He was first in, but I was just after him. And all our family, as soon as they got big enough to 'old an instrument."

"What a pity it had to go. Where did you practise?"

"In the owd Ebenezer."

The Ebenezer had been the village's nonconformist chapel. Now derelict, it had seen use as a Washeteria and a Video Rental, both very short-lived, had been earmarked by the parish council as a Tourist Information Centre, and was now chiefly notable for the two sturdy sycamore trees, which grew through where its roof had been.

Proggle said, "I'm wondering if it's possible to get a band together for our protest march over this European space business. We want to make as much fuss and palaver as we can, marching through town. Maybe through Lincoln as well. Even down London, if we have to. Show that Clagtoft is a lively, busy place that doesn't deserve to be snuffed out."

"Come up here, let me show you summat," Amelia led upstairs and opened a cupboard on the landing. There were about a dozen silver-plated band instruments of all sizes, up to the biggest tuba. And two cardboard boxes, one containing uniform tunics, and a smaller with printed music.

"Everything kep in working order," she said. "Even mothballs in among the jackets. All we need is people to put in 'em and blow the instruments."

"How many Clagtoft people can still play?"

"There's me for a start."

She took down a cornet, wiped the mouthpiece on her apron, then trilled up and down a couple of scales. "Don't play ivvery day. Two or three times a week, just for old times sake."

"Anybody else?"

"My son Tom, as wocks for Cletches. Two of Big Rube's grandchildren, they learned at school at Dogstead. Then there's Josh Kelter and Tich Ounge, base and trombone. Sid Sneck ewsed to be a cornet player but he's lame and couldn't march."

"We could have the band on a lorry or trailer. What about a big drum?"

"There is one but it wants mending. Was left in the Ebenezer too long, the damp got at it."

"Could Abe Chimble mend it?"

"Ain't seen owt he couldn't mend yet. He ment the big tuba when somebody chucked a firework down it on the Friendly Societies Parade."

79

"Not very friendly was it? Did it burst?"

"No, the firework nivver bothered it, but Kelter thought they'd got him, dropped it and run. Next behind was a gret fat horn player borrowed from Dogstead. He trud on it."

"Right. Well, Abe's busy with his digging machine just now but when he's done I'll ask him to look at the drum. Would you go round, see if you can recruit enough to make a band?"

"I'll have a go. Wouldn't need a long programme would it?"

"Anything lively and noisy. That one with bollocks in they whistled in the film…"

"Colonel Bogey."

"…And the Lincolnshire Poacher, would do for starters. And I would like to get a practice march through Clagtoft on the first of August."

Proggle hadn't given herself much time and as she left Amelia's house she remembered another thing; banners. She had acquired enough Hessian to make two big ones; it was old backcloths left in the village hall by the now defunct (it had lasted nearly a year) Clagtoft Theatrical Society. Their one production, Waiting for Godot, had to be turned into a semi-reading because half the cast was busy harvesting on the evening.

She remembered her intention to ask Liz Otmill to paint the words on. As she pedalled round Waddie's corner she saw Liz striding across Cut-throat Paddock with her sketch-pad, heading towards Lollycock Bridge. It was a windy day and a harsh push to the junction with Conker Drove. As she approached the bridge she spotted Liz again, now on the opposite side of the Drain and heading for Clagtoft Hall. If she gets into that wilderness, thought Proggle, I'll have a job to find her.

Already breathless, she zoomed over the hump of the bridge and swerved into the notorious cycling hazard of Silt Lane. This was an unmade road for most of its length, its surface consisting, according to weather, of either deep, hard tractor-wheel ruts or deep, squelchy mud. Today it was rock-solid. After a few yards she got off and walked. When she got to the wild growth surrounding the Hall, Liz had vanished. She left her bike against a tree near what had been a drive entrance, fighting her way through the tangle of brambles and hawthorn towards the building.

Just before she reached, she was stopped abruptly. Liz stepped out from a hiding-place, fingers to lips, beckoning Proggle into cover. "Listen," whispered Liz. They were quite close to the house, not far from a gaping hole where there had once been a window. From inside came the sound of voices. Male and female. The words could not be understood and were punctuated by giggles anyway. Little imagination was needed to surmise what was going on.

"It's noted for it," whispered Proggle. "Big Rube once used to say four bastards in Duchess of York Drive all started in there. Then a gang of travelling people took it over and…"

"Look!" hissed Liz. A figure had appeared at the opening, a man with his back to it. Naked at least to his waist, bending and struggling, evidently climbing back into his trousers. They were still talking but without the giggles. The storm had blown itself out.

"Let's get away from the house," whispered Proggle. "I've a sneaky feeling I know who that is."

They took a wide arc round the side of the Hall and found a path somebody had hacked out, leading back to Drain bank. "Old Olive Ossack comes in and picks the brambles," said Proggle. "Makes some of the best bramble jam known to mankind."

"I was hoping to get some sketches of the house", Liz said. "See if I can concoct a picture of what it might have looked like in its heyday." She opened her pad and studied the bits of roof visible above the wilderness. As she did so, the voices could be heard again and two figures emerged from the bushes. Violet Wask and George Hunking.

"Thought so," said Proggle. "It's our parish clerk. Local government ain't what it used to be."

The couple saw the two women, hesitated a moment muttering to each other, then came towards them. "Afternoon ladies," said George. "Admiring the stately hall?"

Liz said, "I was just hoping a big strong man'd come along, produce a monster chopper, and remove all the trees on this side. So I could get a decent sketch."

George's eyes widened slightly. "Hah. Can't oblige I'm afraid. But we can give you and Miss Proggle a bit of interesting news. I went into the Hall with Violet, er, Miss Wask, to see if there were any clues as to, er, date of it and so forth. And we made a great discovery."

81

Violet was holding a torch and a small quantity of yellowish papers, which she held up for them to see. "In a cupboard behind a fireplace. Pushed in behind a recess, so the cupboard looked empty to whoever wanted to clear it. Just old bills and letters but the dates go back to mid 1800s. Chewed by mice in places but readable."

"The really interesting one," said George, "Is about the castle."

"What?" said Proggle, "Clagtoft Castle?"

"Show her."

Violet brought a letter to the top, held it up. "You can just about read it."

Proggle read aloud: "To Messrs. J. Transom and Sons, Builders, Pyewipe Lane, Iggleby. Dear Sirs, since our late conversation on the matter, I have consulted Mr. J.S....somebody, architect, and... something..."

"Commissioned, maybe," said Violet.

"Yes. Er, plans for alterations to the castle building. Castle building! Hey, there's something! A long time since anybody saw that on paper, authentic. What date is this?"

"1819. Not all that long ago, and there's no clue as to the age, or size of the building, whatever it was. I was hoping for a plan or something, but there's nothing else."

Proggle looked again. "J. Transom and Sons. D'you know, there's still a Transom, retired builder. Ernie Transom, down the Fen. Name like that, he must be one of the family. Same trade. Soon as I get a minute, I'll go down there and see him."

The four parted company in pairs again, George and Violet no doubt still discussing deep archaeological matters, Proggle detailing the wording she wanted Liz to put on banners.

# Chapter Nine

At breakfast, William deMondford Wassing could hear the steady puffing of Chimble's monster machine and the occasional clanking of its tracks as Abe manoeuvred it around. The sounds were sometimes accompanied by slight tremors of the floor, as trees were uprooted and toppled out of the way of the projected moat. Waiting for the work to begin, William had experienced periodic little swellings of the breast, from pride that the last of the Wassings was showing the stubborn resistance to injustice he imagined characterised the long ancestral line.

When the work began, however, he started to have second thoughts. Was he not guilty of an act of wanton destruction himself? Would not one of the early Wassings (Marmaduke. The Colonel had told him, was the father of ten mini-Wassings) have severely censured the destruction of these fine old trees? William had to check himself from rushing out, waving his arms, telling Chimble to stop.

Perhaps Marmaduke, living in a more robust age, would have set forth on hourseback, sword at the ready, and confronted whoever threatened his home. Maybe even cut him down without a hearing. These days, confrontation was less common; everything was done by remote communication; words, words, words. Dammit, he wasn't that good with words, but if only he could contact whoever had told him…

He took his second cup of tea, crossed to the study, and picked up the telephone. It took some argy-bargy with the fools at Directory Enquiries before he even got to speak to anyone at Brussels, and then he could scarcely understand their fractured English. The only thing he got out of it was another number to ring, that of the European Space Agency in Paris. He wrote it down wrongly, however, and spent several confused and expensive minutes talking to a massage parlour in Bordeaux, whose English just about matched his French, and who beseeched him to be there within half and hour otherwise he would miss a golden opportunity. Perhaps mercifully – at least for the health of his next phone bill – the conversation was terminated when Chimble swung his jib with extra enthusiasm and brought down the telephone line uniting the Manor House with the distant house of delights.

Chimble was enjoying his new toy so much, he didn't notice what had happened. He wondered for a second why his stoker, Clive, was waving and pointing, but so engrossed was he in holding the next monster scoopful, wondering how many fourteenth-century labourers it would have taken, and how long, to dig that lot out, that the signals went unheeded.

Clive was thinking it a great adventure, and even left his guitar in Chimble's van to carry a succession of buckets of coal down to the Manor House, using the yoke from Chimble's Hardware.

Henrietta Hammel was enjoying it too, and had slipped into the mental aberration in which Clive had again become Laurence. She had secretly laid in a store of treats against such a day, and whenever Clive appeared to have a moment free from duties, she plied him with cakes, chocolate biscuits and cups of Mr. Wassing's favourite cocoa.

The line of the original moat had been carefully traced and marked out by Violet Wask, but Wassing had forgotten to tell Chimble of it. Considerable modification to the shape and size of it was now taking place. The 21$^{st}$-century version looked like beating the 14$^{th}$ by a factor of three in both depth and width. What with the moat itself, the spoil-heap, and the area devastated by the machine's tracks, the view from the house windows resembled something like a moonscape.

At the height of the fun, Brangle's car drew up in the remnant of the drive. After a brief word with Wassing, Brangle walked to where Chimble could see him, and beckoned him over. The machine was surrounded by a sea of wet mud; when Abe saw the beckoning he looked down for a place to alight, saw nothing but mud, and put the machine into reverse. Steam pressure was well up, everything hot and working freely, and within seconds machine and driver had passed through a 150-year-old yew hedge and appeared in the middle of Squadderby Road. Chimble got down and Brangle met him at the drive entrance.

"Not leaving it there are you? Blocking the road again."

"Onny for a minute. I'll shift if anybody wants to come."

"I came to ask if you'd spare a few minutes to come with us. Myself and the geologist from the oil exploration company. He wants to see the place where the oil appears. He's in my car."

The man got out, spread a map on the car bonnet, and was explaining the subtleties of oil exploration to Clive. "There is an oil area, but very deep. The seismic survey done in 1962 does show a definite fault, roughly parallel with the Lincoln cliff…"

Brangle and Chimble came up. Clive said, "We ain't deep enough for any oil yet, Mr. Chimble. I'll keep fetching coal, keep her going till we get to it."

The oil-man glared at him. "Tell 'im I'm the village idiot Mr. Chimble."

Abe pin-pointed the spot on the map, where Proggle had measured her length in Glugwell Creek. "That's where most of it was, real thick on top of the watter. Cassie had a ketchup bottle filled but she dropped it when she sluthered and went in. She said it tasted like burnt porridge."

The place was half a mile from the nearest road, so the digger was driven back through the gap and the three set off on foot along Snogging Lane, followed by Clive. On the way, Chimble pointed out patches of oil on the surface of the creek, and grass on the bank sides soaked with it. When they reached the place, Chimble said, "This is where it was thickest."

The oil-man studied his papers again. "Mmm, Some distance from the fault, but that's no great… You see, there has to be pressure down there, coupled with rock-movement at some time. And it's a long way down, if there is oil."

Brangle said, "You could drive a road straight across there, coming off Squadderby Road. No sense trying to upgrade this path,"

The man smiled. "I wouldn't hold out as much hope as that. We're not in a Texas situation here."

There was a distant shout, and they turned in its direction. Clive had wandered off to look at a clump of trees a hundred yards away.

"Probably gone to do a quick flash, ignore him," said Chimble.

But the shouts continued and the boy was persistently pointing into the clump of trees.

"Might be a gusher," said Chimble. "I'll go and look."

The oil-man's shoes were already dirty, so he went across as well, stepping gingerly between rows of sugar-beet. When they got there, all was explained.

An old farm-track led to the place from the direction of Clagtoft Fen, and somebody had used the cover of the trees to hide a dumping-ground for used engine-oil. There were at least a dozen large drums and several smaller ones, and many were old enough to be rusting way, the oil oozing out and soaking into the ground.

The oil-man folded his papers and stuffed them into his pocket. "Yes, well, evidently this is going down to the field drainage and out into the Creek. A criminal offence of course but it hardly concerns a geologist. I would advise you gentlemen to inform the police." He set off walking briskly back across the sugar-beet.

"Will somebody git done Mr. Chimble?"

"Easy might," said Abe. "Want to watch out it ain't you."

Clive took a kick at the nearest drum and another forty gallons began its last journey.

* * *

In common with most landlords of pubs in small villages, Jack Grunsell was unable to make a full-time living out of the Stamping Cat. In past times in the fenland, pub-keeping had been coupled with a smallholding, or with a trade such as blacksmith or saddler. For Jack's top-up, he had a part-time job driving a furniture van for a shop in Stumpleton. First coming to Clagtoft a few years back, he had high hopes of turning the Cat into a fashionable out-of-town venue for townies and others who liked to take their leisure well away from home. He saw this, his first licensed premises, as a stepping-stone to higher things, maybe even hotel management, Skegness or elsewhere.

It went wrong from the beginning. Clagtoft did not want a plastic-and-chromium Stamping Cat with outdoor tables and umbrellas; it wanted just what it had always had. If anybody wanted to drink outdoors, there were always cabbage-crates to sit on, or even the churchyard wall across the road.

86

Jack had rapidly put his foot in it by erecting a large sign at the junction of Stumpleton Road and the ramper: 'Stamping Cat 1½ miles. Gallstone's Beer, Full Cuisine, Entertainment. Coaches Catered For.' We'll give him full cue scene, was Clagtoft's reaction. One dark night three figures left the village, one with a spade on its shoulder. Within two hours the sign was in a hundred small pieced distributed among the coalhouses and wood-sheds of half a dozen houses.

While Jack was away on his furniture van, three days a week, the bar was looked after by his wife Edie. It was also rumoured that while Jack was away, Edie was looked after by a regular customer, Harry Gozzard. It was true. When things were going easy on the land and in the pack-houses, Gozzard had plenty of time in the middle of the day. His liaison had begun when she wanted a barrel changed, and he'd offered to help. From the cellar to the living-room was a short step, and a few days later it was an equally short step upstairs. As a bedroom entertainer, she discovered Harry was in a totally different league from her husband.

On one afternoon however, the entertainment was interrupted when Edie heard a car stop outside. It wasn't opening time. Harry went to look.

"It's a police car. It's Flagon. What the 'ell's he want?"

"Who's Flagon?"

"Sergeant Flagon, from Dogstead."

Their clothes were going back on almost as fast as they had come off. Harry was first downstairs. On the way to the door he picked up a sweeping-brush.

"Now then Sarge."

"Hello Harry. Part-time job?"

"Could say that."

"Getting a bit slack on the land, is it? Is Mrs. Grunsell in?"

Edie showed her face.

"A word with you in private, Mrs. Grunsell, if you don't mind."

"See you tomorrow then," said Harry, and set off towards his van, still with the brush in his hand. He paused and looked at it, then tossed it into the van and got in after it. Be a reason for calling back later.

"About your son Clive," said the sergeant. "Two things, the complaint against him, and his non-attendance at school. Both quite serious matters, I hope you agree."

"Well, yes, but what can you do?"

"Mrs. Hovel, who made the complaint, has now made a sensible suggestion. And, I might add, with Clive's best interests in mind. She is entitled to insist on the charge going ahead, and as things stand that means a court appearance. But she will withdraw the charge if Clive goes back to school. She thinks the trouble comes from him having nothing to do all day."

"Might be true. But what if Trudgen expels him again?"

"I'll have a word with Mr. Trugden when I leave you and see if some arrangement can be made."

So it was that on the following Monday morning at nine o'clock, Clive did the 200-yards journey from home to school. And at 9.20 he had slipped out unnoticed into the playground, shown his grinning face at the window where the class could see him but Trudgen could not, and got them all rolling with laughter. This time, he was not sent home. The headmaster took him into his little office, sat him down and talked to him. Not the usual finger-wagging, threatening talk, but making sure that Clive fully understood the options: school and reasonable behaviour, or a court appearance.

Then Trudgen took a risk. "I'm going to leave you alone in this office for half an hour, and I'm trusting you not to interfere with anything. While I'm away, you think about it and tell me your answer when I come back."

The boy sat silent, his dumb expression totally blank, his eyes on a box of books on the floor in the office. Trudgen went, thinking gloomily that perhaps a wrecked office was worth it to get rid of the little sod. He finished his teaching stint on tenterhooks, expecting at any moment to see a fireball erupt, or at least a cloud of smoke. Towards the end of the half-hour he began to harbour a hope that he had slipped away into the village.

He decided on a cowardly approach, went outside first and looked in through the office window. Clive didn't see him. He was still sitting in the same chair, but had taken a book from the box on the floor and was reading it. Trudgen could hardly believe his eyes; he'd never before seen him reading. The books in the cardboard box were not school property, they were a collection of science-fiction paperbacks belonging to Mrs. Trudgen. She had decided not to keep them, and he had promised to deliver them to a charity shop. The one Clive was now glued to was "Best Time-Travel Stories", with a bright, imaginative illustrated cover. The headmaster returned to his duties, thinking deeply.

By the end of the morning, Clive was halfway through the book, and had to be prised out of it and sent home for dinner. Trudgen told him that the book was his to keep, but was unsure whether it registered. Clive started for home, looking at the ground and still clutching the book. Then he turned.

"Mr. Trudgen, what does temporal simultaneity mean?"

"Ah. It… I… er, well." His expression was an advanced state of boggle. "Have you got a dictionary at home? Yes? Well, look it up for yourself, that's the thing to do."

Clive went, still lost in the worlds of the book. In the afternoon, Trudgen arranged a desk apart from the class and sat Clive in it, warning the others to leave him alone. There the boy spent the next three weeks ploughing through a hundred and sixty volumes of science-fiction, taking them home one by one as he finished them.

\* \* \*

When Proggle went to see Ernie Transom, the retired builder, she found herself addressing a man of eighty–plus, but by no means as retired as he was supposed to be. He was in the yard at the side of his house, wearing overalls, sitting beside a huge pile of bricks evidently dumped there from some demolition job, happily chipping old mortar and pilling them ready for re-use.

"Nah then duck. Come for a few bricks? All nicely clen up, let yer 'ev 'em chearp. No sense buying new when they come as good as this."

"My only use for them at the moment," said Proggle, "Would be to take them to Paris and let fly at the office windows where they thought this scheme up."

He put his hammer down. "Is that true then, about Clagtoft coming down?"

"They think it is. They don't realise yet what they're up against. When they meet the barrage of arguments we're putting up… not to mention the barriers. D'you keep any guns in your house?"

"No. Well, I say no. There is an owd twelve-bore in the shed. Me rattin'-gun as I callt it. But I wouldn't dost fire it now. Not bin clent for donkey's years."

"You might need it to defend your house when the bulldozers turn up."

He laughed wheezily. "I doubt if it'd bring one o' them down."

"Maybe not. But it might send the driver scuttling home for a change of trousers. Anyway, take a look at that." She passed him a photocopy of the letter found at Clagtoft Hall.

His eyes almost popped out. "I'll be damned. J. Transom and Sons, Pyewipe Lane, Iggleby. Bugger me."

"Not just now," said Proggle. "Is that your family?"

"It'd be me granddad. Or is it? No, he was George. He might have been one o' them sons. By, this is going back a bit. I hev some owd paperwork as was me dad's, but I don't think it goes back this far. Where did this come from?"

She told him. "Any architect's plans among your dad's stuff?"

"Could be. Come in the 'ouse, I'll git the box out."

They went through a room where Mrs. Transom and an ancient fat bulldog were apparently asleep. But the dog growled with its eyes still shut, and Mrs. Transom growled "Shurrup Fluff," without opening hers.

Ernie produced an old wooden deed-box smelling of mothballs. "Hev a look through there, while I go find me glasses."

Proggle was about halfway down the box when she found it. A large sheet of thick, heavy paper folded four times, with an architect's drawing in ink. It had been outdoors, and some of the inks had run; the paper was foxed and browned. But the subject was not in doubt. It was a castle keep with four corner towers.

"Hooray! This is it! How about that Ernie? Clagtoft Castle, just as everybody says it was. This'll take old Trudgen down a peg, calling it an old wives' tale."

She got Ernie's permission to borrow the plan, and shot off to find Violet Wask.

* * *

Late on the second day of his moat-digging operation, Chimble had almost completed the job and was working to the bank of

90

Clagtoft Drain, at the point where Violet thought had been a wooden sluice gate used to regulate the filling of the moat. She was right; it was still in place. But the woodwork had almost rotted away and the accumulation of garden rubbish on the house side was all that held it in place. As Chimble's machine ate its way in, the whole structure gave way and the water came rushing into the new moat.

Chimble sat opened-mouthed, hands on levers, as the moat was filled to the brim. And he could see that the drive entrance from Squadderby Road, evidently below water level, was flooding over.

Nor was that the end; the whole garden was evidently below water level, and within half an hour the ancient Manor House was an island. Mrs. Hammel's white face hung out of an upstairs window; she was shaking a fist and mouthing what could have been obscenities.

Chimble drove out into Squadderby Road and got down to look. Clive came up with a consignment of coal. "Crikey Mr. Chimble. That's a lot of watter."

"Ah, well, that's what he wanted. Summat to keep the vandals out."

"'Ow's Mr. Wassing off to get in when he comes back?"

"Is he out?"

"Driv out in his car half an hour ago."

"Ah. The car wheels is a fair size, should be all right on the drive. Might have to tek a leap off the running-board to the door-step. 'E'll git used to it."

"Shall I put any more coal on?"

"Might as well now it's here. Then we'll tek it back to the yard."

Mrs. Hammel's voice floated down from the upper window: "How am I supposed to get out of here?"

"Use yer wellies duck. There's places not too deep."

\* \* \*

On the following morning at about 11 o'clock, Chimble took a phone call at the post office. It was Wassing.

"Damn you and your infernal Machine. My garden's flooded."

"Is it really? Well, the owd moat's in there somewhere, and that's what you ast for. Blame the drainage people, they must have let the Drain git too high. Any come in the house?"

91

"The cellar's flooded. <u>And</u> I've been without a telephone for two days, thanks to you bringing the line down. Then the telephone engineer had to go back for some wellies so he could get in. This will cost me a packet, I can tell you. He walked into the moat and almost drowned at one stage; had to go back a second time for a change of clothes."

"I'll knock a bit off the bill," said Chimble.

"Bill? I… I thought this was part of the defence of Clagtoft."

"That particular job was defence of your house, not the rest of the village."

There was a brief silence, then Wassing's phone went down with a bang. Chimble chuckled; the idea of a bill had occurred to him on the spur of the moment.

He chuckled even more half an hour later, when Wassing phoned again.

"It's happened."

"What? Tide come up or summat?"

"Another call from Europe. From the vandals who are out to desecrate our village. This is the final ultimatum; I have only four days, they say, to get the contents of the house prepared for moving out. They wanted to know how many furniture vans will be needed. They are coming on Thursday."

Chimble struggled to keep face and voice straight. "What did you tell them?"

"I'm afraid my temper was up by the time they had finished and I overstepped the mark. My answer was…" He cleared his throat. "By nature both spherical and plural."

# Chapter Ten

Amelia Chaunter's efforts to bring Clagtoft Silver Band back to active life would, in a fairer society, have earned her at least a medal. She plodded around almost every lane in the parish, knocking on doors and pleading for help from anyone known to possess even minimal musical prowess.

Clagtoft had never been in the top echelon of contest-winning bands; if there had been a League it would have been in Division Eight. The instruments had been bought in 1910, with money left to it by Samuel Dreadnought Maltrouser of Clagtoft Hall. Samuel's hope, perhaps, was that by the time George V was replaced there would be a band able to greet the new monarch with a recognisable performance of the National Anthem. It was too much to hope for; twenty-six years was not long enough; when the time came, the band had ceased functioning for the eighth time. The usual reason for silence was a chronic shortage of cornet players able to reach any note above E without the risk of breaking a window.

Amelia was by far the most competent cornettist they ever had… at the age of nine she had a range of two and a half octaves, and by twelve she could sight-read most of the music arranged for bands. She had practised in the garden shed of the house where she still lived.

At the end of her first day's recruitment drive, Amelia noticed that Ernie Transom's handcart was still in Chimble's yard from the last time Abe had borrowed it a year ago. She commandeered it to wheel all the band instruments down to the village hall, after having bullied Chimble into agreeing to the use of the hall for the born-again band to practice, eleven people were present. Not all were musicians. Proggle came and delivered a pep-talk, saying what a great difference a band would make on the protest marches, showing Clagtoft to be a go-ahead place with a lively interest in the performing arts. She was politely applauded, then the band attempted "Abide With Me", which was abandoned during the second verse due to a sticking valve on the tuba.

Liz Otmill was there, sketching the ensemble and pondering the problem of capturing the colour and texture of the instruments in paint. Clive brought his guitar but was barred from joining in. After a spell of wandering around he was sternly told to do up his flies and leave the hall. Olive Ossack, who issued the edict double fortissimo, had come as a volunteer to bang the big drum.

"We'll git a band yit." Amelia optimistically assured Proggle.

When the second practice session produced only five musicians including herself, she decided on drastic action. Dogstead's band still functioned and she cadged a ride with Chimble in his Robin to see how many of its members she could persuade to augment her own band. Her reputation lived on there; her performances of 'The Carnival of Venice', often heard in the park bandstand in Stumpleton, were still talked of in Dogstead when post-practice beer flowed. The outcome of her efforts was a combination confidently expected to render 'The Lincolnshire Poacher' and the first half of 'Colonel Bogey' in identifiable form.

Sundry industrial accidents, arthritis, and sheer geriatric infirmity precluded the possibility of marching, and the only answer was the use of Diana as a mobile bandstand. As the day of Clagtoft march loomed, Chimble worked flat out to get her fit for service.

"It's these damned injectors," he told Proggle. "They'll work perfectly for an 'undred years, then suddenly stop for no rearson."

Proggle was as sympathetic as anybody could be without knowing what an injector was. On a hot, sultry afternoon she had called at the yard to collect some poles for carrying banners on, and had already completed two big ones for walking standard-bearers. She now wanted a smaller pair for a SAVE CLAGTOFT! Banner to be displayed above the Rolls-Royce at the head of the march.

"Look classy on TV that will," she said. "I'll pop down to the Manor House and try it on the Rolls."

"Ah. You'll mebbe need some wellies. All under flood they are."

"I know. I'm ready. Got my bikini on under this; I want to see William's face when I splash up his drive dressed to kill."

Wassing was at his desk in the study and something caught his eye through the window. He looked up and his eyes almost popped out. He collided with doorposts on his way to opening the front door. She was carrying her banner in one hand, her dress and shoes in the other.

"Cassandra!" he exclaimed. "I really don't know where to look!"

"Look where you like mate. It's all the same price. I've come to try this banner, see if it can be fixed up on your car roof."

The water was almost knee-deep in the yard but it didn't worry the big Rolls-Royce wheels. Dangle backed it out with hardly a ripple, in spite of the double handicap of wearing waders and having the bikini-clad Cassandra to examine at the same time.

After considerable discussion, the three trying the banner-poles through the sunshine roof in different positions, there seemed to be no easy way to secure them. In the end, Proggle decided she would recruit two school-children to ride inside and hold it up.

"How about a swimming party in your moat?" suggested Proggle.

Wassing thought not. "It's Clagtoft Drain water, and you know how that stinks at times."

"Like I did, when Chimble let me fall in at Glugwell Creek."

Hammel was persuaded to provide tea in the dry island of the Manor House, Wassing insisting that his guest resume her dress. "You know how rumours so easily begin circulating."

* * *

Ten o'clock was the time appointed for the first protest march to set out from the Stamping Cat, and Eastern Telly had been informed in writing. At about that time a van containing the roving reporter Gerald Nodder and his crew was leaving King's Lynn and heading for Lincolnshire. Coming along the coast road, Gerald opened his map and studied it. "I reckon it's somewhere in that area." he said, pointing to a large blank space.

"Clogthorpe, did you say?" asked the driver.

"Clagtoft, for Chrissake. You've been reading Keith Waterhouse. Turn left at the next roundabout, then look for a sign, either Clagtoft or Dogstead."

They duly turned, and found themselves running alongside an enormous ruler-straight land-drain, three times the width of the road, that looked like going on for ever.

"That looks familiar," said Gerald. "Reckon I saw it last time." The driver grinned to himself; he knew that the fenland contained several hundreds of miles of them, all looking the same.

After about three miles they reached a T-junction and had a choice of left turn over a bridge, or right turn which apparently led only to the horizon.

"Which way boss?" asked the driver.

"Isn't there a signpost?"

"Nope."

They ground to a halt.

"There it is," called one of the crew, pointing. It was lying flat among the growth of keck on the verge. Gerald got out and picked it up. It carried a single pointer which said, 'Iggleby 3½ .'

"Iggleby bloody Piggleby," snarled Nodder. "Anybody got a coin? Heads right, tails left."

They turned right into a lane that wound tortuously along the bank of a drain that never went straight for more than a few yards. The van was heavy and the driver had to change gear to pull away from some of the bends. Then in the distance Nodder spotted another signpost, this time firmly erect. When they got there, it stood at a junction, again with two ways to go, and again with only a single pointer. It bore the magic words "Clagtoft Fen", but pointed across a field, precisely mid-way between the alternatives.

Nodder sighed deeply. "Same coin. It worked last time."

It was a lane out of a nightmare. No ditches, no bushes, hedges or trees, nothing but plain road with plain soil on both sides.

"Stop at the first house," said Nodder wearily.

Inevitably, the first one contained but one man, and he both ancient and deaf.

"Is this Clagoft Fen? I said IS THIS CLAGTOFT FEN?"

The old head was shaken, the shrivelled features deadpan.

"The SIGNPOST said CLAGTOFT FEN."

Another shake.

"What's this place then, if at all?"

"Squadderby Fen. You come right through Clagtoft Fen."

Nodder took a deep breath. "Where's the Stamping Cat? The STAMPING CAT?"

The old man went inside, then emerged holding a fat tabby, still apparently asleep. "Onny cat as I 'ev. Don't do no stamping, far as I know."

Nodder realised he was having it pulled. "THE PUB. THE STAMPING CAT AT CLAGTOFT."

Apparent realisation dawned among the wrinkles and he pointed leftward to the horizon. "That there's Clagtoft church."

It looked to be about five miles away. "You can tonn round in my gairt," said the man.

The van was already pointing in the direction of the church. "Isn't that the way to it?"

The man walked silently round the van, inspected it critically, kicked a tyre. "It'll nivver do it," he said.

"Never do what?"

"Jump ower the Forty-foot. That's the onny way it'd git to Clagtoft that road."

\* \* \*

Strenuous efforts were going on to get the march ready for ten o'clock. Trudgen had grudgingly released the children from school to join it, but had, perhaps unwisely, told them they could come in fancy dress or on decorated bicycles. The result was closer to a carnival than a political demonstration; several grotesque visions invented by Disney were represented, mingling with the fairies, witches and pixies of the more traditional forms of lunacy.

Fighting broke out over who was to ride in the Rolls-Royce and hold the banner; nobody wanted the job because they didn't like the look of Dangle. Liz Otmill solved that problem by offering £1 each to the takers; the fighting continued for the opposite reason. Wassing sat in the back, looking pale and miserable; he had excused himself from actual marching on arthritic grounds.

Chimble v. Diana's injector had not been decisively fought out, though Abe had the upper hand for the time being. The back of the lorry looked colourful. The borrowed Dogstead players insisted on wearing their own uniforms of red blazers and grey trousers; Amelia had her natives sported the older Clagtoft style, known locally as lion-tamer jackets and ratting-hats.

97

The band's repertoire was severely restricted by two governing factors: 1. whether or not enough copies of printed music had survived; and 2. whether or not, granting survival, the players could master the technicalities. Amelia had sifted with skill, the resulting programme being: The Lincolnshire Poacher; Onward, Christian Soldiers; The Skye Boat Song; The Old Rugged Cross; and the first 36 bars of Colonel Bogey. They went through the programme while they waited for the media to arrive, causing Frank Wowser's dog, which lived at Waddie's Cottage, to start howling, which lasted continuously for three days.

Police Constable Albert Tussock had heard that Clagtoft was due for media coverage, and though scheduled for Squadderby that day he thought he ought to be there when it came on TV. As he approached the Stamping Cat yard his highly trained eye spotted several glasses of beer in people's hands. Ha! Serving drinks outside normal hours. He dismounted and inspected something in his bicycle at close range, shook it and spun the wheel. Give 'em time to hide the drinks. Nothing beats the human touch. Respect tolerance these country lads. When he looked again they were still drinking, and one raised his glass and called, "Good health Constable Tussock!" if that's not defiance, I don't know what is.

"Now, sir, where was that drink purchased?"

"Tesco's."

"You expect me to believe that? In a glass?"

"Oh, no, constable. It was in a tin but I borrowed a glass off Edie Grunsell to drink it out of. Only common people drink out of tins." He produced an empty beer tin, and so did two other people he asked.

"Now, Miss Proggle, can you tell me what this gathering is about?"

"Thought you knew mate. It's about making our voice heard against the wanton and senseless destruction of our way of life."

"Very commendable, I'm sure. And who is it what will hear this protest?"

"Eastern Telly. Be here any minute. Soon as they arrive we shall strike off along Stumpleton Road..."

"Hang on a minute. Do I understand you will be making use of the King's Highway?"

"Queens."

"Whatever."

98

"Of course. A perfectly legitimate use of said highway. Been used for suchlike, many times in these troubled islands, and will be many..."

"Just one point, Miss Proggle. There is such a thing as unlawful obstruction, as I'm sure you are aware."

"How the hell can lawful use be unlawful obstruction?"

"Ah – there, we enter a highly contemptuous area of the law, one which has occupied many an hour of a court's time. What I mean, dear, is that we like to know in advance what your plans are, so we can make suitable arrangements for traffic regulation, crowd control and so on."

George Hunking had walked up and heard what Tussock said. "Perhaps I could lend a hand there constable. I am sworn in as a special constable. At your service any time."

"Right you are lad. Get your badge on. Find out the procession route, then stay ahead of it and stop the traffic at each junction. Any difficulty, give me a shout and I'll come and sort things out."

"Where will you be?"

"Along here, Main Road. Everybody out on the procession, there has to be a watch kept for looters. All these premises empty and unguarded become a happy hunting-ground."

Proggle had initially worked out a route, which included Lollycock Bridge, but when Diana was included as a mobile bandstand it had to be changed. "She's too broad in the beam," said Chimble. "They had to fetch a monster crane from Lincoln, that time the school bus took a short cut that way."

Then a modified route had been agreed, including a turn-round in the drive of the Manor House; it in turn was abandoned when the flood came.

"O.K.," said Proggle, "So it will have to be Silt Lane. Tractors use it, so Diana ought to cope."

"Rattle the band's dentures a bit," said Chimble, "But they can stop for a breather."

So Hunking was despatched to the first junction, and Tussock warned him to watch out for the TV people coming, and explained the route.

"How will I know it's them?"

"Simple recognition lad. A good policeman never forgets a face. Anybody that looks like Martin Bell, Kate Adie, any o' that lot."

99

Little more than an hour late, Gerald Nodder and his crew rolled up and parked across the entrance to the Stamping Cat Yard.

"Can't park theer," shouted Clive. "Possession's coming out that way."

Gerald got out and took in the scene. The ancient Rolls was scowling below its unaccustomed 'Save Clagtoft' banner; behind it towered the Sentinel, shimmering and shuddering as if preparing to take the lead with a mighty leap.

"Lovely stuff," said Nodder, signalling to camera. "Get the decorated bikes."

"There's two damn great banners an' all," Clive told him.

"What do you do?"

"Play the guitar." He demonstrated his strum-and-yodel technique.

"Keep it up son. You might get on the telly one day. Who's in charge?"

"Miss Proggle. She's gone for a piss but there's a queue."

"Tell her to give it a shake. Is that a gypsy caravan?"

"Nah. Post office that is."

The van moved on and stopped at Chimble's yard, where the monster steam dragline excavator slumbered. "Bloody hell," said Gerald. "Must have crossed Stephenson's Rocket with a JCB. We'll have that," he told camera. "And the post office on wheels."

Back at the stamping Cat the band struck up the Lincolnshire Poacher, so the TV crew returned to capture the moment for posterity. Clive gyrated behind the Rolls, under the towering cab of Diana, dancing and yodelling with all his might, with no reference to what the band did. Behind Diana, Proggle walked backwards with her loud-hailer, trying to marshal the raggle-taggle trail of dressed-up children and decorated bicycles.

"Get a shot from that school-yard," said Gerald. "With the village hall in background."

The sound man was well placed to capture the rousing strains of Colonel Bogey, but the performance was somewhat overshadowed when Diana's safety-valve opened with a deafening roar.

Gerald grabbed Proggle by the arm and beckoned the sound man over. "This is great stuff, Miss... er..."

100

"Cassandra Proggle. This is only a try-out mind. We're fighting for the existence of our village, and not just with marches. On several fronts – in Westminster, with the Environment people, in Europe itself. Believe me, fen people don't take a threat like this lying down."

"I can see that. What other…"

"If it becomes necessary, we shall totally isolate Clagtoft from the outside world. Using physical force, including firearms, if all else has failed. Of all the places they could land their stupid space scuttles, they have to pick on the richest food-growing land…"

"Can you give us a phone number, in case we have to get in touch love? And we can let you know when it'll be on, if."

"What d'you mean, if? Didn't come all this way for sod-all, did you? Don't you want to see us parading down Duchess of York Drive?"

"Love to, but I think we'll have to get by without. Must press on. Got a murder to do at Peterborough on the way back."

He jotted down Cassandra's number, then he and his crew climbed back into the van and vanished.

Happy that at least the seed of national fame had been sown, the march continued jauntily into Duchess of York Drive, where miraculously the only signs of opposition were a few of last year's conkers tossed into the tuba and a solitary dissenting mini-banner saying "Get Us Some Descent Housing Let The UFOs Have This Slum."

On Stumpleton Road there was a brief pause to allow Chimble to see to Diana's life-giving fire and fetch some buckets of water from Ketchup Terrace, then along Main Road, which by rights ought to have been lined with cheering, flag waving crowds but contained only a sleepy P.C. Tussock. Past the Old Slaughterhouse, were a startled Dr. Mulfry looked out from her deserted surgery, then they turned into Silt Lane. At the junction some heated words were going on between Special Constable George Hunking and Sergeant Flagon of Dogstead police, whose car had been obstructed in the execution of its duty.

The rough surface of Silt Lane and the rigidity of Diana's springs conspired to prevent the band playing without risk of broken teeth. It was no deterrent to Olive Ossack on the big drum; she hammered on relentlessly, her expression registering bliss at the discovery of a way to make loud noises without going hoarse.

The first sign of impending trouble was when the Rolls-Royce came to a stop in a mud-patch. Where Silt Lane passed the grounds of Clagtoft Hall, some large trees hung over it and there was an area of almost perma-mud. Dangle's old face lit up at the challenge; he was thoroughly bored by grinding along in a low gear, and fed up with the complaints of one of the banner-holders saying she wanted to go to the lav. His Italian blood responded to the situation; he called down to the car's old engine-room for maximum power, let in the clutch and leaped forward with the agility of a startled stag. Mud spurted up from the rear wheels; Clive and Diana were plastered from top to bottom.

Chimble climbed down from his lofty perch, laughing like a maniac, waving to the white, panic-stricken face of Wassing who was looking back to see what had caused the leap. The banner-holder dropped her side, shot out of the car, removed her wet pants and flung them crossly into the undergrowth, then headed home on foot with an air of indignation.

Chimble surveyed the mud-patch. "Nivver git Diana through that. Sheer weight'd tek her down, even at full pelt."

Proggle said, "Can you detour round it? It's dry on the field."

It was dry, but it was set with cauliflowers within a day or two of maturity. "Could do," said Abe, "If Kelter don't mind a few mashed caulis. I'll aim for that patch where here ain't any growing."

Diana lacked the athletics grace of the Rolls, but she was willing. "'Old yer 'ats on," Chimble told the band. "We're going cross-country." He opened the regulator wide; Diana took a deep breath and charged the caulis, the band bumping up and down holding on to their instruments.

When she reached the bare patch, her flight ended abruptly. Her front wheels suddenly dropped into a hole created by the weight; her hind wheels lifted and were turning in mid-air. The band slid gracefully forward and finished up in an untidy pile of instruments and players behind the cab.

Proggle came running across as Chimble climbed awkwardly out of the tilted cab. "Anybody hurt?"

Apart from minor bruising, it seemed nobody was. The rest of the marchers came across to look, including Josh Kelter, who farmed the land.

"Could'a telled yer not to goo on that there. Allus 'ev to goo round it wi' a tractor."

"What the 'ell is it?" asked Abe.

Josh pointed to some broken brickwork which had given way. "It's the owd cesspool belonging Clagtoft Hall. Gone down a bit fother, you'd a' bin in amongst the last lot they dropped when anybody lev there."

Although they could smell nothing except Diana's smoke, most of the marchers turned away rapidly.

Abe peered into the black hole. "Historic stuff then. Might be some of the great Maltrouser's in there. We'll send that archaeology gel down to look."

There was no way that Diana could be rescued from her predicament, so the remainder of the march was called off.

In the late afternoon of that day, when all the excitement had died down Cassandra got a call from Gerald Nodder of Eastern Telly.

"We'll have to come again when you do your next march love. Sorry, but we can't use any of this morning's footage."

"Why not? Did something go wrong?"

"Technically, nothing. Everything came out fine; some lovely shots of your march. Just one little detail we didn't notice until we got back and ran it over. Your guitar-player had his plonker swinging out all the time. Can't put that on at family viewing time."

Chimble fired up his track-laying digger and rescued Diana by towing her back to the yard for repair. Kelter wasn't concerned about his mashed cauliflowers; he had already sold the crop as a job-lot to a soup manufacturer.

# Chapter Eleven

Violet Wask had to leave the village for a few days, which delayed Proggle showing her the architect's plan of the castle. Meantime, it was shown to almost everybody else.

When they finally got together, Proggle insisted on going to the site before producing it.

"Four gigantic towers. That's the story, right?"

"So I understand," said Violet.

"And a lot of people are doubtful that it ever existed, right?"

"Rightly so. Scepticism is the safest attitude in archaeology. Speculation, certainly, but until tangible evidence is revealed…"

"There you are then. Tangible evidence, if ever there was."

Violet took the plan and studied it carefully for a long time, Proggle standing by looking quietly triumphant.

"Mm," said Violet eventually. "An interesting drawing of a pretend castle."

"What d'you mean, pretend?"

Violet imitated Oscar Straddle's description of 'four great towers, visible from Lincoln Cathedral.'

Then she tapped the plan. "You probably wouldn't see these towers from Iggleby church. They're only ten feet high."

Proggle snatched back the plan and glared at it. She hadn't bothered to look at the figures. It was plain enough; the height from the base to the top was given as 10' 1½". Is that a code of some sort?"

Violet shook her head and pointed to some text at the bottom. "It's not easy to read but it says that the materials to be used are teak and oak or imported mahogany. 'Construction shall be jointed throughout, and all interior surfaces planed smooth.' And there is the main clue…" she indicated more writing on the opposite side. "For Samuel and Mildred Maltrouser, something, something, children of

S. D. Maltrouser Esquire of Clagtoft Hall. Bless their hearts it looks like. So what you have here is an elaborate children's garden toy. A wooden Wendy-castle."

Proggle threw the plan down and took a kick at it. "Bugger you Ernie Transom. I'll stuff him when I go down there."

"Hang on," grinned Violet. "Never throw anything away, a golden rule of archaeology, until you've wrung the last ounce of information out of it." She retrieved the plan. "Look at that bit, along the top."

There was a silhouetted view of a village.

"Didn't make sense," said Proggle. "Just smudges."

"It's the other way up." Violet glanced around. "If you were standing, say, on Pudding Lane, half a mile from Clagtoft and looking towards it – see? Trees round the pond, almshouses. This might be two hundred, two-fifty years ago. Church, undoubtedly that one; different windmill, but perhaps on the same site as the brick one. The Manor House there. And, hey presto, Clagtoft Hall and a ruddy great castle, just to the right."

"I'll be damned. So what d'you think? This was a wooden model of a real castle?"

"I'd be guessing, wouldn't I? How about this: Old Sam Maltrouser imagined there was, and being a practical joker he goes round telling yarns about it. Tunnel to Tattershall, all that. Folk-stories like that go echoing around for yonks, and some people believe them."

"So much for our delaying the Europe scheme..."

"On the other hand, that silhouette might have come from an old, perhaps pre-photographic view, and was used by Sam to give the architect an idea for his children's toy."

"The only thing I want to know, can it help the campaign?"

"It could. I'll take a walk along Conker Drove, get everything lined up by this silhouette and see if the castle comes where everybody says it was."

"Then start digging?"

"Then start investigating. There's a geophysics team in the county at the moment; if I go to Lincoln with a good story, I might just bag their services."

"Oh, to hell with it. I'll leave it to you. I'm not banking on the castle anymore." She strode away with an air of urgency.

* * *

105

On a hot afternoon in the school holiday, Clive took his guitar and wandered along Snogging Lane, wondering if those drums of black oil were still there. Glugwell Creek, he noticed with some satisfaction, was now a complete oil-slick nearly up to where it joined Clagtoft Drain. An idea crossed his mind, an idea for some time later in the holiday. Involving he rest of the oil and a box of matches.

Around the clump of trees, nothing had changed. The drum he had kicked was now empty but there were still plenty more, both large and small. Within half an hour he had them all oozing into the ground, either by kicking through their shells or by unscrewing the bungs. He watched the fascinating result for a few minutes, then decided it would be a good policy to return to the village by another route.

The rough farm-track leading away from Snogging Lane was unknown to him, so he explored it. At one place along it was a heap of strawy material, his nose telling him it was pigsh. Definitely pigsh. He'd been in Clagtoft long enough to distinguish between pigsh and cowsh. He broke into a trot until he got to the windward. The track ran for a short distance alongside dry dyke, then crossed it on a bridge of old railway sleepers and turned abruptly towards Clagtoft Fen. On the way was a solitary brick barn to explore, a disappointment as it contained only a heap of rotten hessian sacks.

On the near horizon was something more interesting; apple-trees. He could see the fruit on them, some of it mouth-watering red. There were buildings to the left of them, but reckoned if he approached across a potato-field he could get there without being seen. He wasn't that keen on apples but the possible triumph drew him on. There was a tractor at work, near enough to mask any noise he might make.

A thorn hedge guarded the property, but the trees hung over it into the field. One large green apple was enticingly low but found it hard, and sour enough to make his eyes water. The red ones looked the best, but they were higher. He noticed a dead, half-fallen tree, and reckoned he could reach if he climbed on to it.

He laid his guitar down near the hedge and began scrambling up. The tractor engine stopped abruptly. The sudden silence froze him for a moment, realising he was making quite a noise himself.

Then he heard a woman's voice coming from quite close, near to the buildings.

"Well, yes, but not with oils, which is what I'm using. Water-colour's different, you can't faff about with it much afterwards. Damn. Dobbin's moved again."

Then the man's voice, but Clive couldn't hear what was said. Very cautiously he moved to another horizontal branch, from where he might see past a row of runner beans in the garden. It was that artist woman from out of Duchess of York Drive, standing at her easel with a little table beside it, working rapidly and chatting. The subject was still hidden, so Clive reached up to an apple-tree branch to raise himself high enough to see over the bean-row.

It was Kelter's horse, harnessed to a single-furrow plough; and in the ploughman's position was Harry Gozzard, naked.

Clive hung on, goggling at the spectacle, until his arms would hold him no longer. He dropped heavily back on to the fallen tree-branch, which broke with a sound like a gun-shot, sending him crashing down on to the thorn hedge. He let out a screaming howl as a hundred thorns did their appointed job on his skin, then rolled off on to his guitar, which snapped in half under his weight. He scrambled to his feet and shot off across the potato-field at a speed he had never before attained. It wasn't until he reached the footbridge into Squadderby Road that he paused, panting, and realised he had left his broken guitar behind.

\* \* \*

Clagtoft Parish Council held its monthly meeting in the kitchen of the village hall. The kitchen had been the temporary meeting-place since 1938, when the new hall was erected. The fund had fallen short of expectation by £18, so the councillors of the day nobly agreed to forgo the luxury of a separate council-chamber until sufficient money had flowed in. It didn't; the villagers, having got the hall they wanted, saw nothing wrong with councillors sitting in a kitchen. The spare corrugated iron earmarked for the council chamber had long since vanished.

Present at this meeting were Councillors Herbert Brangle (Chairman), William deMondord Wassing, Abraham Chimble, Mrs. Glenda Hovel, Miss Cassandra Proggle, and Fred Cletch. The

Parish Clerk, Mr. Geo. W. Hunking, was in attendance. In the public gallery (formed by bringing your own chair in from the main hall) were Mrs. Olive Ossack and Miss Violet Wask, Community Archaeologist.

Coun. Brangle declared the meeting open and extended a welcome to all. He explained that Miss Wask had to return to Stumpleton, so he proposed dealing with archaeological matters early in the meeting.

But first, an important announcement had to be put before the meeting. Notice had been received from the Commission that, in view of the impending purchase of land by the European Space Agency, the construction of a runway, and the consequent removal of all buildings in Clagtoft, a proposal had been put forward for the reorganisation of local government.

"I won't read out all the gory details," said Brangle; "We shall all get our own copy in due course. This is the first written notice we have had, and if the proposal is adopted it means that this council will cease to exist. Local government in what is left of Clagtoft would be merged with Squadderby to the north and Iggleby to the east. If anybody had told me six months ago that Clagtoft was due to join the ranks of the Lost Villages, I would have called him mad."

Coun. Miss Proggle said, "Mad is the operative word. We are dealing with lunatics. However, the loonies don't always win the day. Calm, rational common-sense often prevails, and if we shout long and loud enough and raise enough hell and hubbub in the right places, it will prevail this time."

"Hear, hear." Said Coun. Fred Cletch. "I propose a vote of thanks to Coun. Proggle for the vast amount of work she has already done."

"Write that into the minutes George," said the Chairman. "Put somebody's name in as seconder. Chimble's will do; we'll tell him when he wakes up. Now, can we move on to the business concerning Miss Wask? I believe she is ready to tell us what she has found up to date."

Violet had prepared a map, a copy of which she passed around to each. "Using an old silhouette sketch of the village which Miss Proggle tracked down, and which included the castle, I took a sighting of alignments and found that the probable site of the castle was some distance south-west of what people think of as it. The area shaded on the map is where it seems to have been."

108

Proggle shook Chimble awake and pointed at the shaded are. "Ah," said Abe. "Back to the owd railway question are we? Where to put the station? Don't tell me we got an answer from the L.N.E.R. at last."

"For Chrissake drop off again," said Coun. Mrs. Hovel. "Let's get on with the business."

"Please proceed Miss Wask," said Brangle.

"I contacted Lincoln, knowing that a geophysics team were in the north of the county. It was a lucky shot; they were just due to move to Norfolk, and were able to spend two and a half hours at Clagtoft on the way."

"Was that them I seen 'obbling about on Zimmer Frames?" asked Olive. "Onny youngsters, an' all."

"They weren't Zimmers," said Violet. "They were latest technology for detecting things below ground level. They surveyed all of Cut-throat Paddock and part of Bosh Green. I have a print-out of their results, but it needs experts to read it so I won't bother the meeting with it. The main positive result is some clear responses, likely to be foundations of ancient walls, at the places marked "A" and "B" on the map."

"Good Lord," said Brangle. "That's right alongside my property."

"I'm afraid so, Mr. Brangle. In fact, the alignment suggests that Goatskin Hall is built right over the site of, well, whatever it was. Which makes total excavation impossible, and would need your permission to work in your garden, even for a partial investigation."

Brangle cleared his throat thunderously. "How… how deep would the, er… excavation have to be?"

"Whatever it takes. We wouldn't know until we got to it. Certainly not less than a metre, perhaps a lot more. We might have to use machines."

Proggle said, "That's no problem. We have it right here in Clagtoft." She jabbed Abe in the ribs. "Abe? Abe? Might want the Chairman's garden dug up. That O.K.?"

"What? Oh, Herbert's garden, sure. Another moat is it? Let's all have one. Moats a speciality. Estimates free. How about Woad Farm Fred, while I 'appen to be in the area?"

Brangle called the meeting to order. "The possibility of there having been a castle is, of course, only one nail in our… I mean, one weapon in our armoury. There's the healing properties of the water in Gandle's Pit..."

"That fell flat on its face." said Proggle.

"Like what my Auntie Meg did when she went down theer." shouted Olive going off into raucous laughter.

"Mr. Chairperson," said Coun. Mrs. Glenda Hovel. "May I remind the meeting that, while we are resolved to fight to the finish to save our village from extinction, we are also committed, as a demonstration of our resolve, to go on discussing the long-term future of it. Defeatism, it was seen in wartime, is the most insidious..."

"Hear, hear," said Coun. Wassing. "As one to have had the heavy hand of Europe and defied it..."

"Right," said Brangle. "But just before we move on I would like, on behalf of the Council, to thank Miss Wask for her, er, informative report. And to wish her success in her... investigations."

A mild outbreak of clapping followed Violet as she murmured her thanks and left the chamber.

The Clerk of the Council, Mr. Geo. W. Hunking, followed her out, no doubt to hold open the outer door for her.

Brangle went on: "What we see, over there on the draining-board, is Coun. Mrs. Hovel's suggestion for the development of the Piggery Lane area into the shopping precinct. Mrs. Hovel tells me that the model was made by her son, and I think great credit is due to the lad."

"The only parts missing," said Glenda, "Are the entrance to the multi-storey car-park off Slodger's Pad, some parts of the roof-garden on top of Debenham's, and the new flagpole on the forecourt of the Town Hall."

"My fault I'm afraid," said Proggle. "I volunteered to transport it on my handlebars and the jolting was too much for the glue."

"Nevertheless, I think it gives the Council plenty to... er, think about and discuss." said Brangle.

Discuss it they did, until very late evening, latterly in the bar of the Stamping Cat. In those few hours the village was promised a fountain, a free car-wash, a public swimming-pool, and a bronze statue of Coun. Miss Cassandra Proggle, "Doing a similar job to that there one in, where is it? Amsterdam, or Copenhagen or somewhere."

110

* * *

Wassing never joined the post-meeting parties at the Stamping Cat; he hadn't the stomach for a lot of drink. He kept a bottle of rather expensive sherry at the Manor House, mainly for visitors, but the contents of his own glass often went back into the bottle when visitors had gone.

On that particular night he was also worried about what Mrs. Hammel might be up to in his absence. Perhaps unwisely, he had told her about the second phone call, warning him to be packed ready for the furniture vans arriving. He had impressed on her the absolute necessity for defiance; but she had an inbuilt fear of officialdom and was sure that if they were not ready they would find themselves thrown into a dark Continental dungeon. A dozen times already, he had caught her filling cardboard boxes with household good, and had spent most of his recent time watching and restraining her.

As usual, Dangle stopped the Rolls precisely too far away from the doorstep for him to comfortably step over. And as usual he attempted a semi-leap from the running-board and failed to make it, dipping one foot into the murky drainwater. When he opened the door it would move only a few inches; in the way was a massive cupboard, which Hammel had somehow dragged from the kitchen and placed ready for quick loading.

It took ten minutes of shouting before he was rescued from his doorstep island; Dangle had gone round the back of the house, and Hammel was busy packing upstairs somewhere. She eventually heard him, and managed to drag the cupboard far enough for him to squeeze through. "Just imagine if the house had caught fire." he told her.

He went into the study, switched on the electric fire, and placed his wet shoe and sock to dry. Then he went on with his next letter to Claud.

"My Dear Brother, At the moment of writing I am in the study of the dear old Manor House – yes, it still stands, though for how much longer God only knows. It is once more a moated manor. I contracted a local man for the restoration of the original moat but unfortunately the mechanism controlling the level of water had rotted

111

away and the garden was flooded. It is now virtually an island-house.

Poor Hammel is timid at the prospect of defying authority and insists on preparing for departure... every time a vehicle is heard she rushes to a window. The expected Public Enquiry has not yet been heard of, and I suspect the European people are sabotaging the process behind the scenes, hoping no doubt for a coup de grace and the satisfaction of seeing the village prone and lifeless before the democratic machinery is even set in motion. One thing, which may yet forestall the day of doom, is the archaeologist's discovery of remains which may be those of Clagtoft Castle. A complication is that they are in the garden of my friend Herbert Brangle of Goatskin Hall. He told me in confidence that an excavation there might influence an independent valuation, should he be compelled to sell. His instinct is to get the highest possible price for it – quite unselfishly. I may add, since this would be guarding the interest of his heirs and successors.

As if I hadn't troubles enough, the long-lasting feud between Hammel and my chauffeur has flared once more. How I envy you, your simple, idyllic rural life on your dairy-farm! On Saturdays, when I release D'Angelis from duty, he spends much time at his allotment. Now that some intervening trees have gone, Hammel can see him there and has noticed that he spends long periods inside the shed with five or six other men. I expect they just sit chatting about things to grow next season, and so on, but her mind dwells on sinister things. Yesterday, without my knowledge or consent, she rang Dogstead police and told them about it.

The upshot is that I shall be having a Saturday visit from them, so that they can make their own observations and act as they think fit. I have told them not to take D'Angelis away for questioning, as I am totally dependent on the Rolls for mobility. My arthritis being what it is, I took part in our recent 'protest march' in it. That affair was to have been seen on TV news, but for some undisclosed reason it was suppressed. I tell you, there are ominous secret forces at work in this old country!

Must put down my pen. Will continue tomorrow. An exhausting day; I can hardly keep my eyes open."

* * *

On Saturday afternoon, Wassing stood at the landing window and watched Dangle leave the granary, wearing his Wellingtons and make his way along the Drain bank, over the footbridge, and into his allotment shed. So far, Mrs. Hammel had been right. Shortly after, a knock on the Manor House door was answered by Mrs. Hammel. It was P. C. Tussock, and he was apologising for bringing his bicycle right up to the door, because of the flood-water.

The three mounted a vigil on the landing, Mrs. Hammel telling her story all over agin, and decorating it with her opinion of men in general and Italians in particular. "Look," she said. "There's two on 'em, as allus reckons to come."

Jack Grunsell from the Stamping Cat, followed by Harry Gozzard, crossed the footbridge and headed for the shed. Grunsell carried a plastic supermarket bag. A minute later, Abraham Chimble came, glancing around furtively before opening the door. Within five minutes, eight Clagtoft males had been swallowed by the little building.

"Worth while 'aving a look," said the constable. "No evidence of lawlessness at the moment but as the lady says, there's enough furtive behaviour…"

"I'll come with you," said Wassing. "As my servant appears to be involved in… whatever…"

"As you wish, sir."

Suitably wellingtoned, Wassing went out the back way while Tussock remounted and pedalled round by the road. The policeman made a silent reconnaissance around the shed. The window was decisively curtained on the inside and a constabulary eye at several possible peepholes revealed careful precautions against any such investigations.

From inside came the sounds of intermittent music, with some canned voices, and an occasional burst of real-life male laughter. Tussock pointed out that an overhead electric cable, supported halfway by a sycamore, ran to the shed from the nearby Bramble Cottage. "Got a telly in there," he whispered. "Illicit video shows, that's what it is."

"Er, pornographic will that be?"

"Bet your last dollar. Lot o' trade in that there, in Stumpleton."

From inside came another roar of laughter, and a voice, probably Gozzard's, "Cor, look at that one!"

113

Tussock took a deep, duty-inducing breath and tried the door. It was secured on the inside. He banged his fist on it. "Police! Police! Open this door!"

There was a scuffle inside and the TV sound went off. "Hang on a minute," came a muffled voice. Tussock repeated his request.

The door opened and Chimble's face looked out, rather flushed. "Ah! Police-constable Tussock, how are you? Good afternoon William."

"What goes on in 'ere?"

Chimble opened the door wide to reveal the company sitting around on a variety of chairs facing the television. "Clagtoft Gardeners' Club," said Abe. "Just in the middle of a session on the gentle art of growing geraniums."

On the screen, Geoffrey Hamilton of 'Gardeners World' was busily pruning away at his blackcurrant bushes and explaining how to do it.

# Chapter Twelve

Dr. Fanny Mulfry's main practice was in Stumpleton, but on two afternoons a week she loaded her car with patients' records, a few medications she knew would be needed, and a practice nurse, said "Heigh-ho for the Old Slaughterhouse", and set off for her Clagtoft surgery. She enjoyed the break from routine and had quickly found herself more nearly in tune with the rural wavelength then with the urban.

She even enjoyed the house visits she did in the fen. They were necessarily house visits in most cases; some retired people on her list were more than five miles from the village and had no transport other than a bicycle. And she was endlessly fascinated by glimpses into the life-style of these sturdy, independent people, as far removed from her own as if they lived on another planet. Returning one day from a remote call, she saw Violet Wask plodding around in a small grass paddock. Not pressed for time, she stopped and went in.

"Looking for another castle down here?"

Violet laughed. "Not very likely. Two hundred years ago this was raw fen. Nobody about but slodgers, slodging around catching their dinners. About half of them suffering from frequent attacks of ague, and never a doctor in sight. Cured themselves with opium, grown on their own patch. No, what I'm following up is a reference to a windmill supposed to have been in this area."

"They did some corn-grinding?"

"No. It was an early drainage mill. There's some peat here, which Shrunk to a lower level when the water left it. To keep it dry they would need to lift the water up to the drain behind that high bank. Having a silt bed it wouldn't be subject to shrinkage."

The doctor looked around her. "It all looks so simple and tranquil. But when you learn about things, it's almost as complicated as the human body. Have you found anything?"

"I think so. Look carefully, there's a depression coming this way from the drain. I think that was the man-made channel down to where the mill-wheel would pick up the water."

"Any sign of the mill?"

Violet shook her head. "I hardly expected any. It would be a post-mill; just a tree-trunk stuck into the ground and the mill hung round it to rotate."

Mulfry looked at her watch. "Must get on. Have to pick up the nurse and take her back to Stumpleton. Can I give you a lift?"

"No thanks. Got a borrowed bike here. I'm of down to Slaumy Gowt next. A campaign meeting to see if it might be made a Site of... what is it?"

"Special Scientific Interest. Great idea. I've heard it's a twitchers' paradise."

They went their separate ways.

\* \* \*

Slaumy Gowt was a pocket of Clagtoft Fen which had escaped the attentions of the Adventurers, the men who had by financing drainage work turned wilderness into fertile plain. About 20 acres in extent, it received human intervention only around its fringes, where it threatened to interfere with the growing of crops. Inside, it teemed with wildlife both in and out of the stretches of water, which punctures its scenery. There were plants and trees in profuse variety, populated by birds of every possible size and shape. Rabbits, big, strong and healthy on the diet kindly provided by local farmers, regarded Slaumy Gowt as their refuge.

The party due to examine the place came by three means: a Mercedes containing Herbert Brangle, Glenda Hovel, Roland Clunch, M.P., and Mrs. Clunch; a Robin containing Abraham Chimble and Cassandra Proggle; and a borrowed bicycle carrying Violet Wask. Only two of them had ever visited the place before; as a boy, Chimble had fished in one of the pools and in the deep freeze of a bygone winter, Proggle had skated on one. Both remarked, on

116

seeing it again, that it was far more heavily overgrown than they remembered it.

"Here we have something we believe to be unique," boomed Brangle. "The fen as it was before drainage. A place where men walked on stilts and crossed wide creeks by pole-vaulting over."

"Are you gong to demonstrate?" asked Proggle.

"I might have, fifty years ago. I think Miss Wask is the only one built for it today."

They had parked on Tupdyke Lane and walked to a point about a hundred yards inside, to where the way forward was blocked by a large pool surrounded by massive willows, its fringes guarded by tangles of thistles, brambles and aggressive nettles.

Mrs. Clunch was terrified. "What a fraightening place. Can't your council get it cleared up Mr. Brangle?"

"We did have plans for it. Right up to early this year, we discussed its possibilities as a tourist attraction. I must admit, we were working from maps. The reality looks quite something else."

"This was to be the road in," said Chimble. "Car park over there to the left. Café and toilets over there, between this pit and the one beyond it, which is the biggest."

"Really!" said Mrs. Clunch. "I'm afraid you wouldn't get me here as a tourist."

"You stick to Bournemouth," advised Chimble, flicking a turd aside with his toe. "Got the squirrels toilet-trained there."

Roland Clunch said, "Maybe I've got this wrong but somebody mentioned this as a possible S.S.S.I. Wouldn't have thought tourists would be encouraged, if so."

"Dead right," said Proggle. "Slaumy Gowt Wildlife Centre was the first idea. We noticed that Peamoor Water, in Dogstead parish, attracts twitchers, plus crowds to watch water-skiing and all that nonsense. We though we could go one better and attract enthusiasts for four-legged wildlife as well. And jumpers." She prodded a stationary frog with her foot and it took a mighty bound in the direction of Mrs. Clunch, who screamed and hid behind her husband.

Brangle said, "It's this European threat that's changed our minds. We think now there'd be more clout in going down the conservation road."

Glenda Hovel had been prowling away from the party, peering at what was growing, scribbling in a notebook.

"Anything unusual Glenda?" called Proggle.

"Oh, loads of that stuff," Glenda pointed. "Celandine. Sweet nettle, stinking mayweed, silverweed..." she turned a page of her notebook. "Henbane, shepherd's purse..."

"Anything in it?" asked Chimble.

"Horse-tail, saffron, I think, fennel. Oh, and one I can't put a name to. Thought it was hyssop at first but then I saw a bigger one. Might be some sort of flax. Not toadflax, I use that. Not comfrey either!"

"Is there much of it?" asked Brangle.

"Quite a lot. Twenty or thirty plants, all in the same area from here."

They all examined one but nobody could name it. Proggle thought it looked like her granny's aspidistra. They were interrupted by an impatient hooting from the lane and Violet went to see.

"A lorry wants to get past," she reported. "Can't get past the cars."

"Damn," said Brangle. "Perhaps once a month..." They all went to the lane. It was a cross-looking driver with a load of steaming manure, one whiff of which sent Mrs. Clunch scurrying back into the perils of wet-land.

Chimble surveyed the neighbourhood and spotted a cart-track leading off Tupdyke lane. "I'll back my Robin into that Herbert. You can come in front of me with yours."

The Robin sailed in as if born to it, but the Mercedes was less nimble. Tupdyke Lane was made with horses in mind and there was little width between dykes for obtaining alignment. And as Brangle admitted sheepishly afterwards, he was never very good at reversing. After the lorry had gone, its driver smiling broadly, they were left with a trapped Robin, its escape blocked by an immovable Mercedes with one wheel halfway down a dyke.

Roland Clunch had mentioned earlier that he had to be at the Municipal Hall in Stumpleton at particular time for a meeting; that place suddenly seemed incredibly distant.

Their thoughts turned to Chimble, the practical man. "What's the next move, Abe?" asked Brangle.

Chimble stroked his moustache and farted thoughtfully. "It weean't drive out, not from that far down. And the Boeing'll nivver pull it out, even if it was right side on it."

"What's the Boeing?" snapped Clunch peevishly. His pockets and his wife's handbag had been searched for a mobile phone and none found.

"My Robin. Whet we need's a tractor and there's nowt at wock within a mile just when you need it. I'll walk up to Cletch's an' borry one. Me gout ain't that bad. Manage it in an hour."

"Borrow the bike," said Violet. It's Mrs. Grunsell's but I'm sure she won't mind."

Before Chimble set off, Clunch said, "When you get to a phone, have me a taxi sent out would you? I don't want to be stranded here for the rest of the afternoon."

"Dooan't worry maate. 'Ave you mobile again in no time..." A further thought crossed his mind. "Had Diana in stearm this morning, so if I can't git owt else I'll bring her."

He went wobbling off towards Clagtoft, leaving the others to explain to the Clunches who Diana was.

Meantime, Glenda had been back into the wilds and found lots of the unnamed plants. "Some of it flowered earlier this year and I've got loads of seeds. Gets up to my height, apparently, which is higher than most flaxes."

"We'll get an expert opinion," said Proggle. "Somebody who'll declare it as a great rarity not to be disturbed."

"If I can get one up, I'll take it to that horticultural research place. Might be somebody there. But it's got a ferocious root, I nearly burst a blood-vessel trying to pull one up."

The two women raided Chimbles car, found a large screwdriver to dig one up. Brangle paced miserably back and forth, glaring at his shipwrecked Mercedes, while Violet told the Clunches about the archaeology of Clagtoft district.

After an hour a distant whistle brought their eyes to the horizon. A plume of smoke, and the tall, stately outline of Diana picking her way round the serpentine bends at the top end of Tupdyke Lane. Clunch looked at his watch for the hundredth time and told his wife, "We might still make it on time."

He remarked on both the size and the silence of the monster, as Chimble skilfully turned it round in a field entrance and did the last quarter-mile in sprightly reverse. A black-faced Abe climbed down and explained what took so long. "All the blairmed tractors in use, so I had to fire up again."

"What is this machine used for? Asked the M.P.

"Day-trips to Skeggy. Mobile bandstand for protest marches. Owt as anybody wants. Oh and pulling cars out o' dykes." He produced a coil of rope and joined the vehicles. "Stand clear," he warned. "If it happened to break you might git a wallop on the kisser."

It didn't break. A few puffs of the Sentinel engine and the big car rolled on to the road as if weighing no more than a Dinky. Brangle looked anxiously at the back where it had rested on the dyke-side. "Not too much damage." he said hopefully.

Chimble looked. And sniffed. "Smells a bit fishy."

"What does?"

"Smells like brairk fluid." He lay full length and thrust a hand up the tail end. "Ha! Thought so. Pipe bosted. Lost all the oil. Be a towing job I'm afraid Herbert. Using the handbrairk."

"What about my taxi?" bleated Clunch.

"No need for that maate. Jump in with Herbert, tell me where you want to be. Have you there in two shakes."

So the inspection of Slaumy Gowt ended with an impressive procession back along Tupdyke Lane: Diana, then the towrope pulling the Mercedes containing Brangle, clutching the handbrake nervously, the Clunches, still anxiously studying watches, and Glenda Hovel, nursing her unidentified piece of Slaumy Gowt undergrowth; then the Boeing, driven with careful inexpertness by Proggle; and finally Violet Wask, who had opted to retrieve her borrowed bike from the back of Diana and pedal back to Clagtoft.

In the gathering dusk, Stumpletonians were treated to a rare spectacle: a mighty steam wagon making its way to the Municipal Hall, followed at the end of a rope by a car containing their Member of Parliament and his wife. Luckily, there were no policemen around; Diana's licence disc mentioned a date which had appeared in several history-books, and lights were considered a frivolous luxury on such a sky-darkening piece of machinery.

* * *

120

For some time Clive had wandered up and down Main Road without his guitar, looking curiously incomplete. People remarked on it, and asked him where it was. "Lost it." he told them.

But a scheme was beginning to form in his mind. He had seen something he wasn't meant to see, and if he told the village… on the other hand he had been stealing apples. And was already the object of police attention. The question was, what would Liz Otmill or Harry Gozzard or both of them pay him to keep his mouth shut?

The idea had been smouldering for some time, when a surprising thing happened. He was sitting on the churchyard wall when Harry Gozzard drove up in his van and stopped. He got out.

"Just the chap I'm looking for."

Clive's leg-muscles twitched and he almost rolled back off the wall ready to run off. Something in Gozzard's manner held him.

"You let my apples alonn, young Grunsell, else you'll feel my belt round your arse. Understand?"

Clive nodded.

"I grow them to feed me sen, not for thieving young buggers to pinch." He turned to go back to his van, and before he got back there a little surge of defiance arose in Clive.

"I seen you wi' nowt on."

Harry grinned. "Ay? What about it?"

"That… that there woman was doin' a picture, wa'nt she?"

Harry's face beamed. "There's a clever lad! You knew what she was doin'! Go on then, what yer off to do about it?"

Clive sat silent.

Harry came back, brought his big red face within inches of Clive's little pale one. "Yer can do just what the 'ell you like son, as long as yer let my apples alonn."

He went to his van, reached inside and brought out Clive's guitar, the two halves hanging pathetically together by the strings. "How did that happen?"

"Fell on it."

"Where did yer fall from?"

"Out the tree."

"See what I mean? Anybody as goes pinching, they git their comeuppance. That's yer lesson ain't it." He put it on the wall. "Put that one in the bin."

He reached inside the van again, brought out a brand new guitar and thrust it into Clive's hands. "Play that instead. And keep in tune for Gawd's sake."

As the van drove off, Clive's eyes followed it. They were brimming with tears as he turned to examine his gleaming new instrument.

* * *

Glenda Hovel had been faced with a minor problem when she arrived home with the mystery plant from Slaumy Gowt. She intended to preserve it in a pot ready to take it to the horticultural research place a few miles away but the roots were so big and ferociously sinuous that she couldn't find a pot big enough. She planted it in a temporary spot in the garden and kept looking at it through the kitchen window. She had been twice through her library of medical herbs and the boys' books on wild plants but could find nothing to match it.

Gavin suggested, "P'raps it's something Mediterranean, and a migrating bird's brought a seed over."

"Millions to one chance," she thought. "What they eat there passes through 'em long before they get here."

"But even if it is rare, they wouldn't hold up the space program for it would they?"

"Maybe not for that alone, but the job of the Public Enquiry is to add up all the things that would be destroyed."

"They could just move it a bit, to miss Slaumy Gowt." Gavin was looking forward to the spectacle of space-vehicles roaring in. Already he had worked out the direction from which they would appear in the sky and with a piece of hardboard left over from his New Clagtoft he was planning a Lincolnshire version of Edwards Air Base. In it, their house had been spared destruction and was converted as an Advanced Observation Post. He had appointed himself Chief Observer and practised daily with his binoculars.

"Mum, if we did have to move out, what'd happen to all your plants?"

She had given it some thought. "If they gave us a garden at least the same size as this, I'd transplant everything. Then claim for the time it took, and for the value of everything lost. Plus my loss of income through losing touch with customers."

"Would you get away with it?"

"I'd better. If people with big properties can profit from it, as I expect some will, I don't see why we shouldn't have a share in the booty."

"Jumping on the bandwagon, do they call it? Look out, here's The Mouth coming with earache again."

Olive Ossack had come into the front gate. "Nah then duck. I've brought yer summat. Just to say ta for that stuff you gev us last time." She handed Glenda a jar of dark, almost black, jam. "Wild bramble. Out'n last year's crop round the 'All. Don't come better'n them."

"Thank you Mrs. Ossack. "I've heard about your famous jam. How's the earache?"

Olive glanced at Gavin and grinned. "Cleared up in no time. Onny thing was, you gev me two lots an' I got 'em crossed ower." She laughed an ear-splitting laugh. "The other wocked a treat on the owd man."

Glenda hesitated but then joined in the laughter. A thought crossed her mind; "While you're here, would you look at something in my garden, see if you know what it is?"

They went to the mystery herb. Olive took one look and said, "Wadd."

"Wadd?"

"Aye. Dyer's Weed some calls it. Dooan't want that starting up in yer garden – nivver get rid on it."

"You sure about the name?"

"Ought to be. Wocked amongst it, years on end. That's the reason as Cletch's place is called Woad Farm."

"Oh, woad."

"That's what I said. Folks as wocked in it was allus called waddies. That 'ouse next the school, that's Waddies Cottage, where the foreman lev. Run the woad mill, 'e did."

"I see. I found this bit at Slaumy Gowt. No end of it down there."

"Shudn't wonder. Grew it all in the fields down there when I was a gel. Fred Cletch's owd man grew an 'undred acre on it some years, till they gev over using it."

123

"That's settled then," said Glenda. "We shan't stop the Europeans with that."

After Olive had left, Glenda rang Brangle at his office to tell him. He knew about woad.

"Around Clagtoft was the biggest woad-growing area. Woad-mills dotted all over. If anybody had asked me, I'd have said there wasn't a trace left. Hang on a minute Glenda."

He was gone for a few minutes then returned. "Write this down. <u>Isatis</u> <u>tinctoria</u>." He spelled it out. "When we produce this at the Public Inquiry that's what we're going to call it. Latin name. And Slaumy Gowt, we shall say, is the only known site where isatis tinctoria is growing wild."

"Would that be true though?"

"You'll notice I said 'the only <u>known</u> site.' That's makes it true, so long as you don't specify who knows."

# Chapter Thirteen

Proggle made sure the police knew about the proposed march through the centre of Stumpleton. She personally delivered to the police station a large map, drawn by herself, showing starting and finishing points; a timetable of start and finish times; a list of vehicles included (the Rolls Royce and the Sentinel); and the name and address of the organiser (herself). She was determined to avoid the objections raised by P.C. Tussock.

Even so, the man at the desk said, "Hang on a moment madam while I have a look through it." He did so, twice.

"That O.K.?" asked Proggle.

"No madam."

"Why not? We have a perfect right to stage a public protest on this matter."

"Certainly have. Nobody can take that away. The important thing is that the police, as custodians of the public peace, are entitled to know all the details in advance. For the benefit of the protestors, as well as in the interests of the general public."

Proggle pointed to the papers she had brought. "What the 'ell's all that then?"

He smiled a fatherly smile. "It's all the details except one. The date on which the march takes place."

"Oh, sorry. It's a week tomorrow."

"Ah. That's market day."

"Of course. Most people about then. No good marching through half-empty streets."

"True. But it's also when there's most traffic as well. Raises problems that does. However, I'll pass it on to the Chief. Got your phone number on has it?"

"Has it? Oh, no. Something else I forgot." She added the number.

"Right Miss Proggle. We'll be in touch if there's any queries. And best of luck with it."

Proggle went on to do a tour of town centre shops and offices, requesting each to display her poster:

## HELP SAVE CLAGTOFT!

A neighbouring village is threatened with TOTAL DEMOLITION, against the wishes of the people who live and work there. CLAGTOFT is an ancient settlement with a distinguished history which is being TOTALLY IGNORED by the BUREAUCRATS OF BRUSSELS, who want to flatten it for ever so they can rival the Americans in the SENSLESS SPACE RACE. If you are opposed to this, JOIN THE PROTEST MARCH through the Town Centre.

## JULY 18th AT 2 P.M.

## AND PLEASE SIGN THE PETITION!

The petition was Brangle's idea. He had prepared the forms in his estate agency office and got some of his staff to deliver them to friendly shops. On the day of the march the juniors would be in the street bagging signatures.

When Proggle had done all she could, she went to see Brangle and asked him, "What are we going to do with the petition when it's finished?

He chuckled. "I did a bit of arm-twisting, as we were being towed back from Slaumy Gowt. Told our M.P. Clunch, that when Slurriton got their petition up about not wanting a rubber-goods factory on their doorstep, their M.P. took it to the Ministry and got is squashed. 'Bring yours to me,' he said. 'I'll make sure it's seen in the right place.'"

What worried Brangle most was whether he should be seen on the march wearing his chain of office as Chairman of the Parish Council. "It's not strictly a council function. So would I be abusing the office by wearing it?

"You wear it to open Garden Fetes, which are not council functions."

"Ah. But that's done by invitation. This march, it's really a political thing. I'd be a bit uneasy with it on while Mrs. Ossack's up there banging the drum and the band playing Colonel Whatsit."

"H'm. Ask the Mayor of Stumpleton. He might know the rules."

Brangle cleared his throat. "Actually, we are not on speaking terms at the moment. He's still upset over Chimble bringing the steam lorry to the forecourt of the Municipal Hall and blowing the whistle at some length. Thought it cheapened the proceedings. I'll ask the Town Clerk what he thinks."

"I'll leave you to it. Have to get back to Clagtoft."

"How are you travelling?"

"On the Dogstead bus. Left my bike at Iggleby."

* * *

Proggle didn't get to the bus. On her way there she saw Jack Grunsell loading his furniture van outside the shop where he worked.

"Not going near Iggleby by any chance?"

"Off to Squadderby love. Could easy go thataway round, ain't above a mile further."

She sat in the van until he'd finished loading. When they got to Iggleby, Jack said, "Right, we'll put your bike in the van and tek you and it to Clagtoft."

"No Jack – it's only a ten-minute ride."

"I want to do it love. Just thought of a reason for wanting to be in Clagtoft about this time."

"You sound a bit grim."

"Not half as grim as I shall be if summats is happening as I think might be."

As they neared the village he turned into Pudding Lane and went through to Main Road. At the bend near the Old Slaughterhouse he stopped the van and looked ahead. From there he could see into the yard of the Stamping Cat.

"Thought so. I bloody thought so."

She followed his eyes. In the yard was Harry Gozzard's van and she realised what Jack had in mind. He got her bike out then walked up to the pub and slipped into the side door.

127

For a few minutes, all was quite. Then a sudden shouting began inside the Stamping Cat, loud enough to be heard all along Main Road. The vicar came out of his front door; Chimble came out of his workshop and up to the yard entrance; Amelia Chaunter's head came out of her bedroom window.

"What the 'ell's going on up there?"

"I think we might see in a minute." Proggle told her.

Round the corner, the front paths of Ketchup Terrace and the almshouse were dotted with people alerted by the racket.

The front door of the pub burst open and Gozzard came out at speed, The Naked Ploughman all over again except that he clutched a towel round his middle and tried to stem a bleeding nose with the other hand. He stood for a moment as the door slammed behind him and all went quiet. Then a bedroom window opened above and his clothes came hurtling down around him.

For a few minutes the watchers stood in fascinated silence as he hopped around trying to climb into his trousers single-handed. When he finally won, gathered the rest of his clothes and limped across to his van, a rousing cheer echoed over the village.

\* \* \*

As an assembly point for the Stumpleton march, permission had been obtained for the use of the front playground of a disused school just off the town centre. The marchers – more than half of Clagtoft's population, Proggle calculated – arrived variously by car, bicycle or by the Dogstead bus. Wassing brought a Rolls-load, and the Sentinel, favoured only by the brave, carried the augmented Clagtoft Silver Band, including apprentice bass drummer Olive Ossack.

Olive was enjoying her excursion into the new-found world of creative music. Chimble had repaired the drum and tensioned its membrane to a hitherto unattained degree of tension. She didn't always wait fot the band to begin playing; she lambasted it for a few minutes whenever her arm felt the urge. "Keep it up!" urged Proggle as they entered the town. "Let 'em know we're coming!"

After ten minutes of to-and-fro-ing in the narrow street, Chimble decided that Diana was too broad in the bean to enter the playground, so he parked in the street, thus releasing two half-mile tailbacks of traffic, which had awaited the outcome of his tactics.

Amelia Chaunter addressed the band: "Let's have a warm-up." She had now extended their repertoire by the addition of Rule Britannia and Blaze Away and she picked on the latter to rouse Stumpleton from its market-day lethargy. Olive excelled herself; she had a good sense of tempo and could scarcely restrain her legs from dancing at the same time.

The town police were on the ball; hardly a half-hour of traffic chaos had ensued before a constable arrived to sort it out. He began by noticing the expired licence-plate on the Sentinel and the fact that its front number-plate (which had suffered in the cesspool disaster) had been replaced upside down. What he didn't notice was that the rear number-plate bore a totally different set of letters and numbers.

Brangle walked from his office to the assembly point. He wore his chain of office but had compromised by putting on a raincoat which half covered it. The Rev. Crispin Owery had thumbed a lift in Josh Kelter's car; he too was worried about his insignia of office but had decided to bring it in his pocket, ready to pin on if the occasion seemed appropriate.

Jack Grunsell was absent. He had been lying doggo since his encounter in his bedroom with his best customer. If anybody noticed his absence, he decided, he would explain that publicans ought to be aloof from political affairs. And anyway, he drove the van on market-days and couldn't afford to lose the money.

H.W.M. Trudgen had decided against letting his school off this time. He argued that it would be unfair on the town's schoolchildren, who had to attend on that day; in reality, he was fearful of questions being raised about it by the Education Authority. All the same, a dozen truants turned up in their Disney, Dalek and Batman outfits.

Clive now considered himself an honorary member of the band and was provide with a chair and a music-stand with a sheet of music headed Gems from Wagner, for Trombone in G. He gazed intently at the symbols, strumming in time to the noises around him. "At least it keeps him buttoned up." said Amelia.

Fred Cletch was a last-minute arrival, driving a large tractor. Proggle was delighted; "Emphasises Clagtoft's agricultural basis."

Liz Otmill and Violet Wask came together in Violet's car, originally just to watch. When they got among the others they caught

129

the excitement and decided to march. "We can consider ourselves honorary Clagtoftians." said Liz as she loaded her camera.

Proggle decided that in the intervals between the band's numbers she would address the crowds with her loud-hailer, telling what it was all about and asking for letters and phone calls to newspapers, television and Members of Parliament. She opened the top of the Rolls so as to speak from a commanding position, standing on the front seat.

Getting the procession out of the playground in the right order was a chaotic affair, mainly because Proggle directed operations with her loud hailer, which nobody understood. Eventually, the Rolls and Diana began inching towards the town. A larger banner on two poles was due next, to be supported by Glenda Hovel and George Hunking. Chimble had thoughtfully provided a long pole for Glenda and a shorter one for the taller George but it was evident, as they emerged that they had the wrong ones, the banner appearing as a wrinkled diagonal.

"Swap over." called Glenda, holding hers out to George. George lowered his pole with a magnificent sweeping gesture, neatly removing the helmet of the policeman who was holding up the traffic. It bounced once then vanished beneath one of the waiting cars. Because of the band, George didn't hear the constabulary howl, and when the officer bent to look for his headgear under the car he took a step back with the pole and delivered an accurate dead-centre prod at the blue-clad rear.

To the rousing strains of the Lincolnshire Poacher the column entered one end on Market Street and several people paused in their shopping to look and wonder.

As soon as the band paused, Proggle switched on her hailer. "People of Stumpleton. You may be wondering what this protest march is about. It's about people from a village called Clagtoft, only eight miles away, fighting to keep the village in existence. The European Space Agency wants to flatten it to make a runway for space shuttles, something they already have in France. Making one here... stop that... making one here where... git your bloody hand off... will destroy valuable farm..."

Her voice finally tailed off, then a click as the machine was switched off. Standing close to Dangle as she was, he had found the temptation irresistible; he was stroking her leg with his left hand as he drove with his right.

Even without that distraction, the progress had not been as smooth as might be expected of such a machine; his clutch-foot, twelve years older than the clutch, no longer had the fine degree of control it once had. His Italian temperament led him into keeping the engine revving briskly, ready for a quick take-off and to keep the beast in check by slipping the clutch. When the hand on Proggle's leg strayed a few inches above her knee, she lashed out with that leg and knocked his foot off the clutch pedal.

Like a racehorse which has felt the whip, the car leapt forward, stopping less than an inch from a large, red-faced man who had been crossing leisurely in front of it. He walked round slowly to Dingle's open window, put the large red face inside it and called him several different varieties of careless driver. Dangle listened patiently, nodding, then moved on.

* * *

Gerald Nodder and his team were in town, though not solely for the protest march. Eastern Telly was gathering material for a series called Eastern Market, a leisurely look at some of the ancient markets. They had spent some time in one of the pubs frequented by farmers trying in vain to get some of them arguing. Then they heard the band playing The Lincolnshire Poacher and Gerald said; "Come on lads, it's the protest march. Let's see if they've brought Flashing Willy and his guitar."

Halfway along Market Street, Proggle spotted the TV crew lining up, hopped out smartly and tipped Amelia. "Give it some beef this time. Let the world hear what Clagtoft can do."

The band took deep breaths and on the cue from Amelia launched an enthusiastic rendering of Colonel Bogey. Olive Ossack excelled herself; the excitement lent strength to her old arm, and she hit that drum as if it had never been hit before.

At the sixteenth bar, disaster struck. Just as they were coming in range of camera and mike, the drum burst and the stick flew out of her hand and came to rest inside. She stood open-mouthed for a few seconds, then as she drew level with the TV men she put her

131

arm back in gear, doing the motions and yelling "Bang! Bang! Bang! Bang!" at the full power of her voice.

Gerald was still laughing an hour later when he interviewed Proggle again.

* * *

A few days later, P.C. Tussock was riding through Clagtoft, ruminating on the news program on TV the previous evening. A shot of Clagtoft's quaint post office, another of its quaint corrugated-iron village hall, and about fifteen-seconds worth of Proggle with her loud-hailer in Stumpleton, making noises like deep, muffled seal-honks.

"A village condemned to death," said the presenter. "The whole population of Clagtoft, a tiny farming community in the Lincolnshire fenland, marched through the nearby market town to make a protest against a European scheme to bulldoze their village down to make a space-shuttle runway. The leader of the protest, Councillor Charlotte Broggle, told Eastern Telly..."

What annoyed Tussock was that the brief item included shots of at least three town coppers, good enough for the Chief Constable to recognise. In the Clagtoft march, his own efforts to catch the camera had failed. Still, catching the Chief's eye on special occasions is only one way up the promotion ladder. Mebbe good, solid police work takes longer but it's surer. And nowhere was police work solider than in the fens. Crime out here's a lot subtler than it is in towns. There, it's crime reported, then wham, bang, action. In these little places the bobby knows everybody, what they should be doing any time of day. A good country bobby's always alert to changes of behaviour pattern.

That little fracas at the Stamping Cat. He'd seen Gozzard's van outside there heaps of times, had a shrewd idea what went on. No law against two people jumping into bed with each other. Strictly it was Jack who was bookable, for assault. But no complaint had been made, so there it rested.

No, the major crime in the fens now was vegetable-rustling. Townies often laughed when he mentioned it, but it was happening. They came from distant towns and cities, using old vans so as to look like gangmasters. Arrived at dusk, targeted fields with high-

132

value, mature stuff, then shot back before dawn. Next morning, as the owner of the field was rubbing the sleep out of his eyes, a market stall would be all set up, anything up to 200 miles away. Lately, one or two had even broken into cold-stores and loaded a lorry, using the farmer's fork-lift.

Tussock steered into Piggery Lane, looked across a field of ripe caulis stretching to the horizon. Not identifiable by any know method, once away from their native field. A difficult one for the thief but...

He braked suddenly as his eye caught something in the middle distance. Ah! A good instance of where local knowledge is irreplaceable. That's Sid Sneck's cottage and I happen to know that Sid, who lives alone, is in hospital. There's somebody prowling around the place. Could be a relative but you never know. In a town, somebody looking round a house attracts little attention. People are just people. He shifted to where he could see the house through a gap in some elder. Somebody small, could be a boy. They use kids these days. Able to get through small windows.

Ginger-haired feller; none that colour round here. Gone round the back, looking for a window no doubt. He remounted and pedalled quietly to the front gate; dismounted and stole silently over the lawn to the corner of the house. Listened for the sound of breaking glass, or a crowbar in use.

Violet Wask came into view, looking up at the cottage. Tussock suddenly felt foolish, standing there. She turned and smiled at him.

"Now... now then, Miss. Hope I didn't startle you, turning up like this."

"No. It's okay. I saw you coming."

"Not thinking of buying it are you?"

"It's not for sale. Mr. Sneck told me before he went into hospital, he wants to spend the rest of his time in it. My interest is, I thought it might be a cruck cottage."

Tussock blinked. "Hardly likely. Old Sid... D'you mean for storing stolen goods?"

"No, I mean, c, r, u, c, k, cruck. With two big curved timbers each end, going up to a point at the height of the ridge."

"Ah, yes, of course. And is it?"

"Looks old enough, but I can't decide without looking inside. I'll have to wait until he comes home."

"What happens if it is one?"

"Then it goes on the list for the Public Inquiry. A rare building, worth preserving, even restoration, therefore definitely not to be flattened by the European scheme."

"I see. You're behind this campaign of Miss Proggle's then?"

"Absolutely. One hundred per cent."

# Chapter Fourteen

On a clear, still, very dark night, the Rev. Crispin Owery went into a spare bedroom of the vicarage to fetch a book. He took a lighted candle with him because he knew that the electric light in there, which fused several years ago, had not yet got a new bulb. The book he wanted was one of a small collection prudently not kept in the study bookcase alongside the Bible, Pilgrim's Progress and 1001 Sermons. The particular volume was called Fun Without Laughing. It was illustrated with colour photographs.

Before he found it, he happened to glance out of the uncurtained window. What he saw froze him. Across Cut-throat Paddock, through a gap between Duchess of York Drive and Goatskin Hall, was a clear view over the level fenland to Stumpleton. A faint glow in the sky told of the town itself, but there in the centre, looking like a slim silver pencil, was the floodlit tower of the parish church. It was a breathtaking sight and he stood for a few moments feeling waves of spiritual emotion sweeping over him. Then normality returned and he began shuffling through his secret collection. He took three.

During breakfast the next morning a thought occurred to him; if they can have a floodlit church, why can't Clagtoft have the same? He recalled seeing Chimble's yard brightly floodlit last winter, when Abe was at work on a steam-roller. After breakfast, he went across to see him.

"Oh, aye. What you see then was an owd wartime anti-aircraft searchlight. One as I bought chearp at an auction. Four quid I reckon. Onny wanted it for the engine and dynamo but the light wocked an' all so I used it. Too bright really. The church, aye, it'd do that a treat. But not all round it."

"I think from the south side would be best. So that it's visible from the main road, to people passing along at night. They see Stumpleton's, and I think they'd be impressed if they saw ours."

135

"True. There's still fooalks as doan't know we're here, even after all the publicity."

"The important question, Mr. Chimble, how much would it cost?"

"Ah. No more'n a drop o' petrol for the engine. Have to go out and see where's a good place to set it up…"

"I was thinking, this being a means of attracting attention to Miss Proggle's campaign, we might be justified in using the Organ Fund, which would provide…"

Chimble wasn't interest in the financial aspects; while the vicar still talked his mind was designing a bracket to mount the big searchlight on the roof at the village hall. And wondering if any trees would need beheading to allow the beam to pass.

Before the vicar was back home, Abe had put the usual BACK IN TEN MINUTES sign on the post office door and gone off to do a survey. (If people complained of how long they waited, he told them "Yer read it too soon").

By ten o'clock he had scaled the roof of the hall, designed a mounting bracket, borrowed a chain-saw and obtained permission to shorten a conifer in a back garden of Ketchup Terrace. "Tek if off at the ground mairt."

Clive Grunsell sensed that activity was afoot and arrived in time to pull on a rope to encourage the tree to fall into Cut-throat Paddock rather than on a neighbour's glasshouse. "Run when it starts coming," Chimble warned him. He did but made it only by inches.

For a day and a half Abe worked hard, Clive worked hard, Ernie Transom's handcart worked hard and the steam-operated digging machine was strained to its last inch of capacity lifting the searchlight up on the hall roof. The only casualty was an elder tree on the hall forecourt, sacrificed to allow the digger to pass. "Room for one more car to park." observed Chimble.

It was an inspired piece of engineering. Only ten days after the vicar's vision everything was up and running and on the first evening scores of people streamed out along Stumpleton Road or Conker Drive to see their little church bathed in brilliant light.

Word passed around rapidly and within a week a press photographer had been and got some first-rate shots. One finished up in a quality national daily paper: 'Village lights up to defy extinction.'

136

Proggle was delighted and did a house-to-house tour collecting money to buy petrol for the generator. Owery had yet to obtain release of the Organ Fund from the churchwardens.

On the sixth evening, a police car travelling from Dogstead to Stumpleton had reason to detour through Clagtoft and as it passed the Stamping Cat and rounded Waddie's Corner the driver got the light full in the face. He crawled to the source where Chimble and a few others stood round the engine.

"Would you cut that light please?"

"What's up?" asked Abe.

"Creating a severe driving hazard I'm afraid. Somebody could get killed. Couldn't see a thing as I rounded that bend."

"Ah. I'll rig up a shield. Be done fost thing tomorrow." He stopped the engine and the light faded out.

"You got planning permission for this I suppose?" said the copper.

An uneasy silence.

"If not, I'd advise you to apply before you use the light again."

He got back into the car and drove off. After a discussion lasting long enough for the car to reach the ramper, a mile and a half away, the church of St. Dismas was brightly illuminated once more.

\* \* \*

William deMondford Wassing had spent a restless night, surprisingly, because he had thought the physical exertions of the previous day would bring perfect sleep. He had instructed Dangle to fill the gap in the bank of Clagtoft Drain, in the hope that the front drive at least would then dry out. The Italian was scarcely equipped, either by muscle or temperament, to execute such a job. He had tossed a few spoonfuls in, then disappeared into the granary to recover.

William knew very well what his ancestor Marmaduke would have done; hauled the man out by an ear, thrust the shovel into his hands then stood over him with a hoss-whip until the job was done. William hadn't. He had picked up the shovel and begun working himself.

And had found himself quite enjoying it. After many years of citing arthritis as a reason for not doing physical things, he

137

discovered that actually doing them could be exhilarating. He had even hauled up some tree branches and other debris and thrown them into the gap. Having got the dam up to water level, he had taken a brush to the front drive, intending to push the water away, and found Mrs. Hammel there already doing the job. Shows the difference, he thought, between an Italian servant and an English. "Nice work Mrs. Hammel." She had almost fainted.

Although his limbs ached pleasantly, sleep had evaded him for several hours. And when he did eventually slip into a light sleep, he was wakened by a commotion downstairs. Oh, God, was it them coming after all? At dead of night, to catch him unawares? Had they been watching, waiting for something to be done about the water?

He groped in a drawer and found his father's ancient revolver. It was not loaded but it was something to stand behind and frighten people with. A blue light was flashing outside, so perhaps they had brought police with them. Maybe they had a warrant to enter and remove all his goods…

He could hear Hammel's voice, and a man's. Putting a dressing-gown on and slipping the gun into the pocket, he went down. Two policemen were inside the front door.

"What's going on officer?" he realised his voice was half an octave higher than usual.

"Received a 999 call sir. Did you make it?"

"No."

"Is anybody else in the house?"

"Only myself and Mrs. Hammel here. The chauffeur lives over the garage."

"Does he have access to a phone? An extension?"

Wassing shook his head. "We've had trouble with the phone lately. The wire got brought down, and had to be restored."

"Wouldn't dial three nines on its own. May we look around inside? The tide seems to be up out there."

They tramped all over with torches but found nothing wrong. "Everything secure sir as far as we can see. Leave you to finish your sleep."

"Well, thank you, off…"

"And by the way sir, wouldn't advise you to carry a gun. Should have been handed in by rights."

138

William laughed feebly, patted his pocket. "Oh, that's not a real one. At least, it is, but it's only a souvenir. First World War y'know. My father's."

"Still liable to make a hole in somebody."

William had locked the front door, crept back to bed and lay shivering, miserably awake, until morning.

Now, he could hear Mrs. Hammel moving around downstairs. He washed and dressed hurriedly and went down.

"Can you explain to me how the police came to be called?"

Her chomping stopped for a moment and she looked blank. "Police?"

"Two policemen were here, talking to you, in the early hours of this morning."

"Oh, aye. I was wondering about that meself. Hed to leave Laurence to see what they wanted."

Sudden panic gripped him. "L… Laurence? He was here?"

"Bin wi' me most o' the night. Aye, I remember now. He could hear somebody moving about outside. The water was swishing. So I went and did 999."

"It was you then."

"That was right, wan't it? 'Mergency number, 999?"

"Mrs. Hammel, that was why the police came. They were answering an emergency call from this number. Now I shall have to ring and explain, apologise. Why didn't you tell them?"

Her mind had wandered off again; she picked up a cloth and began needlessly polishing the spoon she was holding.

He said, "Where's Laurence now?" though he knew the answer.

"Be in the village somewhere. He'd gone when I wock up."

He turned wearily to go to the phone. Something had to be done about her. Perhaps the police would give him some advice.

* * *

Liz Otmill was deeply sympathetic with the village's struggles to rescue itself from oblivion and in rational moments she knew that nothing done up to now was likely to have much effect. She was sure the confrontation had to be much wider and more political than these local marches and meetings. She had written several letters to newspapers, one of which appeared in a national daily, but had a nagging feeling that somebody in a prominent position ought to be taking up the cause. She wrote a curt note to the M.P., Roland Clunch, suggesting that a question in the House might help, but she didn't really expect anything to happen.

What was really engaging her mind was her plan for a series of pictures telling stories of what landwork was like in the fenland, earlier in the twentieth century. While people like Olive Ossack, Amelia Chaunter, Josh Kelter and Frank Wowser were around and still in good remembering form, she ought to push things along in case the worst happened.

In Harry Gozzard's barn was a veritable museum of all the implements and gear that would be needed for the tableaux and though she was slightly (and a little excitingly) uneasy about what his terms might be for the use of them, she intended to take the risk. On the day he posed for the Naked Ploughman picture, so abruptly interrupted, she saw some evidence of his possible thoughts.

The foundation of Clagtoft's agricultural prosperity was potatoes. The rich silt land was uniquely suitable for the crop and could with ease nurture a second or even third crop of brassicas or salads within the same year. She decided that one of her first efforts would be called The Tairtie Riddlers. Almost every one of the oldie landworkers, asked about what they used to do, had mentioned tairty-riddling as a tough, uncomfortable winter job. In those days the main crop was lifted in late summer and autumn and stored in clamps, or tatie-graves. These were elongated heaps of the tubers, run along field-edges adjacent to lanes. They were built by muscle-power and when about five feet high were covered with a layer of straw to protect against frost and the straw held down by soil.

Chimble had told Liz: "If you'd seen all them clamps from where we was, up top o' the church, you'd see bloody miles on 'em, all added together."

Tairty-riddling, it occurred to Liz, was a unique time in the landwork calendar. Most other work had the workers spread out across a field, so that normal conversation was difficult unless you had a voice like Olive's. At riddling time they came together as a social group in a small area. It was usually a mixed group, men doing the heavy humping and loading, women the riddling and weighing. Loading the lorry or wagon was by hand too; two on the ground with a hicking-stick to hurl the full bags up and one above to

140

grab it and manoeuvre it into position. They were one hundredweight bags too; none of your prissy 25-kilo paper wrappings.

Olive set the scene as well as anybody. "When it was real cowd we allus 'ed an 'essian screen round to keep the wind off. As you wocked along the clamp you 'ed to keep moving everything – screen, scales, weight, riddles, bags, twine, needles, to the next place. Scales was heaviest; took two men to move them."

"Did you stop work in wet weather?" asked Liz.

"Gawd, no. Farmers used to like the wet. Thick 'essian bag, soaked wi' rainwater – owd man Cletch used to say he was selling a half-gallon every time we weighed one. You was supposed to put a bag under the weights but it was often forgot."

"What was riddling for?"

"To get rid o' the little 'uns. Them as went through wasn't allowed to go for eating. They was pig-tates."

"Did anybody cheat?"

"All the time. Mainly using the wrong size riddles. Cletch nivver did that; stopped on the right side o' that law, even if he strayed a bit ower wages."

Liz already knew that land-workers' pay, lowest of any job needing skill, was supposedly protected by law. It seemed that some of the farmers, even in the prosperous fens, paid even below that.

"What did you wear for riddling Olive?"

"Owt you had but it depended on the weather. Really bitter earst wind, and the field gate left open, you packed on as much as you could wock in. Bit of owd bag round your waist for an eppon. Didn't matter if you looked like a scar-crow, cos all on yer did."

So Liz arranged with Fred Cletch to use a corner of one of his fields, got together a gang of ex-riddlers and constructed the authentic scene. A mock tatie-grave was built by Chimble with his dragline machine and a few potatoes put on it for effect. A hessian screen was put up and Gozzard brought a van-load of the real gear, vintage 1920s.

"Dress up as if it was cold weather," Liz told them "I can paint in the red noses to suit,"

When the time came, she said, "Shan't keep you long. I'll take loads of photos first and there'll be a copy for everybody. Then I'll do some sketching. The painting I'll finish later but you'll all get a look before I pass it on to my agent. I'll try to make everybody look young again. Josh, can you hide that high-tech watch? I'll bet you didn't have one on forty years ago."

"Onny watch in our gang," said Olive, "Was the foreman's. it was a five-bob Ingersoll kep in his weskit-pocket."

They all thoroughly enjoyed remembering the things they had to do, down to the real-life going behind the screen for a pee. "It was that damn cowd at times," said Olive, "You'd wonder 'ow it nivver froz on the way out."

\* \* \*

On the day after the tableau of the tatie-grave, Proggle called a council of war. She summoned Fred Cletch, Violet Wask, Abe Chimble and Glenda Hovel, and got them to meet in the front of the Manor House, where Wassing was waiting.

"This is crisis time," said Proggle. "It appears that some work on the runway scheme is about to begin. A friend of mine who lives near Peamoor Water has seen a French magazine with an article about the runway and a map of where it will be. Or where they think it will. It runs parallel with the East Forty-foot Drain. Her house is actually marked on the map. Clagtoft, she says, appears as a church and a little cluster of about twenty houses. So evidently they are using information which is years out of date."

"Or else somebody's deliberately cheating," said Glenda.

Proggle went on, "Anyway, that's not the real crisis. They have fenced off a compound next to the Drain and are filling it with machinery of all shapes and sizes – diggers, cranes, bulldozers, lorries. And some portakabin offices and canteens. Obviously, some big works are imminent."

"Been nothing in the newspapers." observed Cletch.

"Won't be, will there? The media will be excluded, you can bet on that. Took us two protest marches to get even a mention on telly and then it was thirty seconds of rubbish. When the first shuttles come zooming in, that's when media'll be here in full force. This now is merely people's lives being wrecked; that's not news."

"Well said," responded Glenda. "So what's our reaction to this activity at Peamoor Water?"

142

"First we'll have a look from a distance. I reckon whatever it is will be visible from the top floor of the Manor House. William, can we have your permission to go up? I've brought my binoculars."

William led them upstairs, the eleventh step going off like a pom-pom as their feet descended on it. Mrs. Hammel disappeared into her bedroom like a rabbit and slammed the door; they could hear something heavy being thumped against it. She thought 'they' were finally coming to get her.

"There you are!" cried Proggle. "That much heavy machinery you can't count 'em!" she passed the binoculars around.

"It's demolition stuff all right," said Chimble. "Three bulldozers in a row this end. And yon crane on the right's got a swinging ball on. Enough stuff there to flatten Clagtoft in a few days."

Proggle said, "They must think we're simpletons, leaving it that near. No doubt they'll be kicking their heels for a few days, waiting for some big-wig in Paris to blow a whistle..."

"Brussels, isn't it?" said Wassing.

"European Space Agency is in Paris," said Glenda.

"I'm sure the man who phoned me the first time said Brussels. Then when I... yes, that's true, they gave me another number. But it turned out to be a false one. Some young lady in Bordeaux."

The party stood in silence for a moment.

"William," said Glenda gently, "I think those calls you got were hoaxes. Somebody playing tricks."

"But he said..." his jaw dropped an inch. "Oh. You mean it wasn't..."

"It was somebody in Clagtoft."

Another silence, then Violet Wask said, "Well, is this is an action meeting, or what? Are we going to let the air out of all those tyres?"

"Ah," said Chimble. "That's one possibility. Take 'em ages to put it all back in. We could leave 'em a bike pump, as a gesture."

"That's only a delaying tactic," said Cletch. "They'd just ring for a mobile compressor."

"Delaying tactics is the first move," said Proggle. "A warning shot across their bows, to put it in military terms."

"Naval," said Violet. "What about oil? They all depend on oil for operating the hydraulic arms and things."

"Now there's a thought," said Chimble. "All the drain-plugs out, and chucked into the middle of the Forty-foot. Tek weeks to replace 'em all and git topped up again."

# Chapter Fifteen

"My dear brother," wrote Wassing, "There is so much happening here in your old village that I scarcely know where to begin. One thing I mentioned previously – why our chauffeur D'Angelis (the villagers call him Dangle) entertains men behind the closed door of his allotment shed – is no longer an unsolved mystery. With my personal assistance, the police investigated. They suspected at first that video shows of a pornographic nature were being shown, but on gaining admittance, found that the show was of a perfectly respectable gardening programme! More power to their (the men's) elbows, I say! I only wish D'Angelis would put more of his knowledge to use in the Manor House garden.

I am happy to report that the water has now largely gone down and we are once more able to walk dry-foot up the front drive. To achieve this I had to literally roll up my sleeves and build a dam to keep out the waters of Clagtoft Drain. Now, as long as we steer clear of heavy rains, it's matter of waiting for natural seepage and evaporation.

Thankfully, threats of our early removal and demolition seem to have receded. On the occasion of a second telephone call from Europe, my temper was raised and I used uncharacteristically strong language. That, coupled with the physical deterrent of the moat (I suspect they have a spy network), has led them to stay their hand. A few Clagtoft people, seeing me still in situ, have drawn the mistaken conclusion that the calls were not genuine.

The overall threat still hangs over the village and a recent sinister development has been the amassing of a large fleet of demolition machines at Peamoor Water, a remote area, where there is nothing to be demolished as you may remember. It is only a mile away; we went there fishing several times. And were warned off because we didn't have licences! They may think they have put the machines where nobody will notice but Cassandra, bless her for her wisdom, has an informant on the spot. The campaign workers conspired in secret (here!) to raid the park and sabotage the machines. This I believe would be the first act of illegality since the movement began. Needless to say, I shall not personally be involved.

Poor old Hammel has deteriorated sadly and I fear it to be a matter of mere days before she has to go. For some weeks now she has suffered hallucinations; earlier in life she lost her only child shortly after birth and now images that a lad in Clagtoft (referred to with some justification as 'the village idiot') is her son returned. Equally disturbing is that she has begun ringing 999 on the telephone (our emergency service; is yours the same?) and then forgetting she has done so. The police turned up at dead of night on one occasion. I explained the position to them and they are sending a social worker to interview the poor old dear and assess her condition.

Under normal circumstances I would already be discreetly advertising for a replacement, as life at the Manor House could simply not go on without a housekeeper. But what can I do? I tell you, I find myself waking at night in a fever of panic over what the future holds. I don't for a moment grudge you your good fortune but at times I wish you were here as a helpmate. Perhaps it is selfish of me to burden you with these perpetual tales of woe but there is simply no-one else. Except dear Cassandra of course but in these turbulent days she is far too busy to pay attention to me. According to my personal diary, it is three weeks since we last enjoyed one of our secret 'cocoa evenings'.

"I must break off from writing – I hear ominous clattering and must see what Hammel is up to."

* * *

The raiding party consisted of Proggle, Chimble and Glenda Hovel. Chimble brought a torch and a universal wrench with which to unscrew the drain-plugs on all the hydraulic reservoirs and Proggle shouldered wire-cutters in case of difficulty entering the compound. Glenda had prepared a herbal concoction, wrapped in a succulent slice of beef which she said would stupefy any guard-dog for up to six hours without causing permanent harm.

146

The three set out half an hour befor midnight along Conker Drove. Halfway between Lollycock Bridge and Iggleby they turned off into an ancient footpath which took them to the bank of East Forty-foot Drain. Such a route would eliminate the possibility of meeting police, though they had a story ready just in case; they suspected that people in the neibourhood were setting rabbit-traps, and they were out to disarm them.

On meeting at Proggle's house, Chimbel had turned up with his face blacked. "Suprising how a face shows up in the dark," he said. "That's why Commandos do it." He offered them a plastic bag filled with Sentinel soot, which they declined.

"They wouldn't see me," said Proggle, "But with that on my face they'd hear me sneezing."

It was as near to true darkness as it gets; an overcast, moonless night, the nearest urban street-lights ten miles away. Only occasional vehicle headlights pierced the blackness, apart from one solitary outside light on a house, which Proggle thought might be that of her friend who had given the tip.

As they approached the compound they went on the dry side of the bank, so as not to show against the skyline, and dropped their voices to whispers. Proggle had a strategy worked out.

"If it's the usual wire fence, we'll open a crawling-hole on this near side. But before we begin I'll do a full circuit to see if there's a watchman or a guard dog. If there's just a dog, I'll throw the meat over. You two lie down until I get back."

Chimble and Glenda went down and Proggle vanished. The two had a whispered run-over of the procedure; Chimble at work on the hydraulics, Glenda collecting the plugs ready to throw into the middle of the Forty-foot on the way back. Proggle had a tool for removing tyre-valves. If they had time to spare, Chimble would do a similar job on engine-sumps and fuel tanks.

"Ssssh," hissed Glenda. She gripped Chimble's arm. "There's somebody in there."

A figure was moving among the machines, pacing to and fro. They ducked their faces down and held their breaths.

"Where the hell are you?" it was Proggle's voice. "Shine the torch for Chrissake."

They scrambled to their feet and Chimble switched on.

"Come round to the other end. There's a gate, but it's open."

Chimble laughed. "Over-confident ain't they? Think it's so remote they don't need security."

They set to work and soon found they had ample time to do all they had planned. In a short time the whole enclosure was reeking with spilt oil and fuel. Proggle expressed a wish that they had planned a fire to finish the job off but none of them carried matches. In any case, as Abe pointed out, it would have brought fire-crews and police cars swarming in from all points of the compass. Proggle had some chalk and insisted on scrawling SAVE CLAGTOFT! On all walls of the Portkabins and on the cab-doors of the large vehicles.

* * *

Peamoor Water was a spaghetti-junction of waterways. The East Forty-foot, built in mid-19th century when the remaining wild fens were drained, ran past ruler-straight, and withing a few hundred yards of the pool which provided the name, seven other land-drains converged. Some were man-made attempts at drainage, one dating back to the 13th century; others were patently old creeks from when tidal waters came washing over the area.

Eastern Drainage was the official body responsible for maintaining land drainage works in the area. Its offices were in Stumpleton and in one office, that of the Chief Engineer, a meeting was going on between him and senior officials of his department.

"If we grasp the nettle now, I reckon we can tackle the culvert replacement north of Peamoor Water and get away with it. Levels are generally lowest for four years and there may not be a window as good as this for another twelve or even twenty-four months."

"Can we divert the Forty-foot into the river?" asked one man.

The Chief shook his head. "They are adamant they won't let us, other than in dire emergency. So I had a think and come up with something I think will work. If we can do the work within five days, we can divert into Glugwell Creek and thence into Clagtoft Drain. We might spill a few pints in Pulk's Bottom but I spoke to the farmer and he's not worried. Clagtoft Drain is sound from end to end and I've calculated that a week's diversion into it, barring a cloudburst west of Sleaford, will raise the level by no more than four feet."

"Is this sudden decision anything to do with the Space runway thing?"

148

"Nothing whatever. We are assured that their runway will be parallel with the Forty-foot and will not interfere with it. They will do all the works themselves, piping and filling, on the land they are buying and nothing will interrupt our own work. Any queries on site, you can tell people that."

"Are we allowed to use that new compound at Peamoor Water?"

"Nope. That's for a different purpose altogether." He used a pointer on a wall-map. "We'll make our own here, Hogpit Farm. There's a small grass field…"

* * *

It was slowly dawning on Clive Grunsell that there was more to playing a guitar than stroking finger-nails across the strings. His new one was not a professional job but it sounded better than the old, and with a little help from Violet Wask he had begun picking out simple tunes and chords.

Harry Gozzard had resumed his midday drinking in the Stamping Cat on the days when Jack was away at work, but he was careful to quit promptly at closing-time. Edie was secretly disappointed but didn't dare offer a resumption of their afternoon frolics.

Clive demonstrated his new techniques to Harry, who encouraged him to learn still more. He suggested to Edie that a tutor might be found and even offered to pay for lessons. She was reluctant, thinking that Jack might be suspicious of the motive. She was probably right.

Several times in the past, Clive had asked Harry for a ride out in his van to the veg. Fields. Harry had refused in the past, in case the boy's well-known hobby offended any of his female workers. Things now seemed to be improving, so when Clive asked again, Harry agreed.

"'Ave to be at Piggery Lane corner at half-six. Anybody as ain't there on the dot gits left behind. And bring summat to eat and drink; there's no caffies where we go."

He squared it with Edie and she promised to vittle him up and have him out on time.

Next morning, Clive thought it a great world to be in. Up and about while half of Clagtoft was still in bed, the air clean and the sky bright, a bag of sandwiches in one hand, his guitar in the other and a flask in his pocket, he marched off to the end of Piggery Lane.

Three men and four women were waiting for Harry and they had another two to pick up on the way, so the van was crowded by the time the first dropping-point was reached. Some gangers now used mini-buses, but Harry belonged to the old school, who didn't believe in pampering workers. "Ain't off to Butlin's, what the 'ell do they want soft seats for. Think theirsens lucky they dooan't 'av to bike to wock, like folks allus used to do."

Four of the gang were dropped off at a packhouse near Dogstead, the rest were due in a cauliflower field, two and a half miles from Clagtoft.

"'Old yer 'ats on," called Harry when they reached it, and drove off the road, over the dyke-crossing and along the field headland, finishing as close to the working point as he could get. On this particular job he was to supply a tractor driver and was doing that job himself.

"Keep out the road, and be'airve yer sen," he told Clive. "If there's any wock you can do, I'll tel yer."

"Shall I get paid?"

"Course you will. Nobody wocks for Gozzard wi' out pay. Won't be a damn sight, but it'll be tax-free."

The overnight chill still hung over the field, so Clive sat in the van watching the work and occasionally plucking at his guitar. When the sun began warming things up he wandered out over the field, eyeing up the women. "Watch out Sarah," said one. "Got his eye on you I reckon. Be letting you have a quick flash anytime."

"I'm ready. Chuck a wet cauli at it if he does."

It happened. At least, the flash did, but Sarah didn't get a shy at it. Harry had been watching in the tractor's driving mirror, and he jumped down, strode to Clive and took him by one ear. "In the van you, and stop in. I said yer could come if yer be'airved yer sen. Sit there and play wi' it if yer want, but my women don't want to see it."

Clive rubbed his ear. "An' that artist woman don't want to see yourn either. Ow!" Harry's hand had collided with the other ear. The boy sat sulkily out of sight until late afternoon, going-home time.

He brightened when he was in the middle of the gang in the van, entertaining them with his guitar. They applauded generously and encouraged him to keep going. One woman passed him a cigarette

150

and a box of matches. In the hilarity which followed, Clive coughing and spluttering over the tobacco smoke, nobody noticed that he put the matches in his pocket. Nobody thought it odd, either, when he picked up two discarded newspapers from the floor of the van and stuffed them in his bag.

Just before they reached the village, Harry stopped at the end of Pudding Lane to let one of the men off. Clive got out as well. He ambled along the roadside, returning the waves of the women through the back windows of the van. As it vanished into Main Road, Clive turned into the Pound, over the footbridge and headed for Glugwell Creek.

On reaching the Creek he immediately noticed that the water was higher than normal, that it was moving, and that a large quantity of dead, oil-soaked vegatation almost covered the surface. He struck one experimental match and threw it down, but it spluttered out.

He had a sudden, exciting vision of the old waterways, the Creek and Clagtoft Drain, ablaze through the village, past Manor House, alongside Bosh Green, right through to Lollycock Bridge. He took out the two newspapers, sat down on the bank and began reading them, crumpling the pages as he finished them and making a heap beside him.

* * *

Earlier that afternoon, the weekly Stumpleton Chronicle and Advertiser had arrived in Clagtoft. G.W. and R. Hunking's Stores were newsagents and on a good week they handled as many as forty copies of the local. On this particular week, thought Chimble, they might sell a few more, if the story of the sabotage of demolition machinery had broken.

As he came out of the shop with his copy, he saw Proggle approaching on her bike; she had the same thought in mind. They went and sat in Abe's van to look through. "Nowt on the front page." he said.

"Apparently nothing inside either," said Proggle. She was working backwards. "Ah! Wait a minute!" she began reading aloud: "Sale postponed. The sale by auction of obsolete and redundant contractors' machinery by Eastern Drainage, arranged for next week at Peamoor Water, has been postponed. Vandals entered the compound overnight and caused severe damage, rendering every machine unworkable. The Chief Engineer of Eastern Drainage told the Chronicle that the damage is repairable but may take several months to put it right. Police, including a dog-handler, have examined the scene of the crime and state that they have clues which are being actively followed up."

When they finished laughing, Proggle said, "You didn't leave anything behind did you?"

Abe sprang up. "Me bloody torch!" Then he sat down again. "No, it's there on the shelf behind you."

"I know you brought the wrench back. Oh!"

"What's up?"

"Glenda's dog-bait. I threw that away as we came out." She burst into loud laughter again. "It says a police dog-handler. There'll be a police-dog somewhere, on its back with its legs in the air. And a copper trying to wake it up…"

* * *

Clive had discovered that starting an oil-fire on water was not an easy job. A tractor was working on the opposite side of the Creek, so he had to hide everytime it came round. He decided to wander along the lane and take another look at Harry Gozzard's apples. This time he did rather better, eating two at the site and coming away with one in each pocket, all ripe and sweet.

On the way back to the Creek he picked up several substantial pieces of wood and when he got back to the trees where the oil was dumped, there were piles of oil-soaked twigs. There were also remnants of black oil in some of the barrels and these he dragged down to the creek-side. It was almost dusk when he struck his next match and he had no need to strike another. Within minutes a fierce fire was going on the sloping side of the bank and it needed only a prod with a tree-branch to roll it down on to the water.

To help things along there was a steady breeze blowing and from time to time, clumps of dry late-summer growth on both banks flared up, until by dark there was a satisfying line of fire a hundred yards long, slowly creeping and floating towards Clagtoft.

* * *

152

It was Henrietta Hammel's last evening at the Manor House. The social worker had spent several hours with her and listened sympathetically to the stories she had to tell about Laurence's comings and goings. Having first heard the truth from William, however, she had concluded that the old lady needed continuous care and surveillance. A place had been arranged in Stumpleton and Dangle was to take her there in the Rolls on the following morning.

"Have you got your belongings packed?" William asked her several times during the day. There had been no positive answer.

Feeling every bit the benign employer, he went into the kitchen for his nightly cup of cocoa and tried to get her to talk about old times, when the Colonel was still alive. But she was in almost total confusion, talking of events forty years ago as if they had happened that afternoon and even 'recalling' things that happened before she was born. After an hour of trying to steer her into rationality, William gave up.

"Now, if you'll excuse me Mrs. Hammel, I have things to do in the study."

He went towards the door but before he reached it she took a piece of paper down from the dresser and thrust it into his hand. "Before I go Mr. Wassing, 'cording to my reckoning, that's how much wages you owe me."

He stared at it blankly. "Oh, of course. Yes, I must attend to that."

In the study, he stared at the figure for several minutes, then opened a drawer and took out a large book. On the front was written "Servants' Salaries" in the Colonel's handwriting. William turned to the latest entries; the last was three months old, made to D'Angelis. Hammel's was even older and she had the figure right to the last penny. There was a cash-box in the adjacent drawer but he didn't truoble to look in it because he knew it was empty.

On top of the desk was a possible solution to the problem. It was a letter from his solicitors in Stumpleton, saying that an offer had been made for two fields belonging to the Wassing estate, just over 55 acres off Squadderby Road. He knew it was Fred Cletch's offer, Fred being his tenant. And he knew it was well below the going rate of a few years ago.

Prehaps he ought to consult Claud first. But no, Claud had effectively cut himself off from family affairs all those years ago. He reached for notepaper and pen, glancing up at the photograph of the Colonel on the wall and muttering something like "Sorry sir."

"To Messers. Pillage and Rumpas Solicitors. For the attention of Mr. Isaac Pillage."

His pen paused as the thought crossed his mind that he might borrow a little from Dangle with which to pay Mrs. Hammel. He dismissed it and continued writing.

# Chapter Sixteen

Wassing finished the letter to the solicitor, got it ready to post and put it in his pocket. He had instructed them to sell the land at the offered price and in a postsript had asked Issac Pillage if he could possibly make an advance on a personal basis, to be repaid out of what the land made. He urgently needed ready cash and a thousand pounds would tide him over a temporary difficult period. Perhaps old Isaac would charge heavy interest, but what could he do? Again he was tempted to ring Claud and ask his advice, but he wasn't sure of what time of day it was over there.

It was now almost dark outside. He heard something moving outside and went to the window. It was Dangle, in Wellingtons, paddling around in the still wet garden. The Italian saw the curtains open and came across.

"Water come in…" he made an arching movement with one had and pointed to the gap in the bank where the makeshift dam had been built.

William opened the window. "I expect the level in the Drain has risen slightly. There was rain in the Midlands earler this week. We'll build the dam higher… higher," he reinforced the English with a gesture of his own. "In the morning. All right?"

"O.K." The chauffeur turned off and splashed towards the granary. Damn him, thought Wassing. Doesn't say O.K. <u>sir</u>. Would have done to the Colonel. Or 'Very good sir.' Might even have saluted, if he'd had his peaked cap on. Never seems to wear it these days. Must mention it.

As he closed the window a puff of the rising wind blew a cloud of smoke across the garden. Somebody burning stubble he thought. Illegally. Happens every year. He went upstairs to look out and on amazing sight met him. In the direction of Glugwell Creek was a long line of fire; not the bright, intermittent blaze you get stubble-burning,

155

but a dullish red, murderous-looking fire which was belching vast clouds of dark smoke towards the village.

Dangle had not gone back to his granary; he had rounded the Manor House, gone out through the front drive, which was again under water, and turned along Squaddeby Road towards the village. He rounded the bend into MainRoad, glanced around him, then went into the telephone box near the post office.

Wassing had just left his study and got to the foot of the staircase when the phone rang.

"Is Meester Vassing, pliz?"

"Speaking."

"Dees call from the Eurpean Space Agen, Chief Commissioner. About this move away from house where you live…"

"Now you listen to me, Monsieur Commissioner or whatever and whoever you are. This house is my legal property and I shall continue to live in it as long as I choose to do so, unless somebody gives me good reason to move out."

"But Monsieur Vassing, ve have to…"

"You have no legality whatever on your side. If you attempt to lay a hand on my property I shall call on the help of the British Police Force <u>and</u> if necessary Her Majesty's Army to have you thrown out by the scruff of the neck."

He banged the phone down heavily.

Dangle came out of the phone box his old face creased with laughter and tears of joy coursing across his wrinkles. As he walked towards the Manor House he heard the distant howling of a fire engine. Sounded to be coming from the Dogstead road, wrong side of the Forty-foot for Clagtoft. Still, they'd made the same mistake before – fire-engines, ambulances, even the police. Sid Sneck had once lost fifteen pigs in a fire because the fire-engine got wrong side and couldn't find a place to turn round. Then had to reverse back to the end of Pudding Lane because they couldn't get over Lollycock Bridge.

By the time he got to the granary he was coughing and the smoke was like thick fog. He shut his windows and from one of them he could see bits of burning debris floating from the end of Glugwell Creek, some still alight on the Drain level with the Manor House. The stiff breeze was helping it along but he realised that the water itself was for once on the move.

156

Wassing had gone upstairs into his bedroom. He shut the window and sat on his bed acutely conscious of the smokey atmosphere. He had a sudden twinge of claustrophobic panic, which got him to his feet and pacing. Perhaps if he went out, took a walk up Squadderby Road away from the smoke, breathed in some clean air for a few minutes...

He went into the passage and along to the bathroom. When he came out he could hear more clattering in the kitchen. Oh God, she's still at it. Ought to be in her room.

"Mr. Wassing! Mr. Wassing!" she was at the foot of the main staircase.

"What it is?"

"Come quickly! There's water in the kitchen!"

He went down. "Don't worry too much. It's the level in the Drain. The kitchen floor is lower than in the rest..." he followed her into the kitchen. "See, it's not over my shoes. We can get it pumped out tomorrow. And we'll get the gap in the bank built up. Perhaps Mr. Chimble would..." he stared at her. "What's that Mrs. Hammel? Is it yours?"

She cradled in her left arm an ancient, almost bald teddy-bear. She looked down at it and laughed. "Course it ain't. What would an owd woman like me want a teddy for?"

He cleared his throat. "No. I see. Well, you can take it with you in the morning when you..."

She had turned away and was going up to her room. "It's Laurence's o' course."

\* \* \*

Before history began, while Clagtoft Drain was still a wide river with tides racing up it twice daily, Squadderby Road had begun life as an ambankment, an attempt by some Saxon settler, or perhaps even Romano-British entrepreneurs, to render some land salt-free and able to graze cattle or grow crops. It was at length successful. The top of the new bank became a footpath, then perhaps a packhorse road and eventually, in the nineteenth century, a cart-track with its usable width a magnificent nine or ten feet. Land on the tidal side of a bank usually builds to a higher level because of the accretion of tide-borne silt over several centuries. It didn't happen on

157

that particular stretch north of Clagtoft; perhaps the sea was already receding at the time of embankment.

The narrow stretch of land between Drain and road became "cheap" land. It was known locally as "intek" (intake) land, too small and misshapen for economic cultivation. On part of it, somebody had built the Manor House, at this moment, thanks to the assistance of the Eastern Drainage engineers, well below the level of the water in the Drain.

William took the "Claud" file from the study, switched off all the downstairs lights and went up to his bedroom. Perhaps if he attempted to finish off his New Zealand letter it would take his mind off the pending loss of Hammel and the threat from Brussels. Or Paris was it? And the water in the kitchen...

He may have been dozing when it happened. He didn't hear it, or if he did, the sound didn't register. The last remaining scraps of his feeble dam had given way and a surge of black, oily water had rolled across to the rear of the Manor House. It threw itself against the French window, the catch of which had long been feeble. The window surrendered inward, allowing the water to rush in around the furniture. With it came several pieces of the burning wood with which Clive had built his fire beside Glugwell Creek. One piece nestled against the foam-filled settee William had bought more than twenty years ago...

It was past midnight when he woke, still fully dressed, and realised that the Manor House was on fire. It was totally dark and he could hear the roar and crackle of it not far away. He rolled off the bed and found the light-switch but got no response. When he opened the door a solid wall of smoke rushed at him out of the darkness.

"Mrs. Hammel! Mrs. Hammel! Get outside..." His voice failed as he took breath to shout again and got nothing but smoke. He found the stairs on his hands and knees and rolled down, coughing, seeing flames only inches from his face as he went.

When the fire-engine got there the house was ablaze from end to end, standing in a lake of water. In the middle of Squadderby Road lay two soaked figures, grotesquely clasping each other. They were both still alive but obviously poisoned by smoke. In Hammel's hand was a letter-file marked "Claud". In William's, an old, soggy teddy-bear.

"Trouble is," said Proggle, "Folks around here seem dead scared of signing anything."

"Even them as <u>can</u> write." agreed Chimble.

They were sitting in the sun in Chimble's yard, discussing the disappointing outcome of the attempt to raise a thousand-names petition against the demolition of Clagtoft. The number to date was 321.

"Not even the population." said Abe.

"No, but population figures include kids, and you can't count them. Though I don't see why not, come to think. Let's pass it to Trudgen, see if he can get a few added."

"That'd be chearting. Any road, what I've heard, most on 'em's itching to see the bulldozers at wock."

Proggle had brought the petition with her. "What shall I do with it?"

"Do what Brangle said – pass it on to the M.P."

"Can't see that useless twat doing any good with it. Can you Abe, honestly? What I had in mind originally was a great protest march down Whitehall, like we did over battery hens. Or was it the Gulf War? Anyway, knocking on Number Ten and you ambling up with a damn great wheelbarrow full of signatures."

"Ah. Or reversing Diana up to the door, and tipping the buggers off the back... Ay up – looks as if owd Owery's about to git his leg stroked."

The Rev. Cripsin Owery's vicarage was just across the road from Chimble's yard. Once a week without fail, the District Nurse called at the vicarage and stayed long enough to excite speculation among people-watchers. The vicar took every possible opportunity to explain that she came to attend to his rheumatic knee. Speculation varied from a gentle massage with aromatic oils to a rollicking romp on the vicarial bed.

Chimble looked at his watch. "She went in at ten to. Let's see how long it teks 'em. Have you heard how Wassing is?"

After the fire at the Manor House, the Lord of the Manor and his housekepper had been taken to hospital in Stumpleton and were being treated for smoke inhalation.

"They'll survive," answered Proggle. "I rang this morning and they are both conscious and responding. I went down to look at the Manor House and there's scarcely a thing left inside it above the water level. Dangle said it was the burning oil that did it. He went up Glugwell Creek with the fire inspectors and showed them where the dumped oil had been. From what I gathered in semi-Italian, they picked up an empty matchbox and several used matches."

"That'll interest the police. Tek their mind off the vandalised machines at Peamoor Water."

"Oo, yes," said Proggle innocently. "I read about that. Wasn't it awful? Want locking up whoever did it."

"You an' me in a cell together, be just the job. Six months, just set me up."

"Wear you down more likely. Look out – something else happening at the vicarage."

A large grey car had purred up and stopped at the front gate. Its driver, a well-dressed elderly man with long grey hair, sat for a moment sorting papers on the passenger seat. He got out with some in his hand, locked the car, glanced around Main Road, then set off towards the front door of the vicarage. He passed the District Nurse's bicycle.

"Hey, this could be interesting," said Proggle. "I've got a sneaky feeling that's the bishop."

Chimble looked at his watch. "Nearly fifteen minutes, they've bin at it. Time to git one another stripped off, if that's what they do."

Proggle grimaced. "Ugh. Owery naked. Like a bladder of lard."

The bishop rang the bell and stood waiting for several minutes. He took a step back and surveyed all the windows. Then he turned to the left side of the house and went round to look in the garden. From the door at the right side there suddenly emerged the Distruct Nurse, hastily stuffing something into her black bag. Dodging gravestones, she ran across the churchyard and vaulted nimbly over the wall. She smoothed the dress down and walked primly to where her bicycle was parked.

"Bet that was a panic," said Chimble. "Wonder if they got going afore the bell rang?"

"Vicars don't actually do it, do they?"

"Some do. Him we had at Stodgington, knocked five kids off the shelf in about eight years so 'e must have bin up to summat. There's

160

Owery, gone looking for the boss in the garden." He stood up to stretch his legs. "By the way, what happened to Dangle in the fire?"

"He was O.K. The firemen moved him out of the granary, and kept hosing it down until the fire at the house had burnt out. He went down to Glenda's. It was young Gavin Hovel that was watching the oil fire from his bedroom window, saw the Manor House catch light and rang the fire brigade. Glenda's feeding Dangle till he finds somewhere to go."

"Funny that. I mean, Wassing thinking the house had been picked out to be first to go, then it went like that instead."

"Could have been them that did it. Europe I mean. Made it look like an accident."

"Believe that, you'd be as gullible as Wassing. Any road, git that petition sealed up, I'll git it off to the M.P. in today's post."

"How will you address it?"

"To 'Sack o' King Edward Tairts, care of the 'Ouse o' Commons's. If the postman don't know who that is, he's not been reading Harvard. Onny thing that idle sod Clunch ever said in there was 'Can we have a window open in heah Madam Speaker, it's rawther staffy.'"

* * *

On that evening a meeting of Clagtoft Parish Council was held in the Council Chamber of Clagtoft Parish Hall. Present were Councillors Herbert Brangle (Chairman), Mrs. Glenda Hovel, Fred Cletch, Miss Cassandra Proggle and Abraham Chimble. In the public gallery were the Rev. Crispin Owery, P.C. Albert Tussock, Mr. Jack Grunsell, and Mrs. Olive Ossack. The Parish Clerk, Mr. Geo. W. Hunking, was in attendance.

The Chairman extended a welcome to all and said that this was an extraordinary meeting. Proceedings would be entered in the Parish Minute Book and if the planned demolition of the village went ahead, that would become an historical document.

Counc. Proggle took exception to the tone of the Chairman's statement. "In the last war, that would have been rightly condemned as defeatist talk. We are not here to consign the minute-book, or the council, or the village, to the dustbin of history. We are here to prove to the world that a small rural community can resist meddling interference from international finance and meddling bureaucrats and continue its tradtitional lifestyle."

"Yes." Brangle scraped his throat. "I'm sure we are all heartily behind Councillor Proggle's sentiments…"

"Nothing sentimental about it mate. We mean business, as they'll find out pretty sharpish when they send their machinery in."

There was a brief silence in the chamber, as if in an act of homage to brave soldiers who had courageously gone out at dead of night to face an enemy which turned out not to exist.

"Coucillor Wassing is not with us, of course," said the Chair. "On behalf of us all, I'm sure I do right to instruct the Clerk to write to him with our best wishes for his speedy recovery. And our condolences on the loss of his family home."

There was a murmur of approval. Brangle went on, "Our good friend and Constable, Albert Tussock, is with us, and would like to address the meeting first, as he must return to duty."

"Thank you, sir. The officer in charge of the investigation into the fire asked me to enquire if anybody saw a person or persons acting suspiciously in the vicinity of the house, or at Glugwell Creek, during the evening of the fire."

Jack Grunsell said, "Dangle was on his his allotment."

Tussock said, "Thank you sir. You mean Mr. Wassing's chauffeur?"

"D'Angelis, his proper name," said Chimble. "Spends moorst of his spare time there."

"Is he a smoker?" asked the policeman.

"Not likely," said Coun. Glenda Hovel. "Not on his pay, or lack of it. And he spent very little time at his allotment that evening, because he was at my place over an hour."

Mrs. Ossack piped up, "Aye, an' I seen him go in the phone box in Main Road. I was tekking a short cut across Bosh Green."

"Any idea what time that was, madam?"

"Time? I dunno. Gitting on for dark it was. Was dark, time I got 'ome. Fell ower the boody cat goin' up my pad."

Tussock finished writing, looked around the chamber, then snapped his notebook shut. "You've all been very helpful, thank you. And thanks to you Mr. Brangle." He left the meeting.

"This is more in the nature of a Parish Meeting…" began Brangle.

"Which is permissible, under the constitution of Parish Councils," said Proggle.

"Quite. And we next have a brief announcement from our priest, the Rev. Owery."

Owery's red, shining face rose above the meeting like a morning sun in the tropics. "Ladies and gentlemen," he said, then paused for thought and added, "And Councillors. It is, I'm afraid, bad news that I bring. It is the news that your lovely old church of St. Dismas, standing at the centre of your community as it has for more than six centuries, has become a redundant church. It will be closed and locked after next Sunday's service and will remain thus for the foreseeable future."

There was an empty silence. The only person in the room who had attented a church service in the past year was the Chairman. Although a Methodist, he had gone to the previous years's Remembrance Day service, wearing his chain of office, as the sole representative of the Parish Council.

"'Ave you got another job to go to?" Olive asked the vicar.

He blinked and made a rumbling noise.

Proggle said, "I think the Church of England ought to be bloody well ashamed of itself, if you'll excuse the language. It's supposed to stand as the moral leader of the people and defender of their right to live, work and worship where they want and at first whiff of a nudge from some twat of a jack-in-office it leaves the battlefield with its tail between its legs. If Jesus Christ had been a Clagtoftian now he'd have been standing at the door of the church with his sleeves rolled up, roaring 'let 'em all come!'"

"I... I, er, anger is, um, an understandable reaction to this news," said the vicar. "And those who are angered by it have their hearts in the right place. Though in fairness, I must point out that the Europe scheme is not the only straw by which the camel's... it is is one factor, a new one, by which... all things taken into account which include the dwindling congregation..."

"I ain't dwundle, personally," said Chimble. "Kep mesen lean and fit, swarming up that damned tower trying to mek it wattertight."

"Yes, yes, and I'm sure the... the church is grateful to all the good people have done so much over the years to... to..." he was almost in tears.

"What 'appens to the money for the organ fund?" asked Olive.

Owery's face was working grotesquely, so Brangle rescued him. "I expect all the funds attaching to Clagtoft church will go towards the maintenance of other churches in the... the bishops... er,"

"See," said the Parish Clerk.

"Diocese." said Glenda Hovel.

"District," went on Brangle, "And I would like it to go on record that the Council and parishioners are grateful to the Rev. Owery for the sterling work he has done over the years in binding together the spiritual life of this little community of ours. Er... in the sight of God."

"Amen," said Chimble.

Owery had recovered sufficiently to say, "The final service in our church will be next Sunday morning at 11 o'clock. The bishop suggested that for this special occasion, everybody should be invited to bring along for blessing any object they consider symbolises their living and being as members of this ancient parish." He took a deep breath, enough for several more sentences the same length, then blew it out again as Polomint fumes. "I wish you goodnight, and may the Lord's blessing be on you." He went.

Olive's voice followed him through the kitchen door; "Do they git the dole?"

Brangle said, "I have to report a conversation with our Member of Parliamment, Mr. Roland Clunch, when I mentioned that the petition against the demolition of the village had been forwarded to him and I requested that he act with the utmost urgency in placing it before the Prime Minister. However, he thought that as the P.M. is currently out of the country, he had better lodge it with the appropriate Ministry, that of Agriculture, Fisheries and Food."

Proggle groaned. "Trust him. Can't that pillock get anything right? It should have gone to Environment."

"Or better still Defence," said Fred Cletch. "After all, this is invasion of English territory by aliens."

"Ah, to 'ell wi' 'em all," said Olive. "Underlings, that's all them lot is. Go to the boss, I say, send it to Buckin'am Palace. If she waved it at some o' them an' said, 'Ay up, git summat done about this, then they'd son buck their ideas up."

Brangle rapped his pen on the table. "Yes, well, while we are out here, remote from the centre of such things, we have to rely on the man we voted to be our champion..."

Chimble roared with laughter, his moustache flapping like the wings of a tawny owl. "Champion! That's a good 'un. Some champion."

The meeting was persuaded to move on to other matters, among them a report that a team from Eastern Telly, working on the documentary about market towns, would be interviewing in Clagtoft area, seeking people who were regular users of Stumpleton markets.

Brangle expressed the hope that people would turn out in good numbers for the closing service in the parish church and a lively discussion went on about what were suitable things to bring for blessing. Fred Cletch thought perhaps a bank-book. Chimble proposed bringing his Robin, as it was the only thing he cared about which would go through the door. "And it's overdue for a service any road." Olive said she would bring their owd cat because "It's nivver bin the sairm since I fell ower it."

Glenda Hovel thought that if the worst came to the worst and they lost their battle, they should seriously consider burying a time-capsule beneath the village, containing things likely to be of interest to historians a thousand years into the future.

Mr. Jack Grunsell thought that the Parish Council itself would make a good subject for the contents of such a capsule and reminded the meeting that the Stamping Cat was due to close in twenty minutes.

Councillor Brangle hastily effected an adjournment.

165

# Chapter Seventeen

The police regarded the oil-slick fire on Clagtoft Drain as deliberate and a car-load of uniformed officers came into the village asking questions, trying to build on the notes handed in by Tussock. Clive saw them arrive and guessed what they were about. He saw them work through Duchess of York Drive, then come along Ketchup Terrace towards the Stamping Cat. At this stage he decided that it would be prudent to be Not at Home. He vanished. He had told his parents that when he came back from the veg field he had come straight home, but he couldn't tell whether they believed him or not.

Two constables came into the yard and knocked on the house door. They asked routine questions about anything seen and Jack repeated his answer about having seen Dangle at the allotment.

"Can you remember what time it was?"

No, he couldn't.

"Just before dark? A long time before dark?"

He thought perhaps just before dark, but he noticed they glanced at each other and the pen hesitated over the notebook.

"Or it might have been earlier."

"I see. Can we have a word with your son?"

"Sure. I'll fetch him." Jack went through the premises, the yard and the garden. The policmen looked around outside.

Finally, one said, "Not to worry. We'll come back later."

They did come back later. Twice. And the second time was when they had been to every house in the village centre and were on their way back to Stumpleton.

"Y'know what's happened," Jack told Edie. "He's seen them here and kept away. He'll be back now they've gone."

The two remaining customers left, so Jack closed the bar and scouted round the village. He knew the boy spent some time with Chimble, and there was a light in one of the workshops.

166

"Clive?" said Abe. "No mate. Ain't seen him all day, far as I can remember." He put down the file he was using, wiped his hands. "Bit lairt for 'im to be out."

"Never known him this late before."

"Let's git the Boeing out, 'ave a run round."

They took the Robin round all the roads and open spaces around the village centre, pausing to examine the waterlogged, blackened shell of the Manor House. They went the full length of Pudding Lane, out into Conker Drove and over Lollycock Bridge. Abe paused and looked across at the dark mass of trees around Clagtoft Hall.

"Can't imagine him going in there," said Jack. "Nervous of spooky places, he is."

A quick check at the pub, then Abe said, "We'll look at Gozzard's place, down the fen." By this time darkness was total and Gozzard's house, when they reached it, was just as dark as everything else. "Must have gone for one of his meals out." observed Jack as they turned to head back for Clagtoft. They went a few hundred yards, then the Boeing spluttered and came to a stop.

Chimble looked down at the petrol gauge and ran steadily through his normal, everyday repertoire of swear-words. Then he took a deep breath and trawled his memory for a few more, peppered the dashboard with them. The machine did not flinch, and remained silent.

"Let's give it a shake," said Jack. "Might slosh a bit more down the hole."

They seized the little car like a pair of terriers and shook it on its springs until it rattled in protest. The result was another 150 yards of carefree motoring, ending with a noiseless cruise to another halt. The medieval traffic-cone crowning the tower of St. Dismas church, with Chimble's searchlight shining on it looked very small and distant. They took pushing and steering by turns, and by the time they reached the village the turns were about 20 yards long.

A check at the pub, where there was still no sign of Clive, then the last lap into Chimble's yard. When they reached it, Jack collapsed over the back of the Robin, panting. Chimble's external yard-light was shining in through the back window of the car.

"Abe," said Jack. "What's that tin on the floor of the car?"

"That? Ah – that's what I used for the searchlight engine. It's..." he suddenly clapped a hand to his head. "Oh, Gawd. It's petrol, ain't it!"

* * *

Big Rube Fasswelt had taken no active part in the Save Clagtoft! Campaign. She heard all about its activities from Liz Otmill and from Proggle next door but she felt no inclination to join in. Infact, she was beginning to relish the idea of a move. Since Little Rube had gone to live in Stumpleton, where one of her brothers already lived, Mum had harboured secret visions of herself being uprooted and replanted there. Camilla Close would be nice; just aroud the corner from her son and but a stone's throw from that place where they had bingo twice a week. And getting into a supermarket when you felt like it, that'd be nice, instead of having to wait for the once-a-week bus and then getting home and finding something on your list you never got.

She didn't just wish; she sneaked into the council office one week, got a transfer application form, secretly filled it in and posted it. And made sure they knew what she wanted by writing "CAMILLA CLOSE" in block capitals across the top. After all, if Proggle's thing wins and keeps the Europe thing out, she would still prefer Stumpleton. She was born there and whenever she walked through its streets she met somebody she knew, had worked with, or gone to school with.

Out one evening, she saw Brangle cutting his front hedge at Goatskin Hall. Now there, she thought, is a man who has to do with the council. She went across and exchanged good evenings.

"D'you know me, Mr. Brangle?"

"Of course. Mrs. Fasswelt, isn't it?"

"That's right. Yer on the council ain't you Mr. Brangle."

"Yes."

"I got me name down for a bungalow in town, Camilla Close."

"Good. Well, of course, that's the town council. I'm chairman of Clagtoft Parish Council, which is not..."

"Aye, but I'm sure your word carries a lot of weight up there. 'Aving a big business in town, an' all."

He laughed but was visibly flattered. "It can often be the personal touch that tips the balance, that's true, but..."

"Meeting 'em all in the White Swan, I know. That's where the real council business is done ain't it? Same as here, at the Cat."

"Ah, but it's not where housing allocation is done. There's professional staff, working to a points system. And of course, if Clagtoft gets the axe, they'll have something worked out."

"Thought you was off to kill that idea, this Save Clagtoft lark. You're on that an' all, ain't yer."

"Of course. Myself and my fellow-councillors are supporting to the hilt..."

"But I bet yer hedging yer bets an' all. Can't tell me you're not smacking your lips over some o' the properties going through your office."

He laughed. "Human nature, isn't it? We all join in with our community, but we never forget to look after Number One. Self-preservation".

"Some very nice places in town. I know, I used to live there."

He became slightly confidential. "Do you know East Brink?"

"Know it well. Used to do me paper round there. Real posh, them is. You got your eye on one o' them?"

"Between you and me, of course, the end one overlooking the park."

"Blimey. Best 'ouse in town, I'd say. Well, good luck wi' it. Don't worry, I shan't say a word to Proggle or any o' them. Onny don't forget, Camilla Close, that's where I'd like to be. Fost one as comes empty, like." She gave him a wink and walked on.

His mouth opened and shut, but he said no more.

\* \* \*

On the morning after Clive went missing, Jack Grunsell didn't go to his furniture-van job. He rang and told the boss why, then he rang the police and asked if they could help.

Chimble and Proggle were in the post office when a police van arrived containing a sergeant, two men and two women constables. They explained their reason for being there and Proggle responded immediately.

"I'll get my loud hailer. Get a crowd of volunteers rounded up, then you can organise a search. Folks are used to hearing me, so they'll come out to listen."

Within half an hour there were 23 people in the yard of the Stamping Cat, most of them armed with sticks as thoughtfully suggested by Proggle. There was a brief conference, then the whole party set out in three separate lots; one to Silt Lane and Clagtoft Hall, the second to the Bosh Green area, the third to the allotments and Glugwell Creek.

"Look in all the long grass and stuff," the sergeant had told them. "In case he's gone to sleep somewhere. In all the buildings, as far as you can without trespassing. Ask permission first, but don't turn yourselves into coppers. If somebody's obstructive, just walk away and fetch one of us."

They had seen it done so many times on the news, they knew just what to do; walking in line, poking their sticks into things. It was a field-day for looking in neighbours' gardens, sheds and greenhouses.

By mid-afternoon the central area had been well combed and nothing had turned up. The sergeant asked Proggle to call everyone back in, and they reassembled in the Stamping Cat yard. Inside the pub, one of the constables had asked Edie about the large building at the end of the yard.

"That's always called the Old Brewery. Jack said it's where they used to make their own beer, years ago. He allus keeps it locked up, so Clive couldn't get in there."

He insisted on having a look inside, and as Jack was still out searching, she fetched the key out of his bedside locker. The officer took one look, then quickly re-locked it and fetched the sergeant. Then they both went in, and when they came out the sergeant re-locked it and kept the key.

With the searchers back together, the sergeant thanked them all for the work they had put in, and told them he had now requested the help of a helicopter as the most efficient way to search the open countryside.

While he was talking the church clock began to strike. He ignored it and carried on. Then he noticed that some of his listeners were loking up at the church. He realised something was wrong. The

170

hands were pointing to three-twenty-five, and it had already struck more than forty.

"Pigeons, I expect," said Proggle. "No end up there. One got stuck in the works."

All eyes were on the clock, when the minute-hand began moving, waggling rapidly back and forth.

"That's a featherless pigeon," said Chimble. "And I'd guess its name is Clive Grunsell."

He crossed Main Road to the church and it was locked. Owery had been watching the search from his upper windows and was now frozen with fear at the sound of non-stop striking. He had convinced himself that something dreadful was about to happen. When Chimble asked for the key, he couldn't find it. "I'm sure I... let me see, I was in there..."

"Not to worry," said Abe. "I've got the spare in the post office. I'll use it." While he was gone, the waiting crowd were treated to a highly unusual form of entertainment; a boy, apparently wearing nothing except a guitar, strumming, yodelling, and perilously dancing around the base of the church spire. When he saw Abe below he called: "Switch the light on Mr. Chimble."

It turned out that he had nicked the key from the vicarage hall, locked himself in the church, searched the vestry and found a full bottle of sherry used by the vicar to fortify himself before services, and drunk himself to sleep on the horsehair sofa. On waking, he couldn't find the key, so he finished off the sherry and went exporing.

Having supervised his removal, re-dressing, and despatch to the Stamping Cat, the sergeant then turned his attention to Jack Grunsell.

"Now you, sir, are coming for a ride with us to Stumpleton Police Station."

Jack's jaw dropped and his eyebrows lifted, simultaneously. "Can't we talk here?"

"You've got your son back. That job's finished. I want to talk about something quite different."

"Oh, aye? What's that then?"

"The contents of the building, part of your premises, known as the Old Brewery. Said contents being a large quantity of new TV sets, videos, hi-fis, micro-waves, cam-corders, larger white goods, and other materials. Probably stolen."

171

"Not by me they wasn't. If I let out part of my premises for somebody else to use…"

"Then we shall want the name and address of said tenant. And also that of the supplier of a large boxful of videos, suspected of being pornographic in nature. Those, incidently, have already been removed for examination."

"Yeah, I know. Git half the force in, set round watching 'em. Any road, I can explain…"

"Just get in the van Mr. Grunsell. There'll be plenty of time for explanations when we get to the station."

* * *

The band of searchers had watched that exchange from a distance and when the van drove off Proggle said, "Now, I wonder what that was about?"

Amelia Chaunter said, "Reckon I've got a good idea. I saw two of 'em looking in the Old Brewery. I can see straight across there out my bedroom winder. He has stuff goin' in there, middle o' the night sometimes. And coming out."

"What sort of stuff?"

"Lot in boxes, new. Sometimes big stuff, fridges, washing machines. Yer don't 'andle stuff like that at two o'clock in the morning, not if you doin' it honest."

The little crowd was beginning to disperse, when Olive Ossack came bustling round Waddies Corner. She reved up when she saw them. "What the 'ell's going on?"

"Too late, Olive," said Amelia. "Just had a male strip-show, top o' the church."

"Who was it?"

"Onny drawback was, 'e kep it covered up wi' 'is guitar."

"Oh, 'im. Huh. Seen all I want o' that. Any road, does anybody know what's up wi' the gas?"

"Gas, why?" asked Proggle.

"Mine's gone of. Can't git no light. Just asked Rose Hunking, she tried 'ers an' it's gone off an' all. I was off up to the phone box, see if I can find out.

Chimble said, "Hang on. I'll try on mine."

When he came back he said, "They didn't know owt, as you might expect. Off to find out and ring me back. That was supposed to be the emergency service."

Proggle was standing on the top step of the post office entrance and she immediately turned the little knot of people into a protest meeting. "Y'know what this is don't you? It's the start of the Clagtoft shut-down. Might be a bit of trouble, breakdown of machinery or whatever. They'll say it's not worth spending money putting it right. It's only Clagtoft and it'll be gone shortly. Believe me, if it does turn out something like that, somebody's going to get a bloody earful from the Save Clagtoft! Campaign."

Glenda Hovel had just come to the back of the meeting, and heard Proggle's last few words. She held up a newspaper. "I don't know what you're on about Cassie but..."

"Gas. They've cut off Clagtoft gas supply."

"That as well? I was going to show you this in the Lincoln paper. 'Village School Closing. The school at Clagtoft, already threatened by the European Scheme, will be closed in any case after Christmas. The children will be taken by bus to Stumpleton or Dogstead. A spokeswoman for the Education Authority stated that all democratic procedures had been..."

"Democratic bollocks!" screeched Proggle. "Not a single bloody parent in this village has been consulted! Can you folks see what's happening? They're simply shuting you down, bit by bit. We shall end up with a village that's not livable in, then they'll say, 'well, we might as well knock it down'. I for one am not going to stand by and see it happen. I'm going to fight it till I haven't got a breath left."

For once there was a mumour of approval, and some clapping. Something was getting through, thought Proggle. She saw Liz Otmill, slightly apart from the crowd, camera at eye. "Get plenty Liz. Let's send some to the papers."

"Has the Campaign got money in the kitty?" asked Glenda.

"Ah!" said Proggle. "Now that's something I was saving for our next meeting. But in view of these sudden developments, I'll tell you now. And we'll get it out to the media as well. We have an important and influential organisation backing us. One with funds galore to spend."

All the ears pricked up. "Who's that?" asked Chimble, "Monster Raving Loony Party?"

173

"Stop being funny Abe. This is serious. Ukoff."

"Ukoff yourself. I was here fost."

"United Kingdom Opposition to Foreign Finance. Something that's backed by a lot of individuals and big firms, and is opposed to foreigners moving in and buying British property, British companies, and British land. They knew of this European scheme to buy land in the fens, and were already planning a campaign of heir own against it. Then our good friend Liz Otmill there, the artist, got a letter about us in some London newspapers, and they immediately contacted her. They could help. So Liz has become the go-between."

Olive pipped up, "What do we need money for? Thowt we was just off to bash the buggers ower the head when they come."

"Remember our first meeting? We said if it came to the worst, we would cut Clagtoft off from the rest of the world. Live on what we've got here, just as folks did years ago. Put road blocks up, so nobody can get in that doesn't live here."

"What about the milkman?"

"Ah. Now there's one thing the money will buy – our own milking cows. There's not much grazing, but when you count the Drain banks, there's enough. Don't worry, all this has been gone into with Fred Cletch and the other farmers. Our own chickens for eggs, fattening pigs. All-year-round vegetables, there's enough cold-storage space. We'd have to buy and store some flour…"

"How about cooking, when there's no gas?" asked somebody.

"We'll solve that. By sharing, maybe. Or buying in microwaves. We've found that they can't cut our electricity without cutting several other places at the same time, so we should be O.K."

"One thing we could have," said Chimble. "A communal kitchen in the village hall, give everybody one hot meal a day."

The longer they talked, the more enthusiastic they became. Proggle noticed that many of them, hitherto luke-warm supporters, were coming up with some sound practical suggestions. She was reminded of the stories she had read and heard about wartime conditions in Clagtoft, when the old Paddy Huts in Piggery Lane had been turned into a Land Army hostel, and the Ebenezer Chapel was a British Restaurant.

"This is a private war," she proclaimed. "Clagtoft versus Europe. And by God they don't know yet what they've taken on!"

174

# Chapter Eighteen

Violet Wask realised she still had the collection on the history of the Manor House, which Dangle had lent her. She knew of the fire but was unsure whether the Italian had stayed in his granary-cum-flat. When she went to look, the place seemed deserted. Not dressed for wading, she was unable to reach it. The water level in Clagtoft Drain was still abnormally high and the flood water, hiding the whole garden, was withing a foot of the of Squadderby Road.

As she stood surveying the blackened ruin, Fred Cletch came along in his Maverick, and stopped. "Nobody at home, sorry."

She smiled. "No. I understand Mr. Wassing is still in hospital. But recovering well. Actually, I wanted to see Dangle."

"Perhaps I can help there. I don't know exactly where he is but if you go to Social Services in town, they were going to find somewhere for him to live. After the fire, he brought the Rolls down to my place at Woad Farm, very sensibly I thought, and he asked if I had anywhere to store it. Which I had. Then I ran him up to the Social Services office in town and left him there."

"I suppose all his belongings are still up there in the granary."

"They are. He says he'll leave them there until the water goes down. The remarkable thing is that since the fire, he seems to have acquired the ability to speak quite good English."

Violet smiled but said nothing.

"Anyway," went on Fred, "From what I hear, it could take another week before the water goes down. It was supposed to be five days, but then the drainage engineers dropped a clanger, dug a hole in the wrong place and fractured a gas main. That's why we've been without gas."

She laughed. "The folks in the village think it was done deliberately to force them out."

"They wouldn't dare do that. Too risky. And as it is, they'll have to come round and tell everybody when they put the pressure back on, and to make sure no taps are left on. Any road, I must get on; can I give you a lift?"

"Er... no, thanks. I've got my car in Chimble's yard. I thought I'd walk across first and check Dangle's allotment shed, make sure it's all secure. By the way, have you heard yet when the date of the Public Inquiry is?"

"Cancelled. Or, to be more exact, never got off the ground in the first place. Apparently our pillock of an M.P. made a balls-up of it, went to all the wrong people, upset the only ones who might have helped, and ended up with egg all over his face."

"So now it's entirely up to Cassandra and her campaign."

"Absolutely. And thanks to these mysterious UKOFF people, it now seems to enjoy almost unlimited funding. Well, must leave you. See you around." He roared away.

Violet crossed the footbridge, noting that it was only inches above water level, and checked the shed. As she returned she felt the plank lurch slightly towards the murky brown water.

After some enquiries in Stumpleton, she found Dangle in one of the council's sheltered housing units. He was in fine spirits, having been given some spending money, his first for several months, and a promise that somebody would look into the affair of his unpaid wages.

More than that; he was fizzing because he had been to the library, looked again in the reference section and discovered some surprising new things about the Wassings and Clagtoft Manor House.

"He talked of the family in the Manor House four hundred years – is nonsense. Whether Mr. Wassing is knowing or not, his grandfather, the father of the Colonel, was buying the house in 1910. paying five hundred, twenty-five pounds for the house. And the manor – how do you call it?"

"Lordship of the Manor."

"This he bought also, an extra £5!" the Italian was delighted with his discovery – as indeed, as an archaelogist and therefore involved with history, was Violet. But she immediately spotted a mild dilemma: did William know all this? And if not, ought he to be told?

Was he genuinely ignorant, or being pretentious about the antiguity of his background? She didn't doubt Dangle's reading of the Manor's history; he had, as his notebooks had proved, acquired considerable skill as an amateur researcher. And it would be easy enough for her to follow through and check. The Colonel would surely have known the truth of the matter; had he imagined it a kindness to his sons to leave them in ignorance? Maybe so; Violet recalled William saying he had never seen the deeds and had sounded as if he had been discouraged from doing so. She decided to stay aloof from the matter. Dangle, now presumably Wassing's ex-employee, could please himself.

* * *

Back in Clagtoft the TV documentary team, to which Gerald Nodder had been attached, were already getting wind of the intensifying of the Save Clagtoft! Campaign. Nodder rang his boss at Eastern Telly to tell him what was going on. "Not all strictly relevant to the Market Towns thing, but it'd be a pity to miss out on some of this." After an interval he got a message back with a go-ahead to get whatever he thought usable as news or current affairs.

He went to see Chimble, and found him raising steam on the dragline excavator.

"What are you planning to do with this machine?"

"Road–blocks, maate. The way they did all in the villages round here in wartime, onny we're doing it now to keep the Europeans out. And instead of concrete we'sll be using tree-trunks and hundreds o' tons o' muck. When you see this 'ere in action, yer want to hoof it quick or else yer might be trapped in."

"How will the village survive, if no food supplies can get in?"

Chimble looked at him pityingly, and remembered one of Proggle's favourite sayings. "Your trouble, mate, you're a typical member of the Pampered Society. Them as reckons the onny place food can come from is Tesco's. Clagtoft is a producer of food. Clagtoft was independent years ago, an' it will be again very shortly. See them Drain banks? All that green stuff? They call that grass, sunny boy, an' it's what cows and pigs and sheep eat. And all that muck on the fields thats where tairts and cabbages grows. Don't

177

worry, once we're shut off and organised, we'll survive. Folks here knows how to do the wock, and they ain't frit of doing it."

Nodder switched off his recorder and went in search of more preparations. At the back of the village hall, Fred Cletch and George Hunking were busy, with the aid of a fork-lift, removing the searchlight from the roof.

"Is this part of the siege preparations?"

"It is."

"What's it for?"

"Up to now," said Fred, "It's been lighting up the church. When we've done it'll be perched on that windmill tower you side of the Drain, and used at night to detect any advance on the village."

"I thought the road-blocks would take care of that."

"They might use tracklayers, come across the fields."

"When you see 'em coming, what d'you do?"

"Blind the buggers with the light, then start shooting."

"Did you say shouting?"

"Shooting. Bang-bang. With guns. And real bullets. We're not standing by and watching our houses knocked down. Who the 'ell are you?"

"Eastern Telly. Here for a documentary but..."

"Well, put this in your programme, mate. Any employee of any company as is engaged in demolition work is risking life and limb if he approaches Clagtoft. He'd be safer losing his job and signing on. We ain't violent people normally, we're just ordinary farming folk as wants to get on with our job. Our business is producing food and it's no more to do with space shuttles than what yours has with... steady on George!"

A heavy length of steel angle slid noisily down the iron roof and fell with a deafening clang, a few feet away from the expensive shoes of Gerald Nodder. He sprang back and collapsed in the smelly arms of an elder.

He went back to the Eastern Telly van, parked in the yard of the Stamping Cat. The cameraman was asleep in the passenger seat. "Look alive, we want some footage of all this. Could turn good, like people getting shot, stuff like that. What's going on down there?" He point down to the end of the yard, where a large police van had back up to the Old Brewery, and the goods from the inside were being removed.

178

"See what I mean? Sit here zizzing, and things happening under your nose." But his enquiry brought a distinctly off-putting reply from the sergeant.

Olive Ossack put him wise when he met her near Ketchup Terrace. "It's all stole, that there is. Carted Grunsel off to the cop-shop they did, kep 'im there while bedtime."

"Are you going to shoot anybody when they come to knock the village down?"

"Put a gun in me 'and, I'll 'ev a go. Used to be a dab 'and at rattin' when me dad kep chickens."

"Well stocked up with food, are you, ready for the siege?"

"They tell us we don't need to. Filling Cletch's cold–stores up, they are. All bought at trade price."

"Who's paying for it?"

"Some firm called Uck. Uck Off, summat like that. You want to see Liz, that there painter woman, she's 'andling all the money side. Lives wi' Big Rube, down there."

Duchess of York Drive was a revelation to the TV men. "Just look at this lot," said Gerald to the cameraman. "Get some of these Cortinas and things." From end to end the front gardens were littered with old discarded objects, some obviously originating at least thirty years ago. Televisions, beds, radios, cookers, fridges, even, in one garden, a whole three-piece lounge suite.

"Which is Big Rube's house?" Gerald asked a child, and was politely escorted to it. Ruby glared at them through the window first, before opening the door with the security chain on.

"Eastern Telly," said Gerald. "Can we see the lady called Liz, please?"

"Oh, telly." Ruby took the chain off, opened the door wide. "She ain't here just now. Out somewhere. Gits all ower, doing pictures. Not back while dark some days."

"Is she your daughter?"

Rube laughed. "Gawd, no. None o' mine was that clever. Liz just lodges wi' me. Rigged up the back bedroom for a studio, works up there when it's too wet outdoors."

"Could we have a look at it, please?"

She stood aside. "No 'arm in that, if yer interested. Straight up and the door on the left."

179

Gerald and the cameraman went up, Rube lumbering behind. Liz had made room for her easel by tilting the bed on its side and there were finished and partly-finished pictures strewn all over, mostly in oils. On the easel itself, in the full light of the window, was The Naked Ploughman, almost finished.

"Cor!" said Gerald, stopping in his tracks. "Just looky at this!" he stood aside to let the cameraman in. "Any good in here?" the man shifted the easel, tilted it forward, switched on a light. "Might be O.K."

"Is Liz a professional?"

"Oh, aye. 'Ez an agent as sells 'em, down in London."

"Who was the model for that one?"

"Dunno." She looked at it and giggled. Then she looked again, and laughed. "I'm damned. Looks like owd Chimble, the fairce does. Rest on 'im should be a bit skinnier'n that though."

"Somebody told me that Liz would know about Uckoff, the people the money's coming from for the Campaign."

"She's 'andling all that. Summat she put in the paper, and them's took it up. Wanting to keep the Europeans out. Hang on." She went away for a few minutes, came back with a slip of paper.

Gerald read it into his recorder. "United Kingdom Opposition to Foreign Finance. Have you got their address or anything?

"No. Bin done on the phone mostly. Any road, the money's good whoever it is. Comes through a slissiter in town. Proggle's already bought some milking cows and some 'ens. Lorry-loads o' tinned stuff gone into Cletch's sheds. Ivverybody wi' a freezer's gitting filled up."

"How long d'you think you can last out?"

"How long? Long as yer like. My granny lev yon side o' Fosdyke, on the marsh, an' she nivver went nowhere shopping. No buses or owt where she was. Still diggin' 'er own tairts when she were eight-nine. All yer need's summat to eeart, ain't it?"

They left Ruby, and as they walked back to the village centre Gerald used his mobile phone, raised the researcher at Eastern Telly, and asked for information on UCKOFF.

\* \* \*

180

In Chimble's room behind the post office counter, a council of war was in progress. An Ordnance Survey map of the village was spread out on he table.

"One complete, permnent road-block on Squadderby Road, there," said Proggle.

"Hang on," said Fred Cletch, "Go out a bit further; one of my field gateways is just there."

"Right," said Proggle, and marked the place on the map. "And another on Conker Drove, just beyond the end of Pudding Lane, about there."

George Hunking said, "What about if they come in Land Rovers and such like? Won't they go into the fields and round the blocks?"

"That'll be took care of," said Chimble. "I'll put 'em where there's deep dykes on both sides and no way through."

"Down the fen," said Proggle, "Harry Gozzard's borrowing a tractor and pulling two big fallen trees across the road. And finally, Stumpleton Road. Halfway between Clagtoft and the ramper, a proper check-point, manned day and night by people with guns. Nobody except people going to and from work, and essential callers, such as Dr. Mulfry."

"Are we 'aving passports?" asked Chimble.

"I had thought of some sort of permit system," said Proggle. "But when you think about it, in Clagtoft your face is your passport. Whoever mans the checkpoint will know a stranger on sight, even a strange vehicle."

"Are we having one of those barrier things that swing up?" asked George Hunking.

Cletch replied, "The paint's drying on it now. I've used one of the fallen trees from the Manor House and two railway sleepers to mount it. Good as anything they use on the Continent at border-crossings. So long as they don't come cross country..."

"That's what the searchlight's for," said Proggle. "Turn-table mounted on the old windmill tower, rope-operated from the ground, set to light up the land to half a mile radius."

"Well, what are we waiting for?" said Chimble. "I've got stearm up on the owd 'urdy-gurdy. Let's git Clagtoft sealed up. Did you order some stearm-coal for my machinery?"

"Delivery tomorrow," said Proggle. "And some extra diesel for Fred's use of his tractors."

"All paid for by this Ukoff?" asked George.

"That's right. Liz is handling all that. She says they've been told about everything we're doing, and they're with us up to the hilt. Well, to be fair, she did mention up to five thousand. She thought if we topped that they might begin to ask questions."

"That's about what I paid for some land I bought off the Wassing estate," said Fred. "I thought it seemed like a hell of a lot of money but these people seem to spend it like water, whoever they are."

"Anti-Europe," said George darkly. "There's a lot of it about, under the surface."

* * *

Gerald Nodder and his team were preparing to return to base when they saw Chimble's dragline excavator come puffing out of his yard.

"Look at that for Gawd's sake. Like something out of a science-fiction film."

"Or a science-fiction nightmare," said camera. "D'you want it?"

"Sure, it's worth a shot. In fact, we'll tag along, watch him using it."

Since using it on the moat, Chimble had added a water-tank on one side and a coal-bunker on the other. Squadderby Road would have been effectively blocked simply by parking the machine on it. The TV men used their van to follow it, though it went at walking pace.

As they passed the end of Pudding Lane, Gerald spotted another van waiting to come out. "I know who that is," he said. "Hotfoot Press Agency, seen 'em before. Means the London papers'll have got it tomorrow." He began prodding his moble phone. "Bit o' luck, we'll make it in our late bulletin."

After five hundred yards, Chimble stopped the lumbering giant, got down, and began shovelling coal on to the boiler fire.

"Is this the beginning of the siege of Clogthorpe?" asked Gerald.

Abe looked at him pityingly. "Get the name right, mate. Clagtoft."

The press men were clamouring for the story, and Chimble paused on the track of the machine for the photographer.

"Stand clear now. These machines is dangerous." He ducked into the cab, blew the whistle, and began working levers. The huge grab swung round, hovered over the field at the far side of the dyke, then dropped and took a great bite out of it. Lifted, swung back, and dropped the mouthful of rich brown soil plumb into the middle of the road. Abe chuckled gleefully, lifted and swung again.

An hour later, he had constructed the highest hill to be seen within a radius of twelve miles. Twelve feet high, fifteen feet from end to end, and stretching across the road from dyke to dyke.

"That'll settle to about ten foot," he told the newsman. "Give it a year, it'll be green all ower."

"What's the next job?"

"'Nother one the same on Conker Drove. Be done afore dark, wi' a bit o' luck. Next time you come you'll be stopped at Ceckpoint Charlie on Stumpleton Road. Won't be no other way in."

"Shall we need a visa?"

"Easy might. Independent kingdom this, now on. You can tell Brussels to look for another bit, they're not having this. They've shut down our gas, shut down our school, shut down our church. We've nowt left onny the post office, and I guess they'll be on to that next. Back up; I'm coming back that way, flat out."

* * *

When Liz Otmill got back to Duchess of York Drive, she found Big Rube somewhat worried. "Mebbe I didn't ought to have done, I let the TV people look in your studio. Telled 'em you was doin' pictures all round Clagtoft and they 'ad the camera on the one with the bloke, you know, bollock-naked."

Liz laughed. "Good for them. You know, if they show that on telly, it could put another nought on the price when my agent sells it. Rube, don't do any grub for me. Got a taxi coming in ten minutes."

"Ah. Got a date?"

"Could say that I suppose. Actually, I'm off to Stumpleton Hospital again. To see William deMondford Wassing. But don't pass it on. You know how people talk in Clagtoft.

# Chapter Nineteen

"Siege in the Sticks," proclaimed one large headline in a national daily newspaper next day. "Inhabitants of a remote fen village have blocked all roads leading in with huge mounds of soil. Their church, their school and their post office are closed. Their gas supply has been cut off and every single building is due to be demolished to make way for a space-shuttle landing strip."

"Fenland Folk say 'UKOFF' to Space Agency," said another. "A wealthy and influential body called U.K. Oppostition to Foreign Finance (UKOFF) is behind the village of Clagtoft (Lincs.) in isolating itself from civilisation. A six-mile strip of fenland is scheduled to be bought to make a European space-runway. The villagers have vowed to become self-sufficient and to keep the bulldozers at bay – using shotguns if necessary. And a third: "Police stand by helpless as steam-driven monster builds road-blocks."

It was Saturday morning and Chimble had fetched a bundle of newspapers from Dogstead. He, Proggle and Liz were in the van looking at them.

"Haven't shut down your post office have they?" asked Liz.

"Just paid out a pension and sold three second-class stamps. Somebody in the newspairper office med that up."

"Police stand by helpless…" read Proggle. "Did you see any police?"

"No. They stood by helpless eight mile away because they didn't know owt was happening."

Proggle turned to the plan of action she had drawn up for the day. "Fred Cletch and his boy manned the barrier till four this morning, so they'll be off till midday. After that, Abe, can you give Fred a hand erecting barbed wire on the Drain banks?"

"Sure. What's that for?"

184

"To keep our cows inside the parish so we don't have to chase 'em up when they need milking. Fred's got plenty of wire."

"Got the cows already have we?"

"They're due to arrive tomorrow. As are the laying hens, which Josh Kelter will keep at his farm. After that, no more battery eggs – all Clagtoft'll will be eating free range eggs. Paying just enough to cover feed: no transport, no supermarket profit."

"It's a wonder nobody's tried it before." said Liz.

"They did," said Proggle. "Only somebody gave it a bad name. They called it Communism. Right, now Abe – when you go to service the searchlight, can you pick up young Gavin Hovel and show him how it works? He'll be doing a shift on that."

She went out to where her bike was left, still studying her job-list as she mounted and rode off.

"She's been at it most of the night, I reckon," said Liz. "How long s she going to last?"

"Collapse real sudden one day. With a bit o' luck, when I'm there to catch her."

"D'you fancy her?"

He grinned, his ginger moustache bristling in unison. "Not really. I like summat with a bit more upholstery."

"Don't look at me. I've lost half a stone since this has been going on. And by the way, if the telly people do show my Naked Ploughman picture, it's you at the top with a moustache but somebody else below, somebody weighing about fourteen stone."

"Is it all in? I mean, all the details?"

"Is on my picture but I doubt if they'll show it all, not if it's an early evening programme. Still, it should be enough to bring on some brisk bidding, if my agent gets it in an auction. 'As seen on TV' and all that."

"Are you taking it to church in the morning?"

"To church? No. Why should I?"

"Owd bladderface's last service. He wants everybody as turns up to tek summat to be blessed."

"Nuts to him. I fell out with him ages ago. What are you taking, the excavator?"

"Wouldn't go through the door. I'll tek the Robin, it's…"

"I know. It's due for a service. Heard that before."

185

"Brangle asked all the council to attend and bring things. Like an army church parade. It's a wonder he didn't want the band. He'll be polishing up his chairn of office, ready for gitting it blessed."

"Load of codswallop. Has Owery done anything for the Campaign?"

"Nowt as I've noticed. Bin too busy romping wi' the District Nurse. Did I tell yer? Reckon the bishop caught 'em at it..."

\* \* \*

On the Sunday morning, Clagtoft awoke to the realisation that it was no longer part of the civilised world. The Chairman of the Parish Council went to his letterbox for his Sunday Telegraph, usually squeezed through for him by Rose Hunking, and it was not there. Mrs. Brangle looked on the back doorstep and there were no milk-bottles. Already, their very existence was threatened.

Most people had done rather better. Those accustomed to a weekly shop in town by car had done double journeys, often taking elderly neighbours in as well. Freezers were stuffed to capacity, a lot of it other people's goods. They all knew about the Campaign's policy of self-sufficiency but they clung to the familiar shrink-wrapped things as long as possible. A few over-seventies recalled conditions in the war-torn Clagtoft of the early 1940s.

At dawn, the Rev. Crispin Owery was at his desk, re-writing his final sermon for the fouth time. The first three efforts were a pile of ashes in the fireplace; he had an irrational feeling that the vicarage was no longer a private place and that people would come in and examine the clues to his life-stlye. The lurid magazines had already gone up in smoke after a last lingering look at some of his favourites.

He kept having terrifying visions of a church filled to capacity, everybody singing away lustily at their favourite hymns. Which reminded him that he had forgotten to give Lily Chaunter, who played the rickety piano which had temporarily replaced the rickety organ ten years ago, a list of hymns for the service. In fact, he hadn't yet chosen them.

Tears of frustration filled his eyes and his plump, pink face slumped on to the paper and wetted the half-written sermon.

\* \* \*

186

The prospect of a well-filled church was well and truly shattered by Eastern Telly. At nine-thirty their intrepid news-reporter, Gerald Nodder, rang Proggle.

"Don't miss our programme 'Agro-topics' at eleven o'clock this morning. That's if Clagtoft is still receiving British television."

"Very funny Mr. Nodder. Lines of communication are kept open for humanitarian reasons. What's going to be on?"

"All about your campaign. How the brave villagers are Digging for Victory and turning Clagtoft into an independent colony within the Empire."

"Believe it or not, we shall be something very like that."

"For how long?"

"Until the silly twats over there decide to lift their threat of destruction. And you can quote me on that in the programme. Plus you'd better mention that sightseers turning up at the border-points are liable to find themselves facing gunfire."

"I doubt if…"

Proggle slammed down the phone and went in search of her bicycle and loud-hailer. Clagtoft would want to see itself on the small screen and she was quite sure that no more that two or three would normally watch anything with a title like 'Agro-topics'. She dropped her mobile phone nto the bicycle basket and set off."

"Listen on TV at eleven o'clock this morning. Clagtoft's Campaign on TV at eleven. Agro-topics TV programme features the Save Clagtoft! Campaign."

The message echoed around the buildings along Main Road. The vicar found a tissue to dab his eyes and opened a window to listen. "Hats off champagne or d.v. Adeline," it sounded to be saying. Oh, his God, what new development was this? He was heartily sick of Clagtoft, its church, its people and of his mission of ministering to their spiritual needs. They seemed to get through life without spiritual needs. The feeling slowly grew that he would be unable to face a congregation that morning; that he ought to start now, and walk away from it, towards… well, it didn't really matter where to.

Proggle had got to the end of Piggery Lane with her loud-hailer, when she heard the first sound of gunshot from the barrier in Stumpleton Road.

Earlier that morning, the fractured gas main feeding Clagtoft had finally been repaired. The Chief Engineer, smarting a little because his precious weekend had been broken into, thanked the men who had worked on it, though suspecting they might just have craftily prolonged the job into double-time Sunday.

"O.K. John," he said to the foreman. "All ready to turn on."

The foreman cleared his throat. "What about warning consumers."

He had forgotten. The drill was that people had to be warned to check that taps had not been left on when the supply failed. Any domestic explosions would be blamed on him if he simply turned on, and it being Sunday, there were no staff around to do the warning.

He was good a thinking on his feet. "I had an idea," he said, "That we might enlist the help of the Army Cadet Corps, it being Sunday." On his way to the scene of the job, he had seen them drilling outside their hut in Dogstead, and remembered that their officer in charge was himself a gas company employee.

When he got back there, he was encouraged by the sight of a large camouflaged lorry standing by. The officer, a fussy little Captain Main-wearing, was immediately enthusiastic.

"Give us a bit of publicity," he said. "And show the lads that soldiers are for public service in emergency, as well as fighting the enemy. In fact, I'll make it a tactical exercise; stop short of the village, spread out over the surrounding terrain, then enter as if storming the place to flush out enemy snipers."

The Chief Engineer blinked a little. "Well, yes. So long as they get the warnings over. And we usually ask people to check on elderly neighbours."

* * *

The barricade guarding the approach to Clagtoft had been erected near an old implement-shed belonging to Woad Farm, so as to provide shelter if it turned wet – as was beginning to happen that morning. Harry Gozzard had gone on duty that morning at four o'clock an should have been partnered by Nelson Proggle, who had

188

failed to turn up. When daylight broke, however, Clive Grunsell came along, stumming his guitar.

"D'you want a go at being a sojer?" Harry asked him. Clive's eyed rested on the army revolver Harry had brought with him. "Wouldn't mind."

Harry picked up the gun. "Not 'evving that. Anybody attacks Clagtoft, you can flash at 'em. Or shoot 'em with your guitar. I'm off to git forty winks in the shed, so give us a shout if anybody comes."

He found a sheltered corner, improvised a bed with wooden pallets and proceeded to catch up on his lost sleep.

For an hour and a half Clive strutted to and from in the road, occasionally levelling the small end of his guitar at an imaginary enemy and making stuttering noises. He raised and lowered the barrier, waving invisible traffic through. Some early Sunday traffic was stirring on the distant ramper but nothing came Clagtoft way.

He crept into the shed, saw that Harry was fast asleep, and picked up the revolver. He knew how they worked and could see that there were six rounds in it. The safety-catch was on. Outside, he raised it in the accustomed manner, said "Freeze!" to a young sycamore tree, then "Wheeee!" as an imaginary bullet ricocheted off it.

Then he heard the sound of a vehicle and looked towards the ramper. It was a lorry coming this way.

"Harry! Somebody coming. Harry!" he ran to the shed. Harry was still decisively asleep. "Harry! Lorry coming!" still he didn't move.

He went back and saw that the lorry had stopped two hundred yards short of the barrier. From each side, uniformed soldiers were leaping down and fanning out into the fields on either side of the road. An officer had got out of the cab and was calling orders to them.

"Harry! Wake up! There's loads o' sojers coming at us!"

Still no response, so Clive, his heart pounding, ducked under the barrier and advanced towards the lorry. He levelled the gun at it.

"Stop it! Fetch 'em back! They can't come in 'ere!"

His thumb found the safety-catch and he pulled the trigger. The kick from the gun took him by surprise. So did the result; a sudden cloud of steam rose around the front of the lorry and the water from its radiator began streaming out on to the road. The portly officer stopped shouting to his troops and ducked out of sight behind the vehicle.

Harry emerged from the shed, bleary with sleep, wondering if what he was seeing was still part of his dream. Then he realised that Clive, now a hundred yards along the road, had his gun.

"Hey, boy, put that down!"

Clive took the shout as encouragement, swept the gun around a wide arc and pumped off the remaing five rounds. Some of the boys raced towards the horizon; others, remembering the training, went down flat behind grass-clumps or cabbages.

Harry removed the weapon from the boy's trembling hand and went to see what it was all about.

* * *

"The next item comes from an even more exotic location," cracked the presenter of 'Agro-topics'. "Over to the Independent Republic of Clagtoft. No, it's not in the Mediterranean – it's just along the road in the Lincolnshire fenland. The people of the tiny village of Clagtoft, otherwise known as Clagtoft St. Dismas, have cut themselves off from civilisation as a reaction to a plan to demolish the place. The European Space Agency is the enemy; they are buying that particular stretch of flat land to provide a landing-strip for their space shuttles. Why use good fertile arable land for that purpose? Your guess is a good as mine."

Chimble's steam digger came on screen, belching clouds of smoke as it beavered away at the building of the road-block.

"No ordinary village, this. Years ago, it was famed far and wide for a spectacle known as the Naked Ploughman – a local farmer with an eccentric habit. He did all the work on his little farm in the remote fens as naked as on the day he was born."

The lower part of the picture came on, just short of the essentials.

"Oh, sorry – I see now that he kept his boots on."

The shot switched to the top of the picture, again just short, "And yes it's all there inbetween. This is an impression by an eminent local artist, Liz Otmill…"

The programme went on to a more sober discussion of the controversial aspects, including speculation about who exactly was behind the mysterious organisation UKOFF.

But Clagtoft's interest had shifted by now; in almost every house somebody exclaimed "Ay up! That's owd Chimble!" and they'd all gone off into roars of laughter. The moment the Campaign was replaced by the next part of the programme, all the videos were being wound back for another look.

\* \* \*

The congregation in the church that morning numbered just three. Councillor Herbet Brangle came alone because neither he nor Mrs. Brangle had mastered the intricacies of the video timer. She volunteered to stay and recorded the programme so that he could go and get his chain of office processed. Amelia Chaunter, though strictly a Salvationist, brought her cornet to be blessed. She had a grandson spending the day with her so he came as well, bringing a pet rabbit.

The Rev. Owery, his moral backbone temporarily stiffened by a coffee and rum, apologised for the absence of a pianist. The service would have to be brief, as he thought it unwise to attempt hyms without musical guidance.

"This is an historic occasion. People have worshipped here since the first church was built, long before the Norman Conquest. But we live in a materialist society, one in which people's spiritual needs must give way to their, um… things like going into space, for whatever reason…"

He stumbled on for some time before realising he had begun his sermon without preliminary ritual and without mounting the pulpit. He fussed over the pages of a prayer-book, began on the wrong page, apologised, then invited them to recite the Lord's Prayer while he mopped his brow and decided what to do next.

When he got around to blessing the things brought, things began slightly better. He said a few sensible things about local government when he put Brangle's chain through the ritual and more about the benefits of d.i.y. music when he dealt with Amelia's cornet. But when it came to the rabbit's turn it objected, took a flying leap out of the vicar's hands, landed on the communion table, scattered the silverware and disappeared into the choir stalls.

The whole congregation joined in the pursuit, which took longer than the rest of the service. After having left a deposit on the steps of the font, the panting, terrified creature was finally cornered by the boy and returned to the vicar.

Owery performed the necessary rites, during which the rabbit closed its eyes and went to sleep. "What a beautiful creature, to be sure!" he murmured. "A lucky boy you are, having such a companion. I never had a rabbit."

"You can have that one if you like," said the boy. "I've got fifteen o' the 'ungry little buggers."

* * *

Cassandra Proggle just about managed to stay awake through the Clagtoft part of the 'Agro-topics' programme but she remembered nothing about it afterwards. Her son, Nelson Mandela Proggle, was used to self-catering after all the years with a supercharged dissentient mother and he placidly heated and consumed two large pizzas.

She slept on the settee for two hours, went to the bathroom to be sick, then crept into bed fully dressed, sweating and trembling. Nelson looked in several times to see if he could help but got no coherent answer. His unease increased to alarm when she began rambling loudly in what seemed to be Swahili. Finally, he rang Dr. Mulfry's number in Stumpleton and told her all about it.

The doctor was at the house door in twenty minutes, having been recognised by Chimble at the barrier and waved through without ceremony.

When she came back, she spoke to Abe: "Your gallant leader is out of action for a few days. Total exhaustion. I've sedated her and given her orders to stay in bed for four days. She's got her son there but it might be a good idea for others to look in occasionally."

"Seen it coming," said Abe. "Onny surprise is it nivver come sooner."

# Chapter Twenty

For six days and nights, Clagtoft was in a state of siege. Four of its inhabitants had learned how to milk cows, two were enjoying egg-collecting and several children were collecting kitchen scraps to help feed three pigs which Frank Wowser was fattening for the village to eat.

"It's ommost like wartime agen," said Amelia Chaunter. "My mam learnt all sorts o' things then, that she'd nivver tried afore."

Fred Cletch sent a man with a tractor to plough up all the disused Council allotments and Brangle announced that in future they would be rent free. Many people in Duchess of York Drive, whose gardens had sprouted nothing but rusted hulks of old cars for years, had actually borrowed spades and were attacking the potential source of food on their doorsteps. A healthy spirit of self-reliance and mutual co-operation, almost visible side by side, running through the community.

"Hope they keep it up," said Jack Grunsell, whose sales of Gallstone's Bitter had almost doubled. His euphoria was somewhat tempered by the thought of the fine he might have to pay for handling stolen goods.

The first hint of change came on the seventh day of the siege and it came from a totally unexpected quarter. In a roundabout way, from South America.

Liz Otmill and Big Rube were sitting after breakfast, lingering over their second cups of tea and listening to the news on radio.

"The emergency conference of scientists, called hastily in South America, has after only two days issued a stark and frightening warning. The process of global warming, already happening faster than predicted, has taken a sudden and unexplained upward turn..."

"Oooh, lovely warm winters. I'm ready," said Big Rube.

"...And the melting of the polar ice-caps is already making measurable differences to the world's sea levels. The flooding of low-lying areas of land, such as that in eastern England, will happen much earlier than previously thought."

"That means Clagtoft." said Liz.

"Oh, I wouldn't say that. "'Ere to Skegness, it's ower twenty mile."

"Yes, but the Wash is nearer. And we're only on the same level as the marshes."

Rube dropped another lump of sugar into her already sweet tea. "Well, let me now if you see it coming. I noticed Proggle's up and about again this morning."

"A bit tottery perhaps, but she'll cope. Any day now she'll have her bike and loud-hailer out again."

\* \* \*

The big news for the village broke that afternoon and it came initially in a phone call from Roland Clunch, M.P. to Herbert Brangle in his Stumpleton office.

"There's a strong rumour about up here old boy. They're saying the Clagtoft runway scheme is abandoned."

"Are they now? That's good news, if it's true. Our protest wasn't a waste of time."

"Certainly wasn't. Though the official reason being given, of course, is this new emergency report on global warming."

"What's that got to do with the space shuttle?"

"Rising sea-level old boy. They reckon in a very short time all the fenland'll be at the bottom of the sea. They'll be fishing off Peterborough pier."

"Tchah. Heard yarns like that before. Thanks anyway."

Brangle sat looking out of his window for a few minutes, then decided to take the bull by the horns. He rand the European Space Agency in Paris.

The answer was clear and unmistakeable. "Yes sir. The decision was taken late yesturday evening and announced to the Press this morning. Due to the uncertain long-term future of the eastern fenland, the shuttle landing-strip will instead be located near Salisbury Plain."

He left his office early to go back and spread the news in Clagtoft.

* * *

"Dear Claud," Wrote William deMoundford Wassing. "This may turn out to be the saddest letter you have ever received. It is certainly the saddest I have ever written. The plain and simple truth is that the Manor House at Clagtoft no longer exists, at least as a habitable dwelling. A clue to what happened is enclosed with this letter - the remains of a previous one, which I had actually been writing on the night disaster struck. It is, as you see, in a wrinkled state and with some parts barely readable, obviously having been soaked in water.

"That evening had already been eventful. Flood water, due to the rising level in Clagtoft Drain had entered our kitchen. To add to our discomfort, somebody had started a huge oil-fire on Glugwell Creek, with burning, oil-soaked debris floating into our Drain and, they say, reaching Lollycock Bridge. The investigating fire officer thought that some of it found a way into the Manor House and started the fire, which totally gutted the place.

"I recall being blinded and choked by smoke and feeling the intense heat as I went – fell, I think more likely – down the main staircase. After that I remember no more. Though it seems likely that I managed to keep hold of the file with our correpondence in it, and somehow along the way to gather up our dear old Mrs. Hammel and drag or carry her to the safety of Squadderby Road. They found us lying unconscious, clinging together. The abulance crew reached the ludicrous conclusion the she had carried me out of the burning house!

My trusty chauffeur, D'Angelis, escaped the fire as he was in the granary across the yard, which did not suffer. And he had the presence of mind to remove the Rolls-Royce and take it to a safe place. It was stored for a time by a farmer friend (a tenant of the Wassing estate), who had it valued for insurance purposes. The figure was quite staggering – around fifteen times as much as it was bought for; apparently it is a rarity, a collector's item.

It stands outside the window now, as I write this, looking somewhat out of place in the front garden of a council house on a

195

rural estate. But the people around here are amazingly kind; no damage has been done to it. The children stand and admire it, and Cassandra, who has now taken it on herself to act as my chauffeur, allows some of them to ride with her when she takes it to Dogstead for shopping.

Perhaps I should explain. After the fire, I was detained in hospital for more than a week, suffering from the effects of smoke-inhalation. Mrs. Hammel was more than fortunate; she was only kept in overnight and is now being cared for by the authorities in Stumpleton. Anyway, once I came round and was able to recieve visitors, two ladies from Clagtoft came to see me several times – never together but one came every day. In view of the amazing amount of work they had to do (both were involved heavily in running the Save Clagtoft! Campaign I mentioned earlier they made time to come in, sit with me, and keep up my spirits. It was truly a lifeline; after what I had gone through, I doubt if I should have survived without their visits.

One, needless to say, was the lovely Cassandra. As I write, she has just come into the room with a cup of my favourite cocoa. When the time approached for my discharge from hospital, which I had anticipated would have to be into a hotel until I found some suitable place, she said – in such a casual tone! – 'There's plently of room in my house, why not move in with me?' My heart leaped! Of all the wishes I might have prayed to be granted, that would have been top of the list. Albeit dismissed as an impossible dream.

So instead of Cassandra becoming mistress of the Manor House, I have become master of 14 Duchess of York Drive! I hasten to add that this is a temporary arrangement; as soon as a suitable house becomes available I shall buy it as a permanent home for us – 'us', incidently, including Cassandra's son Nelson Mandela, a fine boy of thirteen, who is teaching me to play chess.

Oddly, since the diaster struck, my financial problems seem to have miraculously solved themselves. Some of the estate land was sold at a reasonable price; the tenants of the rest have agreed to a rent rise; the insurance company has accepted the loss of the house and its contents as accidental, and will pay in full. Oh and I shall sell the old Rolls, reluctantly, I must confess, and buy a modern car in which Cassandra will feel more at home as my driver.

196

Out of the storms of disaster, it seems, there shine the first beams of a happy and contented life! Marriage? I hear you ask. Ah! It has been discussed, I assure you. But Cassandra is very much a product of the twentieth century, with strong views about the nature of the relationship between man and woman. No, no, she is definitely not a gold-digger. She insists that I pay no more than the 'going rate' for my lodging here and it seems a ludicrously small sum per week. I go along with what she says and leave all the domestic arrangements in her hands. Though she calls herself a 'supermarket chef', she produces far better fare then poor old Hammel was able to manage. I am heavier already!

On the very day on which I write all this, I am happy to report, still another dark cloud has rolled away. The campaign to save Clagtoft has succeeded beyond all expectation. The European Space Agency is in ignominious retreat, tail between legs and looking for somewhere else to put its ridiculous landing-strip. Out of all the turmoil and heartache of the past few weeks, the old village emerges richer in spirit then ever before. They say it takes war to bind people in comradeship and recent events have shown this true. Just now, our newpapers are full of forboding about global warming ('warble gloaming', Nelson calls it!), but we've heard it all so many times before.

Must break off now. Cassandra has just called (she calls me Billy, like you used to do) to remind me that we are due to pick up Nelson from school (imagine the looks on the other boys' faces) and take him into town to buy some new football boots. After Christmas, he will be going to another school. Will explain later."

* * *

Stringy, pale Abraham Chimble came down the steps of Clagtoft post office, winced at his gout-pain, turned to face Main Road and noticed something move on the church tower. He took off his glasses and squinted up. It was Liz Otmill, looking at the horizon through binoculars.

"Watching for the tide coming up?" he called.

She beckoned him to come up and when he arrived, panting, she said, "The sun's shining on a big stretch of water over there. Could be the tide."

197

He took the binoculars and looked. "Pulk's Bottom." he said.

"I beg your pardon?"

"Place called Pulk's Bottom. Little bairsin o' low land as Glugwell Creek overflows into. 'Appens most winters. Onny floods now because they diverted the Forty-foot. Mek a good picture for you, that."

"Packed all my painting gear, I'm afraid."

"Packed? Not off to leave us, are you?"

"For a short time. The agent wants to arrange an exhibition of all my fenland stuff."

"Including that one as was on the telly?"

"Of course. It's already sold but the buyer has agreed to lend it. Best price I've ever had for a picture that."

She had a large plastic bag at her feet, which she picked up and handed to him. "That's for you Abe."

"What's this?"

"It's a watercolour copy of The Naked Ploughman."

His face lit up. "'Es it got my fairce on it?"

"Yes but the rest of it I slimmed down a bit to suit."

He slid it out of the bag and looked; burst into laughter. "Everything on, an' all, damned if it ain't! I'll 'ang this in the poorst office, 'ev all the women eyeing me up an' speckerlating. Thanks Liz, that's great.

"Abe, there's a suggestion I want to make. I've been looking down at your house roof, where the tree fell. Doesn't seem to be all that bad. Will you let me lend you enough money to get it done?"

"Nivver bin much for borrowing money really." He stood silent for a moment. "To tell yer the truth, I had scraped together enough to git it done. Then this morning I got this bill." He pulled a piece of paper from his pocket and showed her.

"What's this? Machine time, 6 hours; four men, 8 hours each?"

"It's the Highways Department. They couldn't wait for me to git my digger out and shift the road-blocks. They sent a bulldozer and did it theirsens. And sent me the bill for it."

"Hey wait a minute. You don't pay this with your money."

"It was me as put the road-blocks up."

"I know, but it was for the campaign. This is for UKOFF. They'll pay."

"That's all ower now, ain't it?"

"They backed the Campaign and they'll pay this bill. Leave it with me Abe. I'll take it and get it paid."

"How d'you know they'll agree to it?"

"I say they will."

He stood deep in thought for a full minute, then turned to her.

"There's summat fishy about this."

"About what?"

"This UKOFF business. Nobody knows owt about it, onny you. You know what I reckon? You med it all up."

She grinned and said nothing.

"You med it up, an' you bin using your own money, ain't yer?"

"Wrong both times. You're right about something fishy, but it's not my money. These paintings are earning a lot, much more than I usually get, but it's really bread-and-butter money. I go long stretches earning little or nothing."

"Must be the organ fund then."

Liz laughed, shook her head. "We've spent that amount several times over. Listen Abe, I was sworn to secrecy at the begining, but now it's all over, it's bound to come out. UKOFF was Proggle's idea, not mine. The money to buy the cows and chickens and all the rest of it was offered, but the donor said that the source was not to be made public. Cassie remembered my letters in the newspapers and invented a phantom benefactor who followed that up and wrote to me. And it worked."

"Up to now."

"Full marks to Postmaster Chimble, the first to smell a rat."

A long silence, then Abe said, "Come on then."

"Come on what?"

"Tell us who put the money up."

"Can I trust you to keep it under your hat? Until the donor gives the word that is."

"Hang on a minute. Somebody as just 'ad a fire, and is getting the insurance? Just sold some land? Just off to sell a posh car?"

"Right."

"Well, I'm damned." He stood thinking for a while, then suddenly laughed.

"What's funny?"

"I just 'ad a little picture cross my mind. Them two in bed together." He laughed again. "Can you imagine it? D'you reckon they... you know?"

"Don't see why they shouldn't... you know, if they want. Down the Drive, they're already calling him Mr. Proggle."

Somewhere in the village below came the sound of an amplified female voice, echoing off the school and Ketchup Terrace.

"URBLE INBRELLO BALAWARRERE NAGULLA."

"Don't bother to work it out," said Liz. "It's her latest Campaign getting under way. When the tide gets here, she wants to build a sea wall around Clagtoft, turn it into a holiday island."